The Champion's Prize
By M. Francis Lamont

The biggest thanks go to my Morgan, the Princess, for understanding that I was creating something special, but nothing is as special as you. The next name on the (somewhat) long list is Diane. You encouraged me to do this and loved it all as you read it. Laura S. You changed my life and gave me the courage to keep going. Janie, Jessa, Analyn, Wendy, Lila and Katrina (who will never read it since it's not regency appropriate but will display it proudly anyway). You listened, suggested, laughed and rolled your eyes but most of all you supported my dream and helped me cope with the insanity at the beginning. Maraya, your proofreading was invaluable. Lara H. I'll always appreciate your 'big red pen'. Thank-you so much. Gwen, you brought Violetta to life and I treasure the talk we had. Dustin, Dan, Liam and Todd; thank you for playing the hero so well.

The last word goes to the champion of my heart, Manu. With the advice, *"Live with Passion,"* you guided me to this path and rarely does a day go by when I don't write. Thank you for your wisdom, guidance and that fantastic hug. They are never forgotten; the tattoo makes it hard to forget.

CHAPTER 1

"I'm for wine and the warmth of a woman's thighs." Cassian called loudly as he dismounted from the wagon returning him to the ludus, a gladiator training school run by his Roman masters but Hades to those that lived within its walls as slaves and warriors of entertainment. "For nothing reminds a man he is alive like the cries of a passion fueled woman." He knew that it would not take long for the men he called his brothers, his fellow gladiators, to find out just how close he had come to death on the arena sands that day and how much he needed to be reminded that he was still alive.

"Prayers of thanks would see you better served." Remarked the ludus medicus, Arturo, who climbed down from the wagon after him. As a druid from their shared homeland of Britannia, Arturo was often encouraging him to return to a more devout life, with prayers and offerings to the gods of their home. "Your position dictates that you should show more devotion as it will be expected when you make your return to Briton." He would say whenever presented a chance to speak of such things in privacy.

"When the gods give me something to be grateful for besides a life of slavery then, perhaps, they will receive my prayers. I am my own master in that regard at least, Arturo." He shared a long stare with the taller, older man that shared his captivity due to the foolish tactical errors of the young warrior the gladiator had once been. The dark brown gaze of the druid stared back at him and he knew that his own amber colored eyes would be flashing with an anger he rarely felt when talking to his friend. He loved the man like a brother, but this one point was one he would continue to refuse to concede. He was about to add to his declaration when a voice from the sands of the training yard caught his attention.

"You return alive. Does that mean that title is returned as well?"

It was the young Germanic 'pup' Argus that had called to him. The young man admired him, and tried to be like him. He had potential to become a great gladiator if he could calm his temper in the heat of a match.

"Title will follow soon enough, Argus." The fallen champion called in return before looking at the druid beside him "That question will not end until title is returned, will it?" Both men chuckled and crossed the sands

3

to the door to the ludus where Julius, his personal guard within the walls and whenever the lanista took him to the city as a showpiece to garner the attention of the city's elite was waiting for them both.

"What brings such a pleased expression to your face, my friend?" The gladiator asked with a grin as they gripped each other's forearms in greeting.

"I will show you in a moment's time, but your Dominus wishes words with you in the infirmary first." The guard jerked his head towards the open doorway at the end of the hall. "He awaits you with little patience."

He closed his eyes, trying to push his annoyance to the side. After a match he wanted nothing more than his cell and either the solitude it held when he had not earned the reward he craved, which was rare, or the wine and warm company of a willing woman to share his bed for a few hours of the night. "As he commands then." His feet were heavy as he followed Julius and Arturo to the infirmary to see what criticisms the lanista had for his performance upon the sands that day.

Stepping into the room behind the guard he met the cold eyes of his master, Tiberius Tertius. Third man in a line of lanista's to train gladiators beneath the stone roof of the ludus. He was a man as hard as he was fair to those that fought for him with their lives. He was a tall man, towering over most of the men in the ludus, with steel grey hair, a hard-lined jaw with eyes as blue as ice that could peer into a man's soul to discover the truth of his worth. He had chosen more natural champions than any man in his ancestry. He had taken one look into the eyes of the young Celt and declared to everyone in the market that they would one day scream his name as champion.

It had taken only a few short years before he had found his way to the sands and begun to make his legacy known to the city and all who came to the games there. They stared at each other for a long moment, Julius shifting his weight uncomfortably beside him and Arturo, ignoring the lanista who he hated, began to put away the supplies he had brought to the arena in case of injuries.

"You summoned me, Dominus." The champion said, keeping the aggravation from his voice when all he wanted was his cell and the relaxation his body craved.

"Yes. I stand disappointed in that farce of a match you gave today in the games." Tertius said, pacing the small room with an anxious anger. "I was under the impression that you had recovered from the fever and its effects."

"I assure you that I am, Dominus." He said with a tilt of his head towards the Roman. "I was not lying when I told you that I was ready to fight. I also did not pick a match against a man twice my size in the hottest hour of the day."

"I do not want your excuses, Otho."

The lanista purposely emphasized the name that had been put upon him since his fall from status as champion. The name meant: Wealthy, which was another insult to a man that stood a champion, who had once been a prince and had everything he ever valued taken from him. Tertius knew he hated it; having to earn back his own name as well as his title, but Cassian would not give in to the provocation.

"I offer none. Dominus. Just the reminder that I will not forsake my training or my quest to regain my title as champion of this house and this city." His voice was firm with a deadly edge. He could see the exasperation in Arturo's eyes as well as the look of warning to say nothing else to anger the Roman.

"I know that such surrender is not in your nature but the next time you stand upon the sands you will be victorious, or you will meet your end." The lanista said, storming out of the small room leaving three aggravated men behind him.

"Do not give it any further thought tonight, my friend." Arturo said, looking up from the ointments he was tending with a frown on his face.

Julius joined the conversation by putting his hand on his shoulder. "Focus upon other things, Otho." The guard's lip curled as though the false name was as bitter on his tongue as it was to his ears. "Let me take you to your cell so that you can find some rest, if there is no reward waiting for you there."

There was a flash of amusement in Julius's eyes, but before the gladiator could question it, they were walking down the torchlit hallway, passing Hector, another of the guards but no friend to any slave in the house or ludus. He seemed to have just left the solitary passage that led to his cell. Was it possible that Cassian had earned some wine from the lanista despite the loss?

Hector was likely to have taken a part of whatever had been sent but he hoped that something worth having was left for him.

"Unless it is a jug of wine and a woman with nut brown hair as her only ornament there is little reward that could distract from today Julius." He said with a teasing smirk on his lips as they entered the cell and the laughter died on his lips as he realized they were not alone.

"It seems the gods have heard your plea." Julius grinned and opened the cell door to reveal the presence of a woman looking nervously about the small space.

The gladiator paused in the entry and stared at the woman in his cell. Dark hair cascading down a slender back that ended in a narrow waist. Her sweetly rounded hips that would entice any man, curved down to legs that stretched for what seemed miles beneath the swell of tempting cheeks. When she turned, and his eyes met hers the world seemed to stop for a beat of his heart. He could not remember when he had last seen something so beautiful, innocent or so afraid. Her eyes were the same blue as the morning sky and stared at him out of a delicate oval face with high cheekbones and pillowed lips that begged to be tasted and plundered.

He smiled and made his way over to her.

"They answer in one regard but now what of the wine?"

Asking as he let his eyes roam over her pale skin, already imagining the feel of her ripe breasts against his chest but when he reached out to touch her, she flinched and stepped away. Curiosity and amusement both flooded through him, so he matched each of her paces until she was all that stood between him and the cold stone of the wall. He bent his head, letting the sun streaked length of his bronze hair fall over his shoulder as he whispered huskily in her ear, his voice a smooth, practiced, seduction. "You are the first whore to ever flinch from my touch though I assure you; I am not a man that hurts women, especially women of pleasure."

He was surprised when she pressed back as far as she was able, trying to angle away from his touch. When he named her a whore a heated flush rose to her cheeks and she glared up at him with anger written on her face.

Violetta stared at the man who had just been brought to the cell she had been left in an hour earlier. He was the same gladiator she had seen barely escape death in the arena before she had been brought here. It had been a spin on the sands followed by a side-step and a dive that looked more accidental than strategic that had seen him spared certain death by the blade of his opponent. This was the man her Dominus, the man who owned her, had decided to give her virginity to? He was a terrifying brute that still had traces of blood on his arms and a wild look in his eyes that was not like anything she had ever seen before. He stood staring hungrily at her as though he had never seen a woman before. How could she do this? How could she surrender her body which had been kept sacred for the years since she came to be a slave.

She thought she was to be given to a temple as a holy acolyte not gifted to this savage who would take her innocence as though he had earned it. All she could do was numb herself to the reality of her situation. When he did what he was sure to do, she would not let him touch her heart, her soul. She would not let him hurt her, not damage who she was. When it was done, she would go back to the arms of the man that waited to comfort her in the agony that was sure to follow.

"I do not know who you think you are, but I am no whore, gladiator, and should you call me so again you would find yourself in some pain." She stated with a vehemence that belied her size and fearful eyes.

He laughed, a carefree toss of his head, before regarding her with more scrutiny; though the words were brave there could be no pretending she had the courage to see them through.

"Who I think I am is of little consequence if you do not know. If you are no whore then tell me how you come to be in my cell? There is only one reason any other woman has ever come before, and trust me little one, they do." He winked with a knowing grin and stepped back awaiting her response. It was possible that she was not a whore, but she was not a free woman if he guessed right by her dress. He had no idea who she was or how she came to be in his cell, but she intrigued him completely.

"If not for pleasure then why are you here?"

He watched as she swallowed hard and stepped to the side to avoid further physical contact with him, though it would be short lived. He was intrigued by her and for a reason he could not explain, he was drawn to her eyes. His instinct called for him to reach out and touch the skin that looked so soft and bring a smile to her frightened expression. She seemed hardly more than a child. She had eyes of innocence and a body made of temptation.

"I am here by order of my Dominus, untouched, as a gift to you to inspire further victory." Speaking the words aloud brought the blush back to her pale cheeks though not of anger, he thought, but of complete and utter shame.

Realization washed over him; she was a virgin, an innocent and he had treated her as no more than a common harlot. He was a better man than this, he was a champion, above the rest of the men in the ludus he lived in and yet when faced with a gift of a beautiful woman he had reacted like a crude savage. It had been too long since he had been in the company of a woman for any other purpose, not since his childhood in Britannia which Arturo remembered better than he did himself. This was not who he was meant to be, who he wanted to be, suddenly he wanted to be a man who might deserve such innocence as he was being given that night.

"Apologies for previous words. I meant no offence but neither did I expect as a fallen champion I would be sent such a gift." He offered a gentle smile in an attempt to see her fears set aside.

"You need hold no fear of me." He said, attempting to brush a strand of hair from her face and frowning when she flinched from his touch again. "I have never used force to bring a woman to my bed."

"Why ever would such a man need to?" Asked a silvery voice from the doorway where, when they both looked, stood a statuesque Roman woman with warm brown hair and ample curves beneath her silk.

He fought back a cringe as the woman stepped into the room watching her eyes drifting over the slight frame of the girl dismissively. He knew that she was of little concern to the Roman. She had come to be pleasured once again by the titan of the arena even though she knew he was repulsed by her crude tongue and groping hands. The desires of a slave meant little to a paying customer of his Dominus.

"Why indeed Domina." He muttered not taking his eyes off his 'gift' even when the Roman pressed her lips to his shoulder and her hand caressed down to clasp him through the fabric of the subligaria wrapped to cover him at his waist. She disgusted him and each time he was commanded to pleasure her it grew harder not to let his true feelings show.

He could not tell if it was relief or pain that showed on the girl's face, but he would not have her stay as captive audience while he was forced to fuck another woman. He held no desire for the vigor required to satisfy the

Roman and it would certainly all but terrify this already frightened little thing. If he did take her, if she truly gave herself to him, he wanted it to be an awakening of pure sensuality, not a thing of fear closely resembling the rape she obviously expected.

"Go," he said, gesturing to the doorway "I will see to you later, when I have time to teach little girls how to fuck."

He smiled to himself. He had been deliberately crude for he did not want to give the Roman woman a reason to make a target of the girl. It was hard enough that she had been sent here to the ludus for rough use at his hands. He did not think she needed the displeasure of the Domina added to her humiliation. The desire to protect a woman whose name he did not even know was strange to him and he would not have been able to explain it to even his closest friend, but there was no denying the feeling.

Cassian watched Hector, the guard who had escorted the Roman to the cell, move to take the girl by the shoulders and pull her from the room.

"Do not worry gladiator." The guard smirked lewdly. "I will see your 'gift' returned to you."

His hands clenched to fists when she cringed under his hand, Hector's subtle squeeze to her shoulder suggesting that she would not likely be sitting quietly awaiting the summons to return to the cell.

The knowledge that she would be mistreated ate at him, made him want to comfort her. When she gave him a last look over her shoulder it was met with a swift cuff to her head from the guard. She never saw the flash of anger that the assault brought from the eyes of the gladiator while she moved down the hallway or how his lips curled in disgust at the hands caressing his arms and back.

Suddenly he felt all traces of the desire he had managed to summon for the silk clad woman slip from his grasp. He would see her satisfied but not how she expected. If offered the choice he would have kept the gifted girl and sent the other away but no matter what other titles he bore: prince, gladiator, champion, whore, always the one carrying the greatest weight would be slave. With that thought in mind he turned to where she now lay upon his mat and knelt between her legs with a cocky grin.

"To your pleasure Domina." He said and lowered his head.

It was at least an hour later, well after the woman had left, satisfied by mouth and hand until she could take no more and he had washed away the taste if not the memory of her 'pleasure' with the cheap wine given to him by his master, that he asked for his gift to be returned to his cell. "If her Dominus has not already reclaimed her." He was surprised to discover how much he hoped that she was still within the walls of the ludus and paced the packed dirt floor in anticipation.

It was a few moments later that the guards opened the door and brought back the young brunette, the thin fabric of her dress slightly askew with a bruise rising on her cheek and a drop of blood dried on her lip.

"Here is your 'gift' back." Hector spat, shoving her roughly to the floor "The little shit bites."

Cassian glowered at the guards, his status as champion of the house affording him the luxury though he dared not move until the door had been shut and the bolt locked behind their departure. Paying no further attention to the men lingering at the opposite side of the door he stepped towards her and crouched down beside her whispering. "Apologies. You are unharmed?"

She looked up and met his eyes for a moment before casting them down once more. "It is not your fault that he is no better than a brutish dog."

He smiled softly, at least in comparison to the guards she saw him as a better man. The flash of anger in her eyes told him that no matter what they had done they had not broken her spirit and that gave him some peace as he studied his brave little gift.

Sitting up and brushing a strand of hair from her eyes the girl flinched when her hand brushed the bruise darkening the side of her face. It was impossible to hide the tremble in her hand that spoke more to what she had been put to while away from his presence than she would give voice to and the fear radiating from her was not lost on the battle-hardened man beside her.

Drawing a deep breath to bring himself to calm the gladiator released it in a slow sigh.

"Fucking cunts. If I had the power I would see them punished for any offence given to you."

Without further words he reached his arms to enclose her small frame. Cradling her close before standing, her feet dangling over the arm behind her knees and her head against his shoulder felt righter than it should have. He walked to the small straw padded bed that he slept on and lowered her gently down onto the mattress. He saw the surprise in her eyes when he did not join her but instead sat on the dirt floor next to the bed. Handing her a cloth he wet in the bowl of water on his table and watched her wordlessly, waiting for her to speak again. Eager for the soft sound.

She sat up on the simple bed and stared at him with wide-eyed curiosity. "Why do you stay? I have heard stories of you in the marketplace, you could kill them all and escape this life and yet you are here."

Looking up to meet her eyes he scoffed and shook his head dismissively. "Did the guards fill your ears with tales of me while they accosted you? Were they intent on terrifying you to make themselves seem to be better men? Earlier you claimed not to know me but now you speak of tales?" He shook his head as though to brush aside the anger that rose unexpectedly at the thought of Hector forcing the girl to submit to his demands after lying about the man she could not avoid. "Escape is impossible. Even if I did seek it, there is nowhere to go." When her cheeks flushed, and she looked away he knew that something of what he had said carried more truth than either of them liked.

"I... I did not know that you were the man I had heard tales about but yes, they told me that you would break me and that I should be grateful they were gentle. They followed the command that my... that I be left intact for you." A shameful tear slipping down her cheek, she curled her knees to her chest and sighed.

Lifting his hand slowly towards her face he gently wiped the tear away with the tip of his finger. "I will do nothing to you that is undesired. I spoke the truth when I stated that it is not my way to force a woman of any standing. You are safe with me and can rest easy in that knowledge."

Flinching at even that soft touch she met his tender gaze with a hopeful sadness in her eyes. "You would not? But... I am your gift; you have every right to take what you wish from me. That is the purpose of our meeting."

Pain etched itself across his handsome face, that such was the reality of their lives he could not deny but it troubled him that one so young was already so resigned to pain. "Yes, you are my gift," He replied with soft sincerity. "And one that I would not see violated, regardless of any cost to myself for refusing it."

She looked at him with a faint twitch of her lips that hinted at a brief smile from the kindness of his words. "I do not think that refusal is an option for either of us, but I would rather stay here with you than go back to those hounds out there." She said looking over towards the door that separated them from the guards, who occasionally glanced through the window into the room. "I fear that he might kill me if I bit him a second time."

A faint smile played across his lips and he almost laughed aloud for the thought of one so small biting the guards was quite amusing to him. She was wrong about options for there was one that he could choose, one that the result of which he would not tell her. It would have been easy for him to make it appear as though he had taken her, the truth would not have been known until hours, perhaps days later, when she was safely away from the danger of reprisal and he alone left to bear the brunt of it.

The simple act of her jest and the growing ease she seemed to have in his company allowed him to let his eyes wander over her frame once again and he felt the warmth of desire course through him. Leaning close he whispered heatedly in her ear with a smile. "What then would you have me do with this precious gift?" He was rewarded by a light in her eyes at his smile, a sparkle in the captivating blue that suggested something that was confirmed in the next words from her lips, whispered as she leaned towards him and raised a hand to tentatively touch the curve of his shoulder

"Unwrap it and show those that tried to break it how to properly use such a thing." The boldness in her voice faltered and she looked down for a breath before locking her eyes with his again. "The sweetest flower has been left untouched for you to pluck."

CHAPTER 2

There was no question in what she meant, what her heart and soul said. Cassian saw it written plainly in her eyes and the silent but subtle change in her composure. It was a remarkable calm that had settled over her like a blanket and he knew in that moment of peaceful release that she was willing to surrender her virginity to him. He had gained her trust and it was not an act of lust that had caused him to seek it for he would rather have taken the lash than force himself on any woman, no matter what her station. He stood and looked down at her, his eyes offering her another chance to refuse him before he laid himself down on the bed beside her.

When Cassian had settled himself down on the bed, between her and the door, he noticed a slight shiver pass over her body. Was she afraid the guards had spoken the truth? Could she still think he was the primal beast they had painted him to be? He stared down into her eyes and leaned over to apply a line of kisses to her shoulder, letting her grow used to his nearness. His blood pounded when her soft hand reached out to trace the smoothly shaved plains of his stomach causing his muscles to tense and flex beneath her touch.

"Apologies, gladiator... I am uncertain of your name, what you are called in the arena and the stories from the market are different, but I am not sure." A flush crept up her neck and to her cheeks. "I doubt that I shall be up to the standards of those you take to your bed."

He laughed softly and brought his lips down on hers with a crushing and sensual intensity. His tongue was hot and hungry for the taste of her sweet offering. He plundered her mouth to silence any doubt she might have of his desire. Cassian knew what he was doing with a virgin in his bed. She would not be the first that he would teach about the ways of a man and woman. When she opened her mouth to him, accepting his intrusion, and wrapped her arms around his neck with a timid caution he groaned lustily. He tried to hold back the intensity of his reaction so that she was not frightened by the strength and vigor of the desire he held for her sweet enticing body that moved to press against him as though it knew what she did not.

Breaking the kiss slowly, the gladiator feathered his breath across her temple following it slowly with his lips, laying small kisses across her hairline

13

and over the ridge of her cheekbone and down the curve of her cheek. While his lips gently explored her face, he soothingly stroked her back in slow circles unraveling the tension lingering in the frame beneath his palm. "Shh, relax." Cassian whispered. "I am not going to hurt you."

Her breath was heavy and short as he watched her close her eyes, reveling in the gentle touch of his lips and the caress of his hands that seemed to melt her body wherever they touched her. He wondered if she had ever felt like this, it was as if no one in her life had ever truly been gentle with her. Coldness and pain might be all she had ever known from men, but he was not like the rest. She opened her eyes and looked up into his eyes. She nodded, straining her neck to kiss his lips and nod in acceptance of his command.

"There will not be pain, at least not more than is necessary. It takes trust, to surrender to the touch of a man who, despite the situation, is a stranger. Do not think..." The soft heat of his lips grazed the tip of her nose and then pressed to the corner of her mouth, tasting the sweet innocent tremble there. "Just surrender."

Grasping the narrow curve of her waist, he drew her hip against the rigid heat of his lower body for only a moment and then smoothed his hand over her hip and down her thigh to the hem of her dress. The touch of his fingers beneath its edge caused her to draw in her breath in a swift hiss. Had the moment not been so serious Cassian would have laughed but instead he gathered the fabric and began to slowly ease it upwards revealing smooth white thighs that begged for his touch. Slowly moving his lips from her mouth, he began to kiss the point of her chin, then the curve of her neck. Testing the rapid pulse at the base of her throat with his tongue he surprised himself with his body's response; every muscle tightened at the feel of her excitement.

There was a blinding flash of panic in her eyes as he pressed close and his hand crept up her thigh, but it passed as quickly as it came. There was no turning back now. When she rolled her hips into his Cassian smiled, but it was when she, with a sudden boldness, flicked her tongue across the hollow of his throat that he growled lustily, letting her know his need for her.

Her hands began to roam down the chiseled muscled of his torso, the tight bands of strength that were his stomach and reached around to his back, pulling him tighter against her small quivering body. He wanted to have her completely naked with him, soft and as glorious as he knew she must be beneath the fabric of the dress that lay as a barrier between them, even though it was raised to her waist, but he did not want her to look back on this moment with regret. The first time she revealed all of herself to a man should not be like this, an event with little choice.

This frightened little thing deserved something more than this commanded taking in a dank cell with the eyes of his guards peeking through the small window at their will. If this was all that she was to be allowed then he would do what he could to make it as blissful as possible. Looking into her eyes he loosened away the upper portion of her dress, his fingers moving with a well practiced gentility he exposed her upper body as he had wished to since the moment he had seen her.

His entire body strained against the restrictions he placed on himself; to cause her no fear or pain that was avoidable, to refuse himself release until she knew the ecstasy of passionate release. He would show her Elysium. His need for her had become like that of a man dying of thirst while looking at a pure mountain spring. Her skin was soft and smooth beneath the rough callus of his hands, the enticing swell of her breast swelling at his touch as though it belonged in his palm alone.

When she raised herself just enough to trail a line of soft kisses down the line of his jaw before pressing her lips against his, he sensed her desire, touched with timidity and returned her kiss with a tenderness that was starting to grow with each touch between them. The cool air on her skin when he had unfastened her dress sent a shiver down her spine and when the roughness of his palm gripped her breast a moan tore from her throat, the first of its kind that he had heard from her. Moved by her innocent reaction to his hands on her body and the touch of her hand moving from his cheek to thread into his hair Cassian paused. Their eyes met, and she nodded the affirmation of her consent, his chest swelled with a sense of pure victory against the fears created by Romans.

When she nodded her consent, the former champion allowed himself to become lost in the flood of sensation that she created in him simply by lying softly in his arms, allowing him access to all of her, denying him nothing, nothing but her soul, her heart. His muscles clenched with the overwhelming power of his need and he lowered a hand to the linen at his waist, quickly removing his subligaria and the all but final barrier between him and the pursuit of his desire. Gods but he wanted her, needed her innocent surrender to cure past pains and spur him to future glory.

Her trust in him was like a drug and he reveled in her belief that he was more than what he might seem. He had to have her now, in the rising heat of the moment while her determination and will ran hot and swift in her veins. Pushing them together gently he dragged his tongue down the valley between her ripe breasts, separated them with his lips, kissing each nipple, circling it with his tongue before tugging, nipping each bud until it pearled to arousal beneath the experience of his coaxing. He could feel her body shake and it brought a smile to his lips as he continued to play with her, teasing himself as much as her. He could hardly wait to taste more of her, to feel her come apart in his arms.

She cried out softly, her breath quickening she whispered. "Please... do not stop." while her hand drifted down to his waist and when her fingertips grazed the pulsing hardness there, her eyes widened in panic at its size. He smiled when she looked up and asked. "It will not hurt much... will it?"

"No little one. Not much." He whispered in her ear with a smile teasing his lips. If she was to feel the pleasure he meant for her, then her arousal would have to outweigh her fear. He dipped his fingers to brush them between her thighs to feel the heat of her readiness and when he heard her breath quicken it was suddenly all he could think about, being inside her and feeling her tighten around him. He wanted to cum so badly that it hurt, an aching need, burning through him to his core.

Nipping the softness of her stomach he kissed her hips before trailing his tongue lightly over her thighs. When she squirmed with a laugh, he took the opportunity to slide his hands under the soft curve of her bottom to hold her steady. He intended to have her writhing and bucking until she could no longer take what he offered and then he would give her some more. Kissing the hollow of her hips one more time he then moved his mouth to her core and rubbing his rough unshaven jaw against her femininity he slid his tongue inside with long languid strokes, growling as the honeyed sweetness of her greeted his senses, intoxicating him completely.

The girl could not keep still. Shifting and almost giggling when he nipped her, his playful sensuality sending a jolt to newly blossomed nerves, she seemed to blush wherever he touched her, however he touched her. The laughter faded to a moan when his lips and tongue began to explore her thighs but when his hands cupped her still tender bottom she shifted from his touch. He had forgotten in the heat of the moment that she had faced rough handling by the guards in his absence and he knew they would not have been gentle with one so spirited.

"Fuck." He cursed softly, what had he done to cause the discomfort? "Apologies, I..." His voice was tender as he lifted his head to lock his eyes with hers before he spoke. "Look at me." If someone had caused her pain, he would do all he could to push it from her mind, to keep her thoughts right there with him and the passion rising between them. To further distract her from anything but him the gladiator kept his eyes locked to hers, flicked her intimately with his tongue at the same time he winked with an erotic playfulness, daring her to laugh again.

When she looked down at him and nodded, he could see the lust she reflected there. Her eyes blinked slowly, soft and unfocused, so heavy with her first taste of desire. Lowering his head in wordless response to the questions in her eyes he lifted her hips, carefully bringing her against his mouth and once again gave her pressure with the sole intent of bringing her to the edge of carnal bliss. When she was there, breathless and willing in his arms, she would be ready, and he would enter her, claiming something that only one man ever could.

She bucked and writhed in his hands, her back arching with pleasure and uttering a small cry she dug her fingers into his hair, pulling him closer, wanting more of what he gave her; mind bending pleasures. He forgot that the guards outside might see or hear her, forgot what would surely await her when she returned to the home of her dominus. Cassian reveled in the way she gave herself over to the slow rise of pleasure that was building between them like a wave.

It was unlike anything he had ever thought possible in this world, and the look in her eyes, the passion and tenderness there overwhelmed him. Cassian could feel his heart being pulled to this mysterious woman about whom he knew so little.. It was foolish, dangerous and yet unstoppable; as she cried out again, she knew it would be more than her maidenhead that he would claim.

Replacing his mouth with a hand he circled, stroked and teased her until her core was slick with her desire. As he stared in the trusting deep blue of her eyes he slowly, gently worked a finger inside and pushed deeply until he reached her virgin barrier. He was relentless though tender when he broke her; at the same moment covering her bare neck and shoulders with hot open-mouthed kisses, adding small bites to deliberately distract her from the discomfort.

His mouth was hot on her skin, she tasted like honey and for a moment he thought that he would never be able to get enough of the taste of her. Withdrawing his hand, he was quickly against her, the rippling power of his warrior's frame enveloping her small one as he nudged, thick and hard as steel against her soft, delicate folds. Breath hissed from between his tightly clenched teeth as he pushed himself slowly into her, easing into the tightness that had been saved for him.

He flinched, watching tears spring to her eyes before they closed when his lips devoured her skin. Her hands gripped his arms tightly as he adjusted to enter her, he tried hard to make it as easy on her as he was able. When she opened her eyes to lock with his Cassian searched her features for any hint of displeasure as her pale thighs fell open to ease his access, her natural instinct taking over. Her breath came in a ragged inhale as he strained against his control. He would not be the savage animal the guards had told her he was, he would be, for these minutes, what she deserved.

Gliding slowly out only to thrust forward more deeply, taking the move slowly, with an aching sensuality, his entire world, every breath and heartbeat focused on their mutual pleasure. Lowering his head, he took her nipples back into his mouth one at a time, suckling them, nipping and wrapping his tongue around them as he whispered. "Tighten your body around me." Pulling back and returning into her again, each time with more intensity, more passionate need.

He did not understand what it was about this girl that called to him but more than his own release he wanted her to have that blinding moment of ecstasy. Even if it was only once and he never saw her again, this moment was important.

She responded to him as though he had commanded her. Gasping as her body started to move with his instead of fighting against him, bringing a smile to his lips. It felt incredible, so unlike any woman he had been with before. Her hands rose to press against his chest, and he could feel his muscles move against her palms as she raised her hips to press the softness of her body against him. The invitation for more was incredible as she daringly circled her tongue around his nipple just as he had done to her, letting the edge of her teeth graze it and bring a groan from his lips that seemed to delight her.

He stilled completely inside her, straining to remain motionless he let her feel him. Cassian wanted her to develop a hunger, a burning desire for the pleasure of a man buried deep within her. When he could stand it no longer he withdrew slowly from the close contact with her sweating flesh. He savored each contraction of her muscles like a sweet reward before he thrust again and filled her to the depth of her body. His own muscles wrenched tightly in his abdomen barely able to hold on to the control that was needed to see this through to the pleasure of them both.

He felt as though he was drowning in the sweet intensity that the enticement of her innocence offered his senses, and he had no desire to come up for air. His thrusts became more demanding, coaxing her to match the rhythm of his body with her own. The light of the torches glowed in the moisture dewing his shoulders and chest as they strained together in an escalating tumult of passion and fire.

He had watched a fear that he was finished with her flash in her eyes but as he gave time for the sharpness to fade and he began to move again it had been replaced by a hunger, one that he felt growing for her as well. "There is more. Relax and feel. Stay with me." She pressed her hips up to meet his with a moan when his motions increased causing a quickening of her breath between barely parted lips. Suddenly bursting with the eagerness of a younger man he coaxed them both an upward spiral of pleasure. He pushed and rolled his body in a demanding rhythmic thrusting, small whimpers and breathy moans slipping from her lips as he brought him new fire, new definitions of need to pleasure her.

Beads of sweat appeared on her breast as their joining became almost feverish in its intensity. He flicked his tongue across them, tasting her as she had so boldly tasted him moments before. One of her hands dropped from his arms to grip the firm muscle of his backside when he brought a cry of ecstasy from her throat and her head rocked back to the mat, making his already aching cock even harder, bringing him to the edge of pleasure and pain.

Their bodies came together like clamor of thunder in the heavens. The gladiator gave himself to her with an intensity he had forgotten himself capable of. He buried his cock so deep into her heat that he could no longer tell where he ended, and she began. His muscles clenched on him again as shuddering warnings of the rapture to come beckoned him towards the fire of release. A visceral cry he barely recognized tore from his throat as he fought against the urge to succumb so soon, determined to bring her beyond ecstasy with him if not before. Focusing on her face his body began to move with a frenzy of orgasmic aggression, eager to see her in the throws of her first release.

Her sounds of passion filled the air as her body coiled, tightening around him. Opening her eyes, she wrapped her legs around him, meshing her body to his, their muscles moving together as though they had become one being. The tightening in his loins that had begun was almost more than he could bear. When she bit down on her lips, causing the blood there to flow again, he brought her over the edge of climax into a moment of rapturous cries and wild grasping to pull him closer, deeper. He ached with a need that had less to do with sex and everything to do with her.

Over and over he drove himself into her; harder, faster and deeper with each stroke until he was all but mindless with the savagery of his need. The innocent passion of the woman in his arms silencing the cries of her pleasure at his shoulder made him growl loudly with desire to make her do it again and again. Then, suddenly, it came to him like a bright moment of visceral clarity. He came with an internal, pulsing cataclysm, erotic in the euphoria he roared the bliss of his release. Deep inside her with the final shuddering of his body. He had held back longer and given more than he had thought he would ever be able to give again. He stilled and looked down at the beautiful creature beneath him and smiled.

Her eyes had closed in the sweetest surrender of trust, and tension poured out of him with his release as another wave of pleasure shook her.

Gasping for breath she stared up into his eyes, her chest heaving and brushing against his with an undeniable intimacy as she lay beneath him. It stirred his heart in a way he was not prepared for, he wanted to hold her close, tenderly easing her to sleep in his arms but it seemed impossible to move, even to do what he desired. His muscles had been pressed to the maximum and beyond in the climb to mind bending ecstasy, and hers must have as well but, happily, she seemed to have no desire to be gone from his arms.

Struggling to speak, she wet her lips with her tongue and whispered. "I... I never knew it would be... like this."

Cassian dragged a hand through the sweat soaked strands of his hair, pushing them away from his face where they had fallen over his eyes. He watched the woman lying beneath the weight of his ebbing arousal who met his stare with a slow recovery. With a soft, tender, smile full of apology for the primal roughness in his taking he whispered. "Cassian." Before taking her into his arms and rolling onto his side so that they lay facing each other with their heads on the small straw pillow only inches from each other. "You deserve to know the name of your first. The lanista commands them to call me simply 'Otho' but that is not my name, not who I truly am. It is done only as a mockery of the man that used to be a god upon the sands and everything that I have lost."

He brushed a strand of hair from her forehead, twirling the dark tress around his finger and waited to see if she would reveal her own name to him, for he was suddenly anxious to know it.

"Cassian" she replied, with a beaming smile as she laid her head down upon his arm. Reaching a hand out to trace across the chiseled muscles of his chest she spoke softly. "I am Violetta. That is all I have ever been called and, I think, all I ever will be. My Dominus did not change my name when I was taken for a slave though I know many do."

With the fingertips of one hand Cassian traced the outline of her lips and smiled. "Violetta, a beautiful name, for a beautiful woman. Relay my gratitude for such a gift to the one who sent you." Sadness sounded in his voice suddenly, the broad chiseled features of his face showed a rare revelation of emotion that he kept hidden from all those around him. "Where is it that you return to now? To whose house do I owe my debt of gratitude?"

Violetta closed her eyes and replied softly. "I will relay the message. He will be well pleased." She shifted under the heat of his stare which made him wonder if she feared her Dominus. "I will return to his villa here in Velletri. I was brought here from the country for service. You are his favorite gladiator. When Felix Census remembered he had a virgin slave he thought I would be a fitting gift to show his esteem." She lowered her head, a strand of her hair falling across her forehead and pink blush rising to her cheeks.

Fear flashed in his heart when she closed her eyes briefly to hide her emotions from him. The thought of what could await her upon her return now that her virginity had been taken sent a shudder that was hard to repress through his mind and he considered the name of her Dominus, reflecting on what he knew of the man Census. The name was familiar to him, the man had been the editor of many games in recent years, the most recent included.

What reason had seen such esteem been built when he had lost in his first return since having been ill? Perhaps to encourage future triumphs or was there something darker behind the giving of this precious gift? Was he trying to kiss the ass of the lanista or increase the worth of the girl by bragging that her virginity had been taken by the champion? There was, of course, the possibility that the gift was one of true and genuine admiration but the cost to her was dear though not unpleasantly taken. "Apologies." He whispered to her. "We do what we must."

She stared up into his eyes, no doubt trying to read what was going through his mind, but he would not reveal the thoughts that might taint this memory for her. His life was not easy. Living in a place where the man you called a brother could be commanded to kill you in the games of some nobility. It was hard for him to trust those he knew well and yet he felt as though he could confide in her and bare his soul, he let her in as he revealed his secret desires. He wanted her for himself and there was not a single woman since Nala that he had even dared to entertain that thought for. What was it about her that called to the deepest part of him?

"Not all men are as bad as Hector and his lot." His attempt to ease her fears of the men she would now face was a failure because there was nothing more, he could say that would not be a lie, so he changed the subject, asking the more menial question. "Do you serve; the house or as body slave?" He wasn't sure why it mattered, curiosity perhaps? They would likely never cross paths again; she would go back to her Dominus; his gift having been set to the purpose it was intended for.

He had no doubt that, now deflowered, Violetta would be put to further such use by the men in her household, that a woman of her rare beauty had been kept pure so long was nothing short of a miracle and surely there was someone other than Census behind that. Did she know what was to come? That despite the care that he had taken with her the result would be a curse to her future? Suddenly he felt responsible for what would come to her and, teasing his fingers through her hair he moved to take her lips in one last tender kiss.

She met his kiss with a longing for more that he knew she would likely never have, savoring the gentleness that she would never get from the man she would now serve. "I had served the house before coming to the city but now I have been told I will likely serve Vitus, son of Felix, as a body slave." She did not say what they both knew; how the man was known for his temper and his brutal nature but simply lay in his arms, committing these last few moments of tenderness to memory. "If it pleases the gods, I may see you again Cassian, but I fear it would be under different circumstances than this bliss." Her head turned when the same guards that had brought her opened the door to retrieve her.

Cassian stood with a sigh and reached for the cloth he had tossed aside, securing it tightly in place before offering his hand to help her to rise as well. His steel control was what made him the best upon the sands and yet he could not deny the feeling of tenderness he felt for the young woman who had trusted him so completely. It was something he could not explain and so he gave it no thought until the guard opened the door and moved to take her from him forever. "NO!" He cried and before he knew what was happening, he was pressing her back to the wall. He gave her no chance to think or to refuse but kissed her as if he could lay claim to her heart and soul with his mouth and tongue. It was as if his fingers threading through her hair, angling her mouth fully to his would give him the last piece of herself that she had held back when they lay together.

There was a sudden hand to his shoulder and the tip of a blade piercing the flesh at the base of his spine that caused him to give her release, stepping away with a look of complete rage. He was not willing to surrender her to the guards who might take advantage of what he had done. His taking of her maidenhood might have much more immediate consequences than the silk merchant who had sent her. His fists flew without thought, striking the guard that he had thought was a friend only a few hours ago. He would not let her go, not yet and not like this.

Julius struck him back as expected, friend or not he would not take such assault from a slave of any standing. They continued the attack and defense, Cassian trying to stop the taking of the girl and Julius doing his best not to aggravate the injury from the games while trying to subdue a man they both knew could have killed him in moments if he had truly wanted such a thing.

Cassian could hear Violetta's voice, trying to stop them, calm him, but it didn't matter, not now. Hector would hurt her if he got his hands on her again and that was something he couldn't bear. She got close enough for him to smell her but still he and Julius fought with increasing intensity but suddenly there was a sharp cry of a feminine voice in pain.

Looking down Cassian was horrified to see Violetta on the ground with a hand to her cheek where a bright red mark would soon turn into a bruise that would last days. "Oh gods. How did that happen?" He reached down to help her up but there was a sudden cold press of steel at the base of his spine.

He looked at the bleeding guard in utter confusion. What in Hades had come over him? He was not a man to give in to these kinds of urges even if he did feel them. It was not the passion behind the fight that bothered him but the sharp tugging need in the center of his chest that screamed to stay with her as he was moved further away. He could not, would not, let himself, remember the last time he had felt anything like this.

When he stepped back, and she was able to see the steel pressed against his spine, her eyes flashed to his and with a small twitch of her head she silently begged him not to resist further on her account. There was a fear in her eyes that had nothing to do with sex and everything to do concern that he might be put to pain before her eyes. Retying and adjusting her dress the young woman moved calmly with the demanding pull of the guards. With a soft exhale she let her hand run down his arm and across his palm in a farewell caress, her eyes did not leave his face until the wall of his cell came between them as she was led out and away.

He winced visibly when Hector put his hand upon her. The lecherous look in his eyes made Cassian want to rage and rip the man's flesh from its violation of what was his. The sound of the door closing behind her was like a blow to his heart and his hands curled into fists of helpless rage. With a roar of frustration, he struck at the wall where he had kissed her, not caring that his knuckles bled while he made his way back to his bed which now seemed so empty without her in it.

CHAPTER 3

Violetta woke up with a start when the firm hand touched her shoulder. Opening her eyes, she met those of Meridius that offered his, as always, silent sympathy. It was as if he knew the dream that he had woken her from had been more pleasant than the waking world. Five nights had passed since she had left Cassian's arms in the ludus and still each night was filled with dreams of him. The precious hours in her own bed after seeing the desires of her Dominus, Felix Census, satisfied were filled with dreams of returning to Cassian's arms and the happiness she had found there unexpectedly. The dreams were a poor substitute for the man himself, but they dulled the ache in her heart for a short time each day though it returned without fail along with the physical pain from the night before.

It was not that Felix was a man who was especially cruel in his bed, he was kinder than the son she had thought she would serve, but he was a Roman and she his slave, existing to do his will and see his every desire met. She was left as unsatisfied as she was as sore as any slave commanded to bed their master was, with the solitary exception of Meridius. If he ever felt a moment of pain or displeasure at his task it was impossible to tell, and the mute man could not have spoken of it even if he had wished to.

Known as 'The Spaniard' to many, Meridius was the first man to show her kindness and through the years they had become as close as blood. He could not speak to most, his tongue had been cut out years before she arrived in the house, but he had taught her hand gestures that allowed them to communicate. He had told her of his life before slavery as the son of a great Spanish general who had been taken prisoner and sold as a slave, eventually he found himself in the house of Felix Census where it was likely he would live out his days despite having the heart of a warrior like his father before him.

With a sigh she stood. "It is time already? The night passes too quickly." There was no time made for the slaves to offer prayers to the gods during the day as the only god Felix held with was the one that would most likely bless his ventures and grant him greater fortune. Meridius was kind and fatherly to her and so he made sure to wake the devout girl so that she could find the small time needed to offer her prayers and small sacrifices.

Violetta was certain that he had his own devotions at the same time but the only way she could know for sure would have been to skip her own. She was not willing to risk the displeasure of her deities simply to satisfy her curiosity, especially when he went out of his way to make it a private thing. "If Dominus were a more devout man we would not have to wake so early to pray." She muttered aloud but when Meridius chuckled softly she could not help but smile. "I suppose if he were a more devout man there are a great many things that would stand different than they are now."

Taking his arm, they began to walk to the small altar room he had assembled. The fear and respect the other slaves of the house had for Meridius kept it safe from disturbance along with the strange symbols that he had painted around the door frame. Once inside Violetta made her way quickly to the corner curtained off from the rest of the room that Meridius had set aside for her use.

He had allowed her to decorate it in honor of the gods of Greece that her mother had worshiped while the rest of the room was devoted to the honor of his strange holy beings. When her simple prayers had finished, she rose to return to the hall where he was waiting for her as always but before she could say a word a muscle in her thigh cramped suddenly, sending her to the floor with a cry of pain.

At the sound Meridius spun on his heel to rush to her side. His face was full of concern and confusion for hers were not deities that demanded the sacrifice of blood without great need. When he crouched beside her, he reached his hand to her thigh while she tried to rub the muscle through the fabric to relax it enough that she could begin her day in the villa above. Violetta tried to brush his hands away; he simply caught both her wrists in his long smooth fingers and ignored her panicked cry when he slowly lifted the material.

Perhaps there was not the need for modesty with him, but what he would see would surely anger him and that was something she did not want. Surrendering, she allowed him to raise the fabric, and he looked down at what should have been white flesh like the rest of her but instead her inner thighs were mottled in bruises of various colors and shades ranging from dark purple to faded green. It was obvious why she had cried out in pain and yet she had said nothing to him, even when he had escorted her nightly back to her own cell.

Cupping her chin, the bright blue eyes silently demanded an explanation she knew she could not avoid now. Wrestling her hands free of his hold Violetta shook her head while she adjusted the material back where it was meant to be. "The hands of Vitus leave their mark. Though he is denied his pleasure by the word of his father it does not stop him from causing pain. They seem to cause him greater pleasure than the body of any woman.

She shuddered in horrified disgust and slowly rose to her feet. "If we are to arrive on time then we should go now." The look in his eyes stopped her and brought a cautious question to her lips. "What has changed? You look as though you have been told to bring me to a fate like death. Am I to be given to Vitus? Has Felix finally granted the wish of his son?" Her body shook with fear that she would be sent to service the man who haunted her worst dreams.

Meridius shook his head emphatically, they both lived with the fear of that day but fortunately for them both the event that had him concerned was far less frightening. Selenia, the daughter of Felix that had been in Rome for the last four years, was to return home for a brief visit. The father in law of Lucia, the woman who had fostered Selenia after the death of Felix's wife, and who now worked to help her find a husband, had died. The funeral and several days after would be for family only so the spoiled young woman was sent home to the house of her father until it was time to return to Rome.

The last time she had been here Violetta had been a servant in the country villa kitchen and not in attendance to be noticed by the woman who was used to getting everything she wanted, everyone she wanted. Meridius wanted to keep Violetta safe from Selenia's lust and desire for amusement in the form of sexual based fear but if Felix was in the mood to indulge his daughter and annoy his son there would be nothing he could do to stop it.

As they slowly made their way to where Felix would be waiting, Vitus not far behind, Violetta was not sure which man she feared more. They both stood as monsters; the father cold and uncaring while the son, though still denied her, was sadist, cruel and hot-tempered. It was not that Vitus was an ugly man, with his strong jaw, full lips and thick dark curls paired with a lean, well-muscled body most women would likely find him attractive until they looked into his eyes. Though dark eyes were usually thought of as warm his were like the depths of Hades; cold and heartless with a calculating gleam that sent shivers down the spine of all those that looked into them.

For six years Vitus had tormented Violetta with hints of what was to come when she was finally available for him to use. More than once he had even forced her to her knees and thrust his cock between her lips as a 'lesson' for speaking without permission. If it had it not been for the watchfulness of Meridius, he would have forgotten his father's command and taken her then and there, but the silent Spaniard boldly put a hand to the Romans chest and scooped her from her knees to carry her back to her cell beneath the villa where he would wipe her cheeks and calm her fears with the fatherly tenderness he had treated her with for so long.

Felix knew he was an attractive man and Meridius could not help but agree. Not as broad in the face as his son but his hair, though a mix of grey and black, was thick and worn longer than the custom of most Romans. His eyes were as bright as they had been when he was but twenty years old and he worked hard to keep his body in a condition to rival the thirty years of Vitus though there was eighteen years between them. Had he needed he could have bested the younger man with a sword but chose instead to use the one between his legs.

With a shake of his head Felix addressed Vitus, barely noticing when the pair of slaves arrived together. "Your sister returns home tonight, and I have the desire for Meridius' strength in my bed after a week of sweet submissions, so I will not deny you the same any longer." His eyes laughed at the eagerness in Vitus' face. "But I remind you that she is not to be broken or marked upon her face, her beauty should always be in condition to be displayed for my pleasure and that of the guests who will come to celebrate the visit of Selenia after so many years gone from Velletri."

Meridius noticed the look of horror flash in Violetta's eyes before she schooled her expression back to meek obedience, but it was impossible to calm her in the company of their masters.

Vitus had watched his father with an angry glare. "Of course, father." He said with a tight smile, and Meridius knew that he would be counting down the hours until he could finally have his fantasy fulfilled.

"Selenia returns tonight? And you intend to host a gathering?" He paused and narrowed his eyes. "Is that shit lanista Tertius invited? With his 'champion' you admire so much?" He scoffed with a curl of his lip "If you wish to fuck the man father then just do so, there is no need to bring the savage into our house."

Felix laughed then gripped his son by the shoulder, a dangerous flash of anger in his eyes that Meridius knew well. "Who I choose to fuck is not your business and that 'savage' is one of the best gladiators in memory. The cost of having to deal with the lanista is what I must bear to have Cassian, or Otho, whatever they are calling him now, here is worth it for the connections made with those willing to come to see him."

Releasing his hold, he smiled smoothly and snapped his fingers for the attendance of Meridius before moving across the room. "Your sister will be home within hours and there is much to attend to before her arrival. You will not cause a scene with the gladiator tonight. Why you seem to hate him so much now, after years at the games, I do not understand."

Turning to speak over his shoulder as he stepped from the room, Felix ran his hand across the bare broad shoulders of his body slave. "Remember Vitus, if you want the girl you will do as I say, or I will find new ways to enjoy her and continue to deny her to you." Walking away Meridius could almost feel the anger from Vitus. Being treated as though he were still a child was one thing that the younger Census could not stand but there was too much riding on the attendance of the fallen champion of Velletri for Felix to bother with coddling his son and risking a show of his temper.

While Vitus stood, slowly comprehending what his father had threatened, Meridius knew he had to get Violetta from the room. With a quick snap of his fingers and the tilt of his head he told the girl to make herself scarce but as she stepped from the room, the Roman called for her to pause.

"Prepare yourself for me tonight, at long last Violetta." Vitus said with a shine in his eyes that made Meridius shudder and Violetta pale at his side. "I fear it will take many hours to see me satisfied enough to sleep."

The laughter of the Roman followed them both out into the hall as Meridius brought her with him to follow Felix.

At the Ludus of Tiberius Titus.

The dawn came earlier than it should have, or at least that is how it seemed as the slivers of light touched the tarnished perfection of Cassian's frame. Even though it was a warm and gentle glow he found no joy in it. The bandage around his wound stood in a sweat-stained contrast to his sun-bronzed skin, an unavoidable reminder of a weakness he should not possess. Denying its existence was a poor reason for his loss. Despite the fevered illness a few weeks ago there was no excuse for what had happened. A fall to the sand should not have brought the vulnerability that caused him to be injured, but truthfully the pain was not what caused him to pause in rising.

If his Dominus, Tiberius Tertius, were to learn the truth of the cause he was certain he would never see the inside of the arena again. Cassian forced himself to stand, clenching his jaw to hold back a scream of pain. He would not let this new wound stop him from what he must do. He had to stand not matter the pain. Perhaps a distraction would help? A memory of pleasure to counter the physical agony he felt? "Violetta." He whispered her name like a prayer. A smile spread across his lips as he rose to his feet like a titan. His eyes pressed closed for a moment before he strode from the cell. Each step managed by the memory of the sweetness of her in his arms.

For hours he trained as though he had no injury, as though his body did not ache for rest and the sweet relief of soaking in the hot water that would be provided at the day's end. He wiped the sweat from his brow and looked at Cirandon who trained the gladiators since the days that an injury had ended his own career in the arena. Cassian held the man as dear as a brother, despite it being Cirandon's wife he had once thought himself in love with until she betrayed him nearly to his death. The idea that his own injuries could see him to a similar position, forever absent the roar of arena crowds, sent a shiver down his spine. He was a fighter and a life that would deny him that was not one he thought worth living.

The dark-skinned man had watched the champion. He had seen the clues to his exhaustion that no one else would notice. "Take to the shade with water and rest a moment." Cirandon whispered from behind him. "Before your brothers see you collapse in the sun."

Shaking his head in protest the gladiator grinned broadly. Sweat coated every inch of his body and each move he made was more painful than he could admit but he would never surrender to his agony. He had spent the morning drilling at the wooden training pallus and the after-midday sparring with the others though the act was mindless due to his exhaustion. Some of the men had teased him that his strength had been stolen by the girl given to his bed, like Samson in the legends of Israel, but he would never let even them know the truth of his injury.

"There are none here that will lay eyes upon that sight." He said with a smirk, tightening the hold he had on the pair of wooden gladiuses he used outside the arena.

"The order comes from a power higher than mine." The dark-skinned former champion glanced quickly up towards the balcony where Tertius observed the training, his eyes fixed on the Celt who had so recently returned to the sands. "Go." The Doctore whispered, pleading as a friend. "Or else see my hands forced to action."

"My body obeys, but the heart..." He wanted to say that he would rather suffer the wrath of Tertius than stop his training. Instead, he released a deep sigh with a brief, but angry, glare towards the Roman observing him and lowered his blades, handing them to the slave who stood waiting to return them to their proper place. This marked the first time he had been given the order to stop training and rest. In truth he was unsure what bothered him more; that he had not argued the point or that his body agreed it was needed.

Cassian had no choice unless he wanted to force his friend to lay violent hands upon him, but still it bothered him to bend so easily to the unfamiliar command. He knew that it was simply the price he had to pay for the loss of his title; his name changed and treated like a dog or the lowest of men until he was once again champion of Velletri and the house of Tertius.

"I want him bathed and scented, now." The lanista called from the balcony as Cassian prepared to leave the sands. "He will attend a feast tonight at my side. Felix Census wishes to see his favor returned."

The unnoticed glare he shot his Dominus would have pierced him through to the wall had it been steel, but Cassian made his way to the baths in perfect obedience even though there were questions burning on his mind. What did Tertius mean that the return of his favor had been requested? Since it was certainly not rest that was on the mind of either Roman for the fallen champion, he had to think that it would be either fighting for private exhibition or to be stripped bare to fuck for the pleasure of their entertainment.

That it might be Violetta he fucked made the idea both appealing and horrifying at the same time. He could not stop them if that was what was commanded. All he could do in that moment, if it came, would be to make it as pleasurable for her as he could so that she did not feel the shame of the act. He would not hurt her even with the threat of injury to himself; he would not let them force him to damage the one pure joy he had given to her. One day he would see them all to Hades but until that day came, he was forced to obedience no matter how hated the act.

Hours later he stood in perfect silence, the image of a god brought to life; torch light gleaming across his chiseled body, every exposed inch like bronze granite and the wound on his thigh well hidden. His hair was braided along his temples to highlight his handsome face, strong jaw and amber eyes. Waiting on word for his purpose to be revealed Cassian steeled himself against what the night might bring. He refused to let this charade be a part of who he was, this was the game of Romans not a gladiator.

There was a faint hope that she would be there; Violetta, the thought of whom sent long forgotten feelings coursing through him. He did not want her to see him like this but still he had to know if she felt the connection that he did or if he was just fooling himself that there was more between them than the gratitude of an innocent girl for a man who had showed her gentleness in awaking her passion and pleasure unlike anything she had likely known.

Even standing in the hall waiting for Tertius he could barely hide the smile that came at the memory of her in his arms. Those bright blue eyes staring into his eyes as though he was a hero instead of a gladiator. The title was really just another name for whore to so many but to her, the look she gave him, made him feel like he could move mountains and like he wanted to protect her from all harm, no matter the cost to himself for the effort.

CHAPTER 4

The sky was a light haze of purple and pink with a few scraps of cloud to catch the colors as Meridius watched Selenia Census step down from the wagon in front of her father's door. She was hours later than expected and her father would be displeased. It would be the driver and not her that would bear the brunt of his anger for she had always been his favored child and it was a thing she often used to her advantage. Thankfully she did not see him as she swept through the doors that opened at her approach. She tossed her head and the long blonde curls falling down her back moved like a curtain of gold as she adjusted her dress, spread her crimson lips in a smile and called down the hall.

"Father? Vitus? I have come home."

Walking down the familiar halls with her entourage behind her Meridius watched as Selenia smiled at Violetta. He froze at the twisted smile that crept to her face, watching the girl who was unaware she was being observed from a distance. He had heard Selenia had enjoyed the available pleasures of both male and female slaves at her 'aunt's' villa in Rome. Now it was his girl that drew her attention and it would be up to him to distract her from the pursuit. It was with a deep frown that he followed the Roman woman into the office of her father, plans forming in his mind as to how he could do what was now so desperately needed.

Standing still, just inside the door Meridius watched as Felix stood to embrace his daughter; his arms wrapping around her while his eyes watched the jealousy of his son. Pulling from the embrace he kissed both her cheeks with a smile. "My daughter, light of my eyes. It warms my heart to have you beneath my roof again though you were expected hours ago. What caused you to be delayed?"

"The journey was overly long due to the driver's caution in avoiding roads that are known to be traveled by some of those who would stand a danger to me and once within the city he refused to listen to directions from a woman." She smirked and raked her eyes over the silent girl who had entered the room to stand beside Meridius. "I think he has left in fear of your wrath, but now that I am home it does not matter. I would however know the name of this sweet little thing. Is she new?" Curling her fingers, she beckoned Violetta to approach, her smile broadening with each timid step she took.

Vitus pulled his sister into his arms, faking a warm embrace so he could rage. "She is MINE" He hissed in her ear before saying louder for his father's benefit. "It has been too long dear sister since we have laid eyes upon each other. You like my newest?" He gestured Violetta to approach and wet his lips hungrily. "A lovely little toy father has given me use of at last."

Stepping free of Vitus' embrace Selenia stared between him, her father and the girl she obviously wanted. Speaking to her father with a playful smile she walked between the girl and Meridius. "I did bring a girl with me. She is currently tending to my things and I find myself in need of aid in attending to a few... needs." She dragged her eyes over the Spaniard before meeting the laughing disapproval of her father's stare.

The Spaniard knew that Vitus was a man who liked to have his possessions admired by others before he denied them their use, keeping them all for himself until they were too broken to be of any use to anyone. Vitus ran his fingertips down Violetta's spine with a smile as he whispered. "You want her for yourself do you not? Or do my eyes forget that look upon your face?"

When he turned to call for wine she said calmly to Vitus. "Of course I want her, and I will have her. Eventually." She taunted her brother with a smile. "If it is not too much trouble, I would have this one escort me to my room, as I assume it is ready for me?" She faked a yawn and looked towards the pair of slaves that her father commanded. She was obviously hoping that he would command one of them to attend her but when he ignored her request, she pouted and asked Violetta to fetch her a glass of wine while Meridius tried to find a way to spare Violetta her company.

While the Romans chattered Meridius watched Violetta shudder while Vitus's finger caressed her spine. Some might think it a sign of affection, but he knew there was nothing in that touch except for lust to cause pain. There was some desire perhaps for her, but Vitus' truest desire was for power and dominion.He wanted what he could not have, and he was more aroused using whatever power he could summon over those that were forced to serve him than he was by even the most willing of flesh.

When Felix nodded towards the wine Meridius could tell Violetta was eager to pour it simply for the chance to get out from beneath Vitus' touch. She moved quickly with a grace that hid her fear completely from those that did not know her as he did. The red liquid filled the cups without a drop spilling to the ground while she avoided the chance for a groping hand from either man without them knowing that she did so on purpose.

Meridius' bright blue eyes laughed silently in approval of her little game but when Violetta brought the glass to Selenia the woman grabbed her arm as though to stop her from running. The large man tensed at the thought of the vicious woman getting her claws into the girl he saw as the daughter he had never had. He had known the Roman most of her life and knew that if she got the chance to have Violetta, she would never let her go until all the damage she wanted to inflict upon her innocence was done.

He had taken a step forward to volunteer to tend to Selenia himself when Felix shook his head. "Your room is ready, and I am sure that you will find your girl awaiting your every desire. See that you are bathed and prepared for tonight. I have invited guests to meet you, the elite of Velletri and some of the finest entertainment that could be devised."

He waved his hand dismissively to them all and turned to the desk spread wide with papers that he needed to deal with before the night's festivities. Meridius then nodded to Violetta to get away as fast as she could without drawing attention to herself and moved to attend the master of the house.

Turning before she left the room Violetta eyes locked with Meridius. The hope that perhaps the lanista and his champion would be included by some miraculous blessing was in her eyes. Meridius thought perhaps he would be able to encourage the sending of the invitation if it had not already been sent. If he could find a way to help bring them together again he would. For even if it was just to lay eyes upon him and the chance to break words she would be forever grateful to him.

Hours later Violetta watched Felix Census survey the party as the family entered the hall flanked by a trio of body slaves behind them; Violetta, Meridius and the golden-skinned Maya that his daughter had brought to attend her. The slave of Selenia stood out among the pale Romans and Violetta could not help but admire the spirals of dark hair that flowed like a fountain from her head. The trio of slaves watched Felix smile at the scene displayed before them all; the elite of Velletri and some even from Rome itself drank and laughed under his roof. The room fell to silence as the host appeared and, taking the cup Violetta had quickly fetched, he raised his hand in a toast to them all "Hail friends, new and old, welcome to the house of Census. I offer humble gratitude for your attendance to celebrate my daughter Selenia's visit to Velletri. I invite you to eat, drink and celebrate for the joy of my household standing complete once again fills me with such happiness that I am certain the gods themselves stand in envy."

Violetta watched Felix' smile falter when Vitus noted aloud that the lanista was not yet among the guests nor was the gladiator he had requested present. If Tertius thought that he could avoid the return of favors owed, he would soon be brought to heel as had any other man who had ever thought to deny the senior Census his wish.

Listening eagerly when her Dominus instructed the captain of his house guard that he would give the man a little while yet to appear before he would send a party of men to provide escort to the event. He intended to have the fallen champion to impress his guests with or without his Dominus to control him. This meant that Violetta would have her heart's desire present, at least to fill her eyes if nothing else was possible.

After ensuring that both Felix and Vitus each had a full cup of wine Violetta slipped away to stand at the wall, taking the chance to scan the room while staying out of the reach and sight of the drunker Romans in the room. It would not be the first time she had been accosted by wandering hands and the lewd comments of men. They knew they were denied access to her before but this time it was different, this time she was not a virgin untouched and reserved from any man's taking.

This type of event was one of her darkest fears since returning from Cassian's arms; that she would be given over to a group of men to entertain so that Census could earn their favor or their business. She had seen other girls being used for the same thing and was not foolish enough to think that she was so special to him that he would pause before offering her if it would see coin to his purse.

The size of the party and the number of slaves brought to attend to the guests allowed Violetta a rare few moments of freedom to wander and observe those whom she was unfamiliar with, which was a larger number of the guests than she had expected. Stepping away from the wall she greeted those she knew with a soft smile and a nod while looking hopefully towards the entry for the household of Tertius to enter.

Suddenly it felt as though she were being watched with a deep scrutiny, looking up she found herself eye to eye with Selenia, the Roman woman's eyes watching her as a cat observing a mouse before pouncing upon the unsuspecting prey. The girl was just about to turn and find a place to hide from her when the woman rose and began to make her way towards her in a straight line that left no room for escape.

Violetta could feel her gaze follow her as she moved around the room, her timid movements seeming to be of much greater interest than the familiar bawdy jokes of her father and brother. How was it that though she was just a slave she somehow captivated the Romans around her? The thought turned in her mind before she looked up to find Selenia closing in on her with a seductively devious smile on her bright red lips. Frozen in fear she watched the older woman pause at the table to take a plate of fruits and to have the cup of wine in her hand refilled before she finally cornered Violetta against the wall, her eyes cast to the floor and her hands clasped in front of her.

"Well now, little one, at last I find you unencumbered by my father and brother, so I have you all to myself. Is that not a lovely thing? Hmm?" As if she was attempting to calm a wild creature, Selenia took a grape from her plate and held it against Violetta's lips but the girl did not move. "Eat, it is alright. I want you to." She said with the same smile.

When her lips parted to allow the grape into her mouth Selenia let the tip of her finger linger for a moment before licking the trace of juice from it. Fighting to repress a shudder, Violetta thanked the gods silently for the last-minute command from Felix that his children not create a scene that would cause gossip. He especially commanded Selenia to avoid pursuing her 'feminine attractions' while in his house as it made attempting to find her a husband an even harder task than it already was proving to be.

"Take some wine too." She said eagerly, tucking a strand of Violetta's long dark hair behind her ear. She was blushing red at being singled out in the room and could feel the eyes of some of those around them starting to watch. "You may not know me but soon enough I expect that we will know each other very well indeed. If you please me, you will have no reason to fear me. Would you like this?" It was not as much a question as it was a command but still, she stared into her face, waiting for an answer.

Violetta had no idea how to react. The woman seemed kind but there was no doubt that had Violetta even tried to refuse there would have been consequences beyond what she could imagine. "Gratitude Domina." She whispered, sipping the rich wine and trying not to cough as it burned her throat. She was dangerous. This was dangerous. Vitus was watching and as he had already been told by his father that she was to be his for a time she could not risk any more of his anger.

The grape was sweet, and it was tempting to believe her kindness was just that, but she was of the family of Census and Violetta could guess what Selenia wanted from her. The angry look on Vitus' face and the satisfied smirk on his sisters told her that she was right; she was being used as a pawn between them. The sudden furrow in Vitus's brow and the way he leaned to whisper to his father made her pause and almost drop the cup. "Apologies, I must go and see to your father's wine, Domina. He is insistent that I attend to him promptly."

She did not wait for permission but ducked around Selenia to almost run so she could fill the cups of Felix and Vitus, flinching as the son ran his hand possessively down her back. Taking no chances that his sister might call his new 'toy' away Vitus kept her by his side until he sat to discuss certain theories of obedience with a few of the men his age. He then drew her down to sit at his feet as though a loyal dog while his fingers played in her hair, caressing then pulling just to hear her whimper of pain while she held his cup.

Violetta became so caught up in trying to anticipate the next tug that she did not hear the lanista announced but when the crowd moved she saw him. Her gladiator was standing behind his masters with the torchlight glimmering across the perfectly defined muscles of his chest. Her breath caught in a gasp that caused all the heads of the men around her to turn to see what everyone else was talking about.

She could hardly breath watching him walk through the hall. With the crowd pressing in close to him it would be almost impossible for Cassian to see her, but she could not help but stare. Tertius and his wife were dressed in finery. He was in a crisp white toga and she in a rich copper-coloured silk gown with emeralds in her hair, ears and around her neck. To most they would have been an eye-catching couple, admired by all present, but it was the man who came behind them stole the attention of the entire room; Cassian, champion of the city and an Adonis in the flickering light of candles and torches.

His hardened muscles looked as though they had been carved for a temple in the likeness of the gods themselves, the oil on his flesh giving off a shine that was almost divine, but the perfect mask of his face kept the hatred and anger she knew he felt for Romans well hidden. He did not speak or acknowledge those around him but stopped where he was told to when they had reached the center of the hall. His eyes on the ground Violetta could tell his body was full of tension. She wondered if he remembered that this was the home of her Dominus? Was he as eager to see her as she was to see him or was she just one of many happy nights in bed that held neither face nor name of importance?

Felix made his way through the crowd to greet the lanista, a friendly smile on his face as he embraced the man.

"You have come late, my friend. I was beginning to think you had decided to refuse the invitation." His voice hinted at the danger that would have come with refusal, but he then turned his attention to the lanista's wife and smiled again. "But at least you have brought one of the jewels of Velletri with you to make up for the delay."

He placed a kiss on the beautiful woman's cheek before turning his attention to the gladiator that had stopped almost all the conversation in the room.

"I see you have made up for your delay with grand style though. It is an exquisite pleasure to be in the presence of this magnificent creature in all his glory." He let a hand trace across the broad muscled chest up the tense cords of his neck to cup his jaw, turning Cassian's head so that their eyes met.

"I trust you enjoyed the sweet gift I sent for your use, champion." He asked loudly, his voice filled with amusement at the hardness in the younger man's eyes. "Was she a good little fuck for you?" He was taunting the warrior, and everyone knew it.

Violetta's eyes widened in shock, her cheeks and ears burning with shame as Vitus turned to look at her.

Left beside Meridius while their masters moved to inspect their latest entertainment, Violetta took the older man's hand in her own, seeking comfort from the fear and shame the night was bringing to her. Though she was certain that he had feared her being given to Selenia as an amusement for the days she was within the villa, it was beginning to look like there could be worse things waiting at the hands of their masters if Felix was in the mood to cause a scene. The pain of hearing Cassian asked about their night together as though it was nothing of consequence was worse than her fear of the sexual games of the woman. Lifting her eyes to find those of the champion she found no comfort in his expressionless mask.

She could see his hands clenched in fists, it was the only outward sign that he felt anything at all, but it gave Violetta some hope that Cassian felt outrage where she felt fear and shame. They had called him a 'creature' but if he had been standing in the arena with blades in his hands, the ability to strike his own decision to make, there was not a man in the room that would have dared insult him and well she knew it.

Meeting the questioning gaze of her Dominus for a moment the gladiator turned his face to Tertius, seeking permission to answer, when the lanista nodded with a grin he answered.

"She was indeed a pleasure, as all women can be. You have my gratitude, Dominus." He cast a fleeting look around the room, avoiding her gaze, before returning his head to its lowered position of obedience.

Violetta's face fell and she felt as though her heart would shatter when he spoke of what they had shared as though it were nothing but a few moments of pleasure when it had shaken her world in a way she struggled to find words for.

Felix laughed heartily and tossed his arm across the broad but tense shoulders of the gladiator as he leaned close, pretending to whisper in his ear but instead speaking clearly so anyone could hear. "She is a sweet little thing, so soft and warm in my bed each night." With a taunting smirk he beckoned his son to attend him instead of sitting while the rest of the company had gathered around the gladiator. "Vitus come and see the fantastic delight our friend has brought to add to the night's entertainment."

Violetta could hear the laughter in his voice even though she had her eyes once again pointed down to the floor. Her shame was complete. With her former lover's words she knew there was nothing for her in his arms but rejection. How they would have laughed if they knew her thoughts, her hope that she had meant something to him. When her master called his son to his side, she knew that she would have to follow even though it would mean facing this growing nightmare.

Following Vitus as he rose to answer the call of his father Violetta found that her hands were shaking and that her heart thundered in her chest. Would he even recognize her? What if he had already forgotten her face since she meant so little to him? Standing just behind Vitus and Selenia, who had moved to join her family while they inspected the new amusement, she let the breath slip from her lungs and dared to raise her eyes to meet those of the gladiator. Not sure what she would see there, the girl prayed for at least some shadow of recognition while the Romans spoke around him as if he was not a person but a statue. If there was nothing in his eyes that spoke of recognition she felt as though her heart might break into a thousand pieces more than it already threatened to.

Her breath caught in her chest where their eyes met. His were warm with not only recognition but an eager excitement that sent a rush to her heart. Had he meant what he said or was it just words to silence the Romans? Was it possible that he remembered her with enough fondness that she should dare to risk speaking to him again? The beginning of a smile reached her lips, growing broader each time she dared to raise her eyes to look at him

Pulling Violetta's attention from Cassian, Vitus stepped towards the gladiator sipping his wine and circling the statuesque slave standing before him. No one, even the man who hated him, could deny Cassian was a glorious specimen of a man; well-muscled and with the face of a god. Violetta knew Vitus' thoughts about the champion were less than flattering. He thought the champion was a savage, beautiful for his kind but a mindless savage nonetheless.

"So, this is the invincible Lord of the Sands?" He smirked and smacked his lips as though tasting the air around him before a bored expression fell on his face that Violetta and the other slaves knew to be dangerous. When he wore this expression, it was usually followed by a violent outburst, the last recipient of which was still recovering from his wounds.

"I have yet to see his equal, though he is uglier than I thought. I am sure he is worth the coin you have invested which from what I hear is more than you can afford." He arched a brow at his father and left to return to his conversation leaving his sister, Meridius and Violetta with the gladiator and his father's dwindling attention.

Turning to look at Selenia, Violetta found the woman was staring at Cassian with amazement in her eyes. A surge of jealousy tightened her jaw when she saw Selenia brushing her fingers across his chest before she asked breathily. "Does this... divine beast have a name, or shall I just create one?" Violetta's eyes fell to the floor to hide her anger. With her head down most of those around her would not notice that she was barely breathing, and her eyes kept returning to the face of the man who had noticed that she was there but gave no acknowledgment of her presence yet.

When Felix reached out once again to grip the gladiator by the shoulder Violetta watched Cassian flinch under the hold. "This, my dear daughter, gathered friends, is Otho Carius, once called Cassian, the greatest gladiator to grace the sands of Velletri and, apparently, the most expensive." His tone was mocking as he stepped away to join the other Romans that had gathered to see the impressive gladiator. Since he did not hold blades and was yet fully clothed there was little to maintain their excitement, so they turned and walked away as though he and Violetta were nothing more than dust on the floor.

Violetta shuddered in a mix of revulsion, worry and relief when Selenia stepped past her in pursuit of other desires. The woman looked to Meridius and beckoned him with a curl of her finger to follow her into an alcove. Violetta knew he would be commanded to service her needs in private so that Selenia was not chided by her father for her lust and could return to her other pursuits without distraction. The other Roman men and women resumed their discussions but as Meridius left to join Selenia in a chamber not far off the hall his eyes briefly met Violetta's and flickered to the gladiator with a frown as though he did not trust the man not to hurt her even standing in a room full of people.

CHAPTER 5

Cassian wanted to laugh. The stupidity of the son of Census was baffling to him. He had earned the title of champion many times over with glorious victories, blood and other tasks done to completion, no matter how distasteful. A single defeat might have cost him the official title within the city, but he knew who he was, and the loss did not change that.

He had to force his hands not to curl into fists again. The desire to answer the man with pain was stronger than he had felt in years. Sweat rolled down his forehead and his lips twitched to give voice to his thoughts regarding being put to the same tasks and taunting words of nobility without the title of champion that had made it bearable in the past. Every breath he drew here was a mockery. He had to wonder if Tertius had known this would be the plan when he brought him here.

He had been about to slip behind the mental mask that would separate him from all that was around him when he saw her standing still as the departing Romans moved around her, she was completely still, like an island in the sea of enemies. Her beauty sent his heart racing and his breath froze in his chest. She was even more lovely than the last time he had seen her. All else fell away from his thoughts but that she was there, seeing him in the falseness of a title that was no longer his and a name not his own.

Cassian felt his tension grow as the Romans cleared away. Would she remember him with pleasure or fear? He prayed she could see that he had lied to her Dominus when he said she had been nothing more than another body to warm his bed for a time. The voices of the crowd grew dull like the buzz of insects in another room and he found that they were both staring. All the words he had wanted to say slipped from his mind when their eyes met. He was left, laughably. dumbstruck and silent for moments that seemed to stretch into years.

Finally, she took a small step towards him and whispered his name softly so that none could hear her except him.

"Cassian?"

The shake of his head was all but imperceptible, but his voice held a gentle warning to her as he whispered.

"That is no longer my name. I am nothing but the ghost of a champion here tonight. Call me Otho in their hearing."

He could feel the smile in his eyes and dared to let the corners of his lips lift a little with the simple joy of seeing her again. She was a fire in his blood and a drug to his senses. He had to fight every instinct he had so that he did not pull her into his arms then and there. His entire body strained with the need but instead he replied to her whispered words.

"The gods seem to favor me. I had held hope to see you this night and here you stand, the answer to prayers unuttered."

She seemed smaller than he remembered or perhaps it was this place and those around them that caused her to shrink. As though a woman of her rare beauty could hide in this room full of common nobility.

She nodded at the reminder of the name that he would be addressed by until he regained his title. Taking one step closer to him Violetta whispered.

"You do have some memory of me then?"

He nodded, still staring. He wanted to reach out and touch her, take her tiny hand in his so that he could ease the trepidation in her eyes, but too many would see it and the risk would be too great and so instead of a touch he gave her slightest of nods with a brief half smile.

"You are recovering well? Your fever did not leave you with a lasting deficit?"

It was a question innocent enough that it would not attract the attention of anyone that happened to be listening but the look in her eyes and the way that they met his spoke volumes.

"When will you take the sands again for your title's return?"

Anyone that had bothered to watch could tell that there was something more than idle curiosity in the question. The danger of discovery grew with each second, but he could not help prolonging this meeting. Who could tell when another chance would come?

He was surprised. How did she know he had been ill? Had he given himself away when she was in his arms? If he had shown weakness in bed with her it would be a blow to his pride that he did not know if he could recover from. Tonight, there would be no trace of imperfection as Tertius had seen that the utmost care had been taken to hide the bruising with armored coverings on his legs instead of just the linen subligaria. "I will regain the title at the next games, by command of my Dominus and the coin of a man who's name I do not know or care to."

The gladiator searched the face of the girl staring adoringly up at him, the shadows on her face showed the marks of slavery and its strain upon body and soul. He wondered if she would break under its weight or was she strong enough to bear it?

She was so agonizingly beautiful that it hurt, almost as much as the look of complete fear in her eyes. He needed to touch her, hold her close to his body and feel the warmth of her skin against him in the heated ecstasy of their joining.

The memory of her beneath him, around him, sent a flashing bolt of desire through every nerve but against the scream of instinct to pull her from the room and seduce her to his arms he answered in a hushed voice that did not entirely hide his desire. "It is memory of you that aids recovery and the will to push through lingering effects."

"Memory of me? Truly?" A soft smile lifted the edges of her lips when he spoke, and he wanted to make her smile even more. Before either of them could say more, across the room, they both saw Vitus strike the cheek of the girl Maya from Rome who had spilled food onto the table beside him. He watched her hand rise to her own cheek, flinching at the memory of that same touch but when she looked back at him, she smiled, perhaps to let him know that his touch to her cheek was the memory that proved to be more powerful.

She smiled again before speaking in a hushed voice so that no one would overhear "When I saw you fall in the arena; I thought my heart would stop. I... I feared for your life. Though we did not yet then know each other as we do now it is something that haunts dreams." Her gaze slid shyly to the ground and he wondered then if she had heard his words to Census and thought them to be true.

The Romans around them seemed to forget the presence of the champion once the wine and food was served and so when their backs were turned and she moved to stand beside him he dared, ever so briefly, to brush the back of his hand to hers the need for contact so strong that he dared the discovery just to touch her and feel the heat of her skin for a breath.

There was no need for pretending with her. He could be Cassian, not the gladiator or even the prince. She had no expectation of glory, of the 'champion', but just a man who found himself wanting her more than he wanted his next breath and that made him nervous.

The boldness of their touch even in the room of Romans was pure excitement and thrill. He could feel the blood pooling in his lower body leaving him hot and heavy, ready to toss aside reason and care. The need for her was burning inside him like a fire but he could do nothing, not even let her know how much he felt.

"You attended the games the day we met? Apologies for your need to witness my failure." The glare of the younger Census was enough to give him the pause he needed against pursuing his desire, but he could not help the tender smile that met her stare.

She shook her head softly.

"I have yet to see your failure Otho." She said as her knuckles touched the back of his hand in a sweet and innocent contact once again. "What I saw was a man pushed to fight too soon after an illness. Is that not closer to the truth?" There was a faith in her eyes that stirred his pride. He wanted, more than anything in that moment, to be worthy of the adoration she placed upon him.

"It should never have been seen, what happened in that arena, by your eyes or any others. I have no excuse and will not offer one. I will simply say that in my next fight I shall stand victorious or never stand again." He did not have the chance to say that he had sworn an oath to that end because the lanista Tertius shot a look of warning to stand silent before he had to be commanded to it. The man must have caught sight of their interaction but he still offered a smile to Violetta before returning his gaze forward.

Inhaling deeply, Cassian caught her scent, the one that had haunted him since he had held her the first time. It was beautiful, subtle and an intoxicating floral mist over his senses, driving him to the edge of madness with the wish to have it all around him, under him and mixing with his own. "I hope you are not there to see, if the violence frightens you."

Her eyes shone up at him with emotions swirling in the brilliant blue. His lips ached to show her with more than words how much her faith in his ability meant to him. He wished that it was possible for Tertius to purchase her from the merchant. Maybe it was? If he impressed upon his Dominus how the girl inspired him to fight, to kill and to strive for the glory of championship again then the man would be a fool to not at least attempt to see her brought to the ludus

. He was about to whisper his idea to the woman at his side when she spoke again instead.

"Then I will pray for glory. I fear your death is a thing I could not recover from." The words were barely from her mouth when the summons he had feared came from Vitus. She left his side with a sigh to refill the Roman's wine and sit again at his feet with her eyes stealing glances towards him as often as she dared.

Vitus' eyes lit with amusement as he watched the girl leave his side and Cassian knew that, from that moment on, there would be eternal enmity between them. When Violetta sat obediently at the Roman's feet, he had to watch as he let his hand wander over the milk white skin of her shoulder. He was playing with the ties of her dress not caring if it came untied or simply fell. Cassian wondered how he would react if it did? Would he be able to contain his rage, or would it be his undoing?

He noticed that the Roman woman, the female Census, was staring with a similar intensity to his own. There was no worry for the girl in the gaze, instead it was an angry possessiveness that worried him even more. Was there no one in this house that would look out for her? Did his woman stand alone amid the monsters that possessed her? Fury flooded through him when Vitus nudged the fabric to the curve of her shoulder and he could see her shaking; waiting for the humiliation but the man stopped, to the visible disappointment of his friends, and took a grape from the table.

Biting it in half he let some of the juice drip down onto Violetta's shoulder then leaned over to lick the fluid from her skin. The Romans laughed collectively at the shudder she could not repress. The delight they took in introducing innocents to the depravity of the true nature of those that called themselves masters was sickening to him and he hoped that he would be afforded the chance to ease the fear this was surely causing Violetta.

Over ten years as a showpiece and, if enough coin was exchanged, a plaything of the most elite of Velletri Cassian had mastered the ability to hide his true emotions and disconnect himself from the agony and humiliation that was intended to accompany it. Trying to catch her eye he could only hope that she knew that if he were free to act without risking her safety, if their shared slavery did not stop his hands, he would never allow her torment.

He let his mind dream briefly of what he would do if the other slaves around him suddenly surged in a violent rebellion like the legend of the Thracian Spartacus years ago in Capua. Such things were dangerous even in thought so he set them aside, giving way to the thoughts of how he would soothe Violetta if he had the chance.

As if the mockery and touch of Vitus were not enough for Violetta to stand and for Cassian to bear witness to, Selenia joined the crowd once again, smiling sweetly as she crossed the room leaving the tall bulk of a male slave to follow her and attend her father. Taking a seat beside Vitus, Cassian watched as she reached a hand to stroke the dark glossy hair that hung down the Violetta's back and looked up to meet the gladiator's eyes with a silent challenge, daring him to react as she scratched her mark into the shoulder bared by Vitus' games.

Cassian watched the woman beneath hooded eyes. She was no different than her father or brother. The dangerous lust in her eyes was not just for the body but for dominion over the very soul of her target. The tension that gripped him when she dared the gladiator to react with her eyes made him lower his gaze quickly. He was not afraid of her and he would never bow to her will, but if he had held the stare it would have meant a challenge between them that he was not free to meet.

He almost shivered at the ravenous hunger of a predator that was in those cold dark eyes, insatiable in its perversion and so very Roman. The last thing he wanted was to leave Violetta in this house, but there was no clear way to see her removed tonight. She belonged to the monster and though there was some hope that he would be able to convince his Dominus to purchase her just to ease the mind of his fallen champion it would not be accomplished tonight.

He choked back a groan of discomfort, his face never breaking from its mask of composure. God's he needed some relief from the standing for the stillness required brought a pain to the ache in his body that might send him toppling to his knees despite his best efforts. When he looked up it was not the daughter that met his eyes but Felix Census himself with a smile that chilled his blood.

Looking from the champion to the lanista Felix issued a command disguised as a request. "Good Tertius, summon your man. I would see the pallor of little Violetta's skin against the golden stone of the gladiator." He stood unsteadily "Come pose us a pretty picture to gaze upon while we dine." He waved a hand towards the oval decorative pool in the center of the room. It was only a few inches deep and likely was not overly warm, but it might as well have been an ocean for all the danger it might hold for Cassian at the hands of a drunken Roman.

Cassian did not move but looked towards his Dominus and his wife who both looked as shocked as he felt at the request. Was the man serious? A part of him thrilled at the idea of being close to her but how would Violetta feel displayed and exposed before the crowd? He fought the urge to shake his head, but this was not the house of Tertius and of late, he held less sway than he was used to with his master and it would remain so until the title was once again his.

For a moment he had hope that his Dominus would refuse but when Lycithia smiled and set down the cup of wine in her hand he knew that neither man had the chance of having their way for she would have hers, despite any and all protest. Pressing his eyes closed he sighed and prepared for the command that would come.

"Otho attend!" She called, closing her hand over her husbands with a smug, catlike smile, her voice musical while commanding the champion staring at her. "Good Felix would see you displayed before us." His movement at her summons broadened her smile. She enjoyed the thrill of power that came with commanding the gladiators more than anyone he had met, even her husband who had the profession in his blood for generations.

With a breath he opened his eyes, watching his Domina's face Cassian could not understand the command coming from her. Lycithia was not one who had ever enjoyed having the champion gladiator of her house teased and tormented in this manner. She knew better than most what he had been through for the amusement of others.

When he stepped to obey her command, he could feel all the eyes in the room turn to watch as he seethed with each step. The oil made his suntanned skin look more like cast bronze as he approached the pool and the people surrounding it but that did not matter. What was worth was appearing a god when the truth was laughably opposite. When he stood in the middle of the room, just barely out of Lycithia's reach, she pointed towards the pool. "Into the water, as he directs you." Her tone was a warning that was as unneeded as it was mocking. The man would not risk the humiliation or violence that would come with disobedience.

Cassian stepped into the still water of the pool and though he knew it was warm the look on Vitus's face, a desperate hunger, made his blood turn to ice and the champion fought a shiver from the sudden chill. In his own house such things might happen but Tertius was not a man to abuse his slaves for amusement. His wife was a kinder woman who often took the younger female slaves under her protection form the lechery of her countrymen until they came of an age deemed proper. The fearful resignation on Violetta's face told him that Selenia was not so kind and that it had been some time since anyone had raised hand or voice against the torment delivered at the hands of the masters of this house.

"Kneel." Was the command from Felix that broke his thoughts. Following a glare of warning from the lanista Cassian sank to his knees the water quickly soaking the quilted material that covered his legs. He looked to Felix, curious what he would command next in this strange play of power and dominion.

"Violetta, my little flower, come and complete my vision." He snapped his fingers to summon her from where she had become hidden from Cassian's view by the sudden press of Romans around the pool. "Let us have a goddess to the arena's god to pray to." He guided her into the water to stand before Cassian. As soon as her foot touched the pool it was like a liquid fire in his veins.

Felix led Violetta to stand mere inches away from Cassian. He had to hold his breath as she was posed to stand looking down over her shoulder at him with her left hand extended as though to invite his adoration. The Roman then took Cassian's hands, he had to force himself not to physically recoil from the touch but when his palms were placed at rest on Violetta's hips in a pose of pleading embrace. The look of adoration on his face was not forced but came easily as did his silent pleading that she open her eyes that were demurely hooded so that it was impossible for him to see the sparkling blue that he knew would mirror the spark of desire that he had felt since laying eyes on her that night.

He barely noticed that the Roman had stepped clear of the water, vainly declaring himself a great artist as he left the pair of slaves behind him. That was when Cassian's personal goddess opened her eyes to stare deeply into his. When their gazes locked his world shifted and he lost himself in the oceanic blue. He could feel his fingers tighten on her flesh as a hunger built in the depths of his soul. He wanted her. More than he wanted to rise from his knees in the water he wanted to taste her kiss and feel her melt against him.

The elite of the city chattered around them but there was no word that he heard, even his name, while she stared down into his eyes. His breath stilled in his chest while his heart thundered so loudly. He swore she had to hear it and yet she gave no sign of it. Violetta was so still he could not help but wonder if she was affected by this forced nearness. Despite her curiosity, was she afraid of him or immune to their proximity? Her blank expression made him question himself for the first time in years. Had what they shared simply made her, at last, available to a lover here? Was he a fool to think that he might hold a place in her heart after that night together?

Finally, a subtle smile lifted her lips and Cassian felt a wave of relief wash over him when the hand Felix had outstretched to accept his adoring worship lowered to cup his jaw and the soft pad of her thumb stroked his cheek.

Releasing the breath he had been holding as a soft sigh Cassian relaxed in her hand. No matter what the rest of the night brought at the hands and command of her drunken master or his son with the smile of a sadist, he would hold this moment as a treasure. The way she looked at him stirred something so long forgotten he did not recognize it at first. It was softness in the middle of the stone walls of indifference he had spent his slavery building in his heart. It was warm and tender. Fiercely protective of her safety and jealous of the thought that there could be another man she cared for when he wished for all her affections. His eyes widened at the realization; it was love. New and barely budding but pure and true all the same.

There was a beautiful expression on her face. Cassian did not know how she was able to be so serene in the company of so many Romans. They were not subtle about their interest in the scene that Felix had created in the shallow water, but he was grateful at least that, so far, none of them had reached out a hand to touch either body. He prayed that he would not have to watch them molest her, he wasn't sure that he would be able to tolerate it in the light of newly discovered emotions.

Perhaps if they stayed still the drunken Roman's would lose interest in them for a time and they could take a moment to breathe and perhaps exchange a word or two. He swore that if there was a chance, if they were left alone, he would kiss her and erase any doubt between them both of just how strong the attraction he felt was. He would discover if what he felt burning to life in his heart was shared or if he once again would find himself a fool in love with a woman who had no real care for him at all.

He realized Violetta's expression had changed to a fearful panic and the soft rhythm of her thumb stroking his cheek had paused. Worry for the cause brought him to realize that it was a reaction to his own expression which had shifted into a scowl of anger at the memory of his previous folly. He proved himself right when his playful wink and sudden smile were met with a sudden blush to her cheeks as she looked away to the room and then back to him.

Cassian thrilled with pride at the immediate response such a simple flirtation brought. He wondered what it would take to make her entire body flush that same pretty shade of pink. What it would take to make her laugh? He cursed the fates that had placed her in a house so far from his own. He wanted to court her, to show her the worth he held her with. He wanted to champion her awakening, then guide her through the exploration of her sensuality before seducing her body and soul with his own.

He was so busy dreaming how he would make her his, how he would convince her to fall as deeply as for him as he felt himself falling for her, that he did not notice the room had cleared. It was the cough at the door as Meridius closed it behind the departing crowd that seemed to be following Felix out to the garden that had alerted him to their sudden privacy. Cassian smiled broadly and sat back to start at her, uncertain as to what words to break first.

CHAPTER 6

Selenia had risen with the rest of the guests to follow her father out to the balcony overlooking the paddock, but it was not his horses that she was interested in. Stepping close to her brother she pulled him aside as the rest of the company stood at the rail, eager to see the animals. "Vitus, brother dear." She cooed in his ear. "You have something that I want, and I think you know it." She sipped the wine in her hand and watched him carefully. Vitus always played mind games and there was a price to pay, but if she played just as well, they usually both got what they wanted from the situation.

A slow smile spread across his face at her words. He would know exactly what she wanted; Violetta. The only question was what she would have to do or give in order to get her? Though it was not likely he would let her keep the lovely girl as a toy, there were several days before Selenia would be collected to return to Rome and this city had always been dull. She wanted something to keep her occupied.

"What is it that I have, sweet sister, that you could want so badly?" He briefly scanned the girl, Maya, that lingered at Selenia's heel as though she held his interest with her exotically golden skin and spiraled hair but then returned his attention to her. He held up the plate of fruit he had brought from the villa. "Something from the table perhaps?"

Taking a piece from the plate, she returned the smirk and nodded as she bit. "Yes, something from the table, just a little something." The game for the girl had begun and now she was certain that she would have her. It may not be tonight but the next would find Violetta in her room as night fell. Watching the crowd marvel over the horses she leaned close to her brother. "The girl, she is a fresh little innocent. I want to play with her before you ruin her completely with your ways."

Selenia had seen what happened when Vitus was given free rein with a slave. They lived, usually, and returned to their work but they were never the same. It was as if he broke something inside them with his games and tools that he called 'toys'. "How long have you had her? I would not think long, she still has an air of hope about her."

Vitus chuckled and nodded. "She is indeed new to me but has been fathers for some years though untouched up until the most recent weeks. To my deep displeasure I assure you. The animal in the pool with her is the one who she was given to for deflowering. He did a job almost as good as I would have done myself." He described to Selenia how she looked when she returned from the ludus; a bloodied lip and a deep bruise rising on her cheek, fear had radiated off her that would have sent blood rushing through them both with desire.

Selenia thought about how she was back there with the monster of a man now. Surely she was trembling in terror that she was being forced to pose with him touching her. She would smell of fear when they returned and Selenia knew that when she took her to bed, it would be new to her, but she would make sure that she felt no fear. If she was afraid of men, it would not be hard to turn her interests elsewhere just as she had a few other slaves in Rome.

"She is a sweet little thing is she not? Naïve but that will change soon enough." Vitus said in a voice that told his sister how his mind spun with the wicked ways he would play with what innocence remained in Violetta.

Selenia almost shuddered at the look in her brother's eyes. It was as cruel and demented as she knew him to be deep in his soul, if he had one. She knew him well enough to pity the fact that the little beauty would soon be just another one of her brother's broken and discarded conquests. "Then, dear brother, let me have a little fun with her before I return to Rome." She smirked and stared down at their father. "I am sure there is something from our father that I can see done for you."

They began to whisper to each other, bartering back and forth with offers and counter offers until an agreement was reached that saw them both satisfied and Violetta's fate was decided by those that would be her masters. "I look forward to it, dear brother." Selenia said and moved away towards a merchant who had caught her eye earlier, he was rumored to be in favor of several senators including Titus Claudius. It would be a good match if his interests could be piqued and he was a man weak enough that she could easily see him controlled.

Coming back to the gift of the present solitude the Cassian smiled broadly. "Violetta?" He whispered, staring up at her while his hands tightened at her hips. "You stand a true goddess in my eyes, but my worship might bring offence if I were to offer it in the manner I desire most."

His words brought him the reward that he wished. She smiled, so brightly it stopped his heart in his chest, and softly replied, her voice still barely more than a whisper. "Cassian? If I stood as such how could I refuse worship from such a man as you?" The colour on her cheeks deepened when she asked. "What gesture is it that you offer as such?"

She asked the question with such innocence he paused before giving the answer. The last thing he wanted to do was frighten her, but since he had begun he could not stop now. "You would allow me such liberty? Would you be my priestess if you refuse the title of goddess?"

She nodded slowly, staring down at him as though she was mesmerized by his words. He intended to take full advantage of their solitude and rose to his feet. Her hand fell from his cheek at the same moment that his rose to cup her own. Her skin was as soft as he remembered the petals of flowers to be and she leaned into his touch with a smile lighting her face. The flames of the candles about the room gave her a soft, but divine, glow that sealed his decision as though he had no choice.

Stilling her from a possible flight by resting his free hand upon her hip Cassian lowered his head to gently press his lips to kiss her. It was bliss, she was so delicate and warm in his arms. She leaned against him while his hand slid around her waist pulling her tight to his frame and the one at her face slipped into the pinned curls of her hair.

She moaned breathily as his lips moved across her jaw and then down her neck. He could feel her breasts crush against his chest through the thin fabric of the dress she was wearing and suddenly all he wanted was to tear the fabric from her body and sheath himself in her, making waves within the shallow water they stood in. Their bodies would churn the basin into a tempest, and he would bring her to a shattering climax with their cries filling the air.

"They will not be gone long." She whispered in his ear before lighting kisses down the tense muscles of his neck. Her kiss was a delight, but her words cut through his illusion that they had the time to do as he desired, as he was certain she desired too. It was impossible for him to ignore the responses in her body that matched his own. The way she pressed herself close even once he removed his hand from her waist up to slowly inch the fabric of her dress off her shoulder, exposing herself to him in agonizing increments that thrilled him at her allowance of his exploration.

His blood was thundering in his veins and her body was warm and flushed to the touch. How could he stop the spiral they had entered? The Romans had left the room not long ago, surely they had some time in which to share a few more moments together, a few deeper kisses and intimate touches. Cassian smiled and kissed her again.

"Shh priestess. I am at prayer, fully devoted to your worship." With his eyes locked to her he finished sliding the dress off her shoulders. His breath was a swift intake as the light, reflecting off the water, illuminated her upper body beautifully. The affectionate nickname of 'priestess' would certainly never be inadequate to describe the woman standing before him.

"Cassian..." She moaned beautifully for him when his hands eagerly cupped his newly exposed idols. He smiled and shook his head, trying not to laugh when she continued "It is an affront to the gods to compare a lowly mortal to their divinity?"

The concern in her face was so strong that he wondered if this was a woman that had been meant for the temples before she had been sent to him. "The goddesses of my people would be honored to have you stand among them when they descend to walk with men and beasts in the light of a Beltane fire." He growled before replacing a hand with his mouth and tongue, eagerly lapping each bud in turn while Violetta squirmed in his hands.

"So, are you a glorified gladiator, a god of the arena, or a savage Celt of the north? The likes of whom tales are told of their uninhibited passions in bed as well as with their blades?" She asked with a look of breathless wonder in her eyes that made him want to play the part, but not tonight.

"I am all these things and many others little priestess." He murmured, kissing down the soft plane of her stomach while pushing the light linen further down. Her soft giggle sent a surge of pride coupled with desire bolting through him. It was a beautiful sound and he wanted to hear it again and again until it blossomed into a full laugh.

He eased the fabric over the curve of her hips, ready to let it fall to the water he knelt in once again when Violetta reached to catch it.

"We cannot! If it is wetted by the water then they will know, Felix will know, and if he does it will be an unholy wrath that he rains down upon us both."

He caught the fabric, letting it leave his goal covered with just the hint of the dark curls peeking at its edge.

"I would not have you risked for the pursuit of passion Violetta, but neither would I have passion halted by fear when there is still time for us to be together. I would not let such a chance pass us by." He gazed up at her and teased the tip of his fingers up her inner thigh. "Will you trust me to keep you safe? Will you hold faith in me?"

He lifted the material to rest atop his head, leaving him out of her sight but in sight of the object of his lusting desire. Above the skirt of the dress Violetta's hands rested on his shoulders but not to stop him. The encouraging squeeze of her hands was all he needed to begin his sensual plundering. Nuzzling between her creamy thighs he blew hot breath upon her before sweeping her with his tongue.

Cassian smiled when her knees trembled at the first touch and let his hands slide down her legs to assure her that he would not let her fall into the water. Delving deeper she moaned, hot and breathy, making him wish he could see her face once again while he brought her nearer to the edge of release with each clever stroke. Her taste was like honey, pure and untainted by wine or fruits just as she was pure and divinely his.

He devoured her, knowing that she fought to stay on her feet and wishing that he could lay her down, on the floor or upon a proper bed, he did not care but the fire of lust coupled with the spark of newly realized affection was almost more than even he could stand.

When he sensed that she could stand no more he lifted the material back over his head and let it fall against her quivering knees as he kissed his way back up her stomach. Bringing the straps of the dress with him as he sadly covered the body he was beginning to think of as a treasure. He finally reached her lips with a growl of unsatisfied hunger.

He had seen the residual fear in her eyes and wanted to wipe it from her mind,even if it was only just for the remaining moments that they were alone. He would not press his luck much longer, but he had to taste more of her and could not find the strength to break the kiss. Her tongue played back against his, making him smile. He had high hopes for her scope for passion. Would she be the match for him that he thought her capable of being?

Her hands threaded into his hair suddenly and he dropped the fabric in his hand to wrap his arms around her, crushing her to his chest with a subdued roar of passionate need. "Violetta..." he hissed, opening his eyes just as they both realized the train of the dress had hit the water, soaking quickly as horror mirrored in both their expressions. "It was an accident. Fuck,do you think he will notice before it dries?" He asked, bending with her to help wring the water out of the dress and drape it back in place.

Gods help him she looked as though she were about to cry and had yet to speak of it. Would she rage or weep at his carelessness? Or would she try to blame herself for what was his fault? There was a sudden weight in his chest. That his pursuit could have just led to her being punished made him cringe inwardly.. In this house it was not likely to be similar to the strong words that he would have received from Tertius if they had been in the villa above the ludus. Had he, in his haste, destroyed something special that had just begun?

"Violetta?" His voice was a whisper, searching her face. "I will not let you carry the punishment for this, if there is one. I will take it on myself." He did not add that he did not know how he could manage to convince her master to direct his anger at him instead of the girl who was his property. The merchant would not likely be as easily swayed as Tertius by his words, but he had to try.

Tears were pooling in her eyes and his heart dropped to his stomach when she wrapped her arms around herself. It was not in imitation of a tender caress but to try and shield her body from what he could only imagine were the horrors of her memories.

"There is nothing now to be done unless it is to hope that his attention is kept elsewhere until the dress is dried." She told him in a hushed tone. "What drove us to such madness that the dress was forgotten?"

Her tone was full of confusion that played its innocence against his guilt.

"Something that the gods seem to have forbidden me from having. I would not risk your safety to have such again." It felt as though to say such a thing would kill him and yet his heart kept beating and his lungs filled with the air of the room, combining the incense of the roman's celebration with the sweetness of hers. It was a smell he would always remember.

"You have my apologies, little priestess, for my recklessness. It will not happen again." He said with a bow of his head to hide the heartache in his eyes.

"Cassian." He heard her gentle whisper but did not dare to look up and meet her eyes. The pain he might see there would be more than he could take. He had to start to steel himself against her. He must build walls to keep the blossoming affection hidden where it might grow in secret or die a slow and painful death along with his heart.

A soft hand touched his chin and raised his eyes slowly to meet the blue ones that implored him to answer for the hurt that shone at him behind the pooling tears. "It will not happen again? Do you truly have no care for me beyond sweet memories of tender moments gifted by Census?"

She thought he had no care for her? That she was just a memory of bedding to fade and be forgotten? He knew that was what they should be. That he should agree to her words though they might destroy him. He had to let her go for her own safety and yet he could not, would not. He wanted Tertius to attempt her purchase from Census so that she would be safe and under the protection that his favor might bring to her. He wanted her to be his, but would a heartbreak now at the earliest moments be better or worse than one later? After as many moments as they could squeeze from their masters?

Her question had given him hope that he was not alone in his feelings. Reaching out Cassian touched her cheek, holding back a smile when she leaned into his touch.

"Violetta, this could end your life and any chance of your long-lasting happiness. As a gladiator I could fall in any match and the last woman that I believed cared for me has been dead for five years now. Though I would never raise my hand against a woman, her death is on my head. The deed was not mine, but the fault is. I would not risk you to the same fate"

She blinked up at him and pulled away from his hand, instinctively protecting herself from his words and the hurt he knew they had to have delivered to her.

"You do not want me to care for you because you are worried that I may be hurt? Put to death by Felix? Or is it that you do not wish to feel encumbered by one who does not understand the world you live in?" She asked him in an accusatory tone.

How could she think that of him? That the night they had shared was just another night for him and that it meant nothing. Had his words convinced her of that or was there more at play against the sincerity of his actions?

Shame at his failure as well as the likely return of the Roman sent Cassian back to his knees. Now the pleading posture that Felix had placed him in held more truth than he wanted to admit. Seconds later he wished he had not thought the name for the man in question opened the door in return.

The Roman entered the room in advance of the others; his eyes fell upon the slaves positioned in the pool and his chuckle turned into the dark laugh of a devious drunk. It made Cassian shiver and think of all the things he could have done to her with that smile upon his face. Thoughts flooded his mind of what Felix might do now, some more terrifying than others. He could test their resolve, hers the fear of the man and his own to reign in his lust and anger. Would he position them in greater intimacy? Or perhaps a feat of strength and have him lift her and hold her in place above his head? Cassian could practically see the ideas forming in his head as he walked towards them and stopped at the edge of the pool.

He grazed his hands over them both, one to his neck and the other groping the shoulder of the girl standing before him. "What a pairing you would make in passionate embrace." He traced his tongue across his lips and swayed slightly, the effects of a night of wine evident. "I should have commanded her taking to be a display of your prowess before my eyes Cassian. Perhaps I will have it now? You inside her for all to see?"

His eyes glazed with lust at his own words, the desire for the man before him and the girl he knew all too well showing grotesquely in his eyes. Cassian prayed, for her sake and his sanity, that he would keep drinking for hours after the party so that he would not call her to his bed.

The gladiator was sure that Felix revelled in the fear he cultivated in Violetta, but he could not react. They both had to keep their façades in place. His was total detachment, sculpted of stone and iced indifference while hers was nervous, trembling in his worshiping hold. Cassian could tell she was trying not to give in to the panic that came with each touch of Felix' hand.

He hoped that there would be no more once the others began to enter the room. It was hard enough to keep still when it was a private moment but the company of so many others that might join in the torment in their own ways would make it near to impossible to keep from reacting in some way.

When another sound came from the doorway Cassian thought it might be the rest of the party but instead it was merely Vitus following his father. He watched as the man rolled his eyes at the way Felix enjoyed molesting slaves.

Though he could not see her face Cassian could feel the fear in Violetta's body and a quick peek revealed a smile that was deeply sadistic in nature on Vitus's face. The gladiator wondered if he could see that his father had now begun to send his fingers creeping over their exposed skin. If either man saw the protective need in Cassian's eyes, how long would it be before one or both of them started to use their feeling for each other as a weapon in the mind games they played?

Felix was obviously lost in the feel of the skin beneath his hands. The rough oiled skin of the gladiator beneath his right and pale softness of Violetta under his left hand. The contrast of the tanned and pale must have aroused him for as his hand wandered down her chest, moving lower to the damp edge of her skirt, the other moved to the beautiful braided hair of the champion where he twirled a loosened strand around his finger with a tug before beginning a crude verbal assault.

"Tell me, did she cry out beneath your invasions Gladiator? Did she plead for you to stop? Did she weep as she does beneath me? Or did you silence her as you took her?" By now his hand had reached the edge of Violetta's dress and his face showed a sudden surprise to find a dampness there. He must have made some expression of surprise because she froze in his hands.

She was terrified and Cassian could feel it in the speed of her pulse and tenseness of her body. It was a mercy that he had not lifted the material or slid his hand high enough to feel the evidence of the love he had made to her with his mouth. If he had found that dampness Cassian knew he would make a scene even bigger than the one they were already in. Looking up and around he could see that they were no longer alone with just her Dominus and his son yet there was no one to help her. Even Meridius who looked at Violetta with a face full of concern could do nothing to save her from whatever was about to happen. He realized with a deepening dread that the night had just flipped from stolen bliss to promised hell.

CHAPTER 7

Adrenaline rushed with the hatred flowing through Cassian's body, the two leading towards the loss of his composure. A man could only take so much, even in the bonds of slavery there had to be limits. His face remained stoic, but his eyes flashed towards his Dominus seeking the answer to why this humiliation was allowed, was he not wanting the man to return to his status as champion? How was this going to achieve the desired effect? He would rather face a series of nights fighting in the pits where there was no glory and even less rules than having to kiss ass in this manner just to prevent the proverbial ramming of cock to ass.

He moved his eyes to the face of Vitus and his blood ran cold. The man was a monster and it was obvious in the way he stared at the pool that his perversions were deeper set than even his father. If he had or did cause pain to the woman lying next to him, he swore he would one day cause the Roman to cry for mercy that would never come.

Instinctively he pulled his head away from the smooth fingers entwining in his hair and turned his head slightly to meet Felix's vicious question with a stare of disbelief. Had he truly asked him, in front of her, how he had taken her? The man was drunk but completely mad on top of that if he thought that the gladiator would give voice to answer that. The lust in the dark eyes was disturbing and he recognized it for what it could mean.

Tertius was not beyond offering his gladiators for the pleasure of men even if it was not their preference to be with a man but when his expression suddenly changed and the girl at his side shifted Cassian let his eyes follow the path of the Roman's and when he saw the source of the man's delight his rage set fire and the thundering of his pulse overcame common sense and he began to move to defend her before he knew what he was doing, his actions were stopped only by the sight of his Dominus leaping to his feet.

Violetta pressed her hand against his hip, perhaps hoping it would stop him or at least cause him to pause before giving anyone cause to suspect their secret. Vitus did not know and the way he was grinning into his wine said that he still thought that she was terrified to be pressed so close to the man. If he ever knew the level of feeling that was beginning to grow and burn between them the Roman would make sure that her life was an even deeper misery than he had intended already.

He let his eyes flicker towards hers, was she silently begging the heavens to not let this escalate? As his attending body-slave she would know better than most the type of cruelty that Felix was capable of when his anger was raised. Even without the anger it was evident in the way that he asked his question, knowing full well that she could hear it. Cassian was certain that the Roman was hoping to frighten her with the memory of what was supposed to have been a horrifying and painful experience. He could never know the bliss that it had been.

Almost as if she could hear his thoughts Violetta glanced up at his eyes, he hoped that if she understood the hatred and rage there that she would not be afraid, not of him at least.

A slow, devious smile spread across Felix' face as he held eye contact with the gladiator, each of them refusing to back down or lower gaze first. It took all he had not to flinch when Felix called out loudly over his shoulder "Tertius, my friend, it seems your gladiator has forgotten himself and has not yet given voice to answer my question."

He stilled his hand on Violetta and removed his hand from the braid in his hair as he turned to stare expectantly at the lanista. He was determined to have his answer and perhaps more; it was possible that the Roman's desire coupled with his own master's burning need to rise in society could see a great deal of pain metered out, likely to someone who did not deserve it.

Defiance was burning across his countenance and he looked Tertius full in the face even though that was forbidden for slaves in such public scenes. It was too late to care that he was bound to be punished for this, he had been baited and had fallen right into the Roman's trap. His suspicions were confirmed when his Dominus stood with a smooth, if slightly agitated grin.

"He is your man this night, good Felix." Tertius shrugged as if he could not be bothered to deal with the disobedient man who was still calm standing in the water of the pool. When his blood was racing with anger and something else that was dangerously close to possessiveness. Both had him interested to see if it was for himself or Violetta that he was as close to losing his control as a recruit upon the sands. Was it outrage or was it the girl that sparked the fire in him?

"For your pleasure or his own punishment as you see fit. The man needs to be tested." He knew he had committed an offence against the host and his own Dominus, he knew that Tertius would not allow him to be injured so there was little that Census could do to him in so public a forum.

"Cocksucking son of a whore." Cassian cursed under his breath. Glancing once more at Violetta he inhaled a deep breath and eased himself out from under her, every muscle in his body protesting the move. He wanted to stay with her; hold her, protect her and the intensity of his emotion made him nervous. Stepping out of the pool he squared his shoulders and glared darkly at Felix. Let him bring his worst, he had faced harder things than this merchant could come up with.

Vitus looked up at the words of the lanista and grinned as he rose to his feet. He looked between the girl, the gladiator and his father before standing. "Gratitude good Tertius. Punishment shall be a certain pleasure I assure you." His lips spread to a deep and devious grin as his eyes met those of Cassian who returned the stare with one of icy indifference. Slave or not he knew he was threatening in his composure and calm to the point of being unnerving to many Romans. When Felix shook his head at Vitus, he felt the first stirring of hope, the man was completely drunk, unsteady on his feet and slurring his words, surely, he would not allow anyone else to take the punishment and how strong could he be in his condition?

Violetta propped herself up on her elbows, trying to shift her hips away from the hand that rested between her thighs. Her move was met with a harsh barking command to "Be still!" that was followed by Felix's right hand coming down across her cheek in a harsh blow while the other gripped her thigh hard enough to make her bite her lip against the pain. Cassian's hands clenched in tight fists; it was almost impossible not to strike the man for laying wrathful hands upon his woman.

"I am grateful for your gift to *me* good Tertius and it will of course be a pleasure to see things righted between us." He practically purred before locking eyes with the defiant gladiator before him "I ask again, Otho, and you will answer loudly for all to hear; did she cry and scream under your invasions? The way she cries under me or did you silence her as you took her?" he looked from the man to the girl who had watering eyes and whispered, "Answer on her pain." He arched a brow and shifted the hand between her legs, moving a finger in a way that, though unseen, brought a moan of discomfort from her lips.

He regretted his loss of control the moment it happened and the knowledge that she would be the one to pay the price for it now settled across his broad shoulders like a heavy weight that he would have to carry until he could make it up to her, if he ever got the chance. For the briefest of moments his heart seemed to stop in his chest, not out of fear for himself at the hands of Felix but only that he might be commanded to hurt her to make him laugh. Cassian knew he was on the brink of defeat that was far worse than anything he had risked on the sands.

His own actions had taken away any chance of a choice, if he had only been able to hold on to his temper this would not be happening. His muscles tensed to the point of near snapping, but he refused to give more ground than that or to have shame in his voice when he answered; "She made no sound, Dominus." Quickly his eyes sought her and locked on to the beautiful blue, not breaking his gaze in the hope that he would bring her some measure of comfort to ease the pain and chaos he had brought to her.

Their eyes met as a tear slid down her cheek, the sting of the slap must have been harder than he gave the old man credit for, her cheek was red and swelling as he watched. He tried to tell her with his eyes that he blamed himself for this instead of the monsters that commanded it and hoped that she would not hold him to blame for the reaction of his instincts.

He wanted to laugh aloud as the lie passed his lips; she had cried out in pleasure so loudly that she had to muffle the sound at his shoulder; the memory was so vivid that he could feel the press of her teeth in his flesh again and the sounds of her passion echoed through to his soul.

His words caused Felix to pause and his intrusive finger paused its assault, she held her breath until he removed it and straightened to approach the gladiator. When he was inches from the younger man's face Felix paused to smirk, dangerously mocking him "Then perhaps I stand your master there as well," he looked around and laughed with his guests as he crowed loudly "For she cries out under me! Even while he took her maidenhead the man could not coax a sound from her. Rutting like the animals they are no doubt left little chance for her to mew her tender pains." In mockery of the intimacy he had posed them in the Roman wiped the finger that had been inside

Violetta across the lips of the gladiator, daring him to lick his lips and taste her.

After a moment of shared stares, one man daring the other to break Felix turned to take a cup of wine and call to Vitus and Selenia, ignoring Cassian or making it seem as though he was "Come; bring the little bitch as well so that we may enjoy this punishment as a family. He smirked at the pair of slaves in a way that made Cassian's blood run cold.

What would he do and why did he need Violetta and privacy from the gathered company? There was a little relief when he called to the lanista; "Good Tertius of course you and your lovely wife should attend this as well so that you might see how it is that *my* slaves would not dare such a bold action as your 'champion.'"

As they stood to join the family of Census the lanista and his wife began to discuss what was about to happen. "Tiberius! What possesses your mind to allow such a thing?" Lycithia spoke through a hard smile, her question filled with such disapproval that her husband flinched slightly, and Cassian had to hold back a chuckle. The man who wanted to seem so powerful was still controlled by his wife. "End this now, the man is a champion and if Felix or, gods forbid, Vitus lay hand upon him the price will be too high. He has been through enough."

They were not fond of each other, but he knew that it could not be out of any kindness that she did not want this punishment to occur. Was she worried that the fire in his eyes, his desire to win, would be extinguished by this drunken merchant? He knew that he could not avoid punishment for what he had done but he was not going to give up.

The lanista shook his head emphatically and took his wife's hand to press a kiss to her palm. A wicked smile on his lips he nodded towards the gladiator and whispered as though he could not hear him while standing next to him.

"Look at the man. Do you not see the flames in his eyes? The hunger for violence? That is the hunger I would see in his eyes as he takes the sands in the arena next. This is the fuel he needs, and we need him to feel the burn of it in his soul." Tiberius hissed to his wife with his hand on Cassian's shoulder.

This could be the way to give him back the drive he had been missing in the arena, hopefully bring the title of champion back to his name as well as his Dominus' house and the coin that came with it; which is what would truly make the Romans happy. If Violetta was the key to reigniting the passion of a champion in his blood, then she had just become one of the most important slaves in Velletri as far as he was concerned, and his own masters had to see it.

With a warning look sent to Cassian by the lanista as he helped Lycithia to her feet the house of Tertius, slave and Romans, followed their host to a much more private chamber where lounges were quickly being set in a circle. What in Hades did the man have planned? The devious look on Felix's face made the gladiator wonder if the merchant had manipulated everything that had happened that night to get this point, so that he could have the champion of Velletri at his mercy if even for a short moment?

Walking gracefully next to her husband Lycithia smiled and said softly, with a casual glimpse at the gladiator behind them; "Then my love, let us take a deeper pleasure in the igniting of this inferno with the knowledge that its fires shall burn ever brighter for our good fortunes." He watched her cheeks flush as they strolled casually, did the woman feel excited at the thought that he might be commanded to bed Violetta before them? Such had not occurred in years, not since there had been a battle to purchase him from the ludus. He would pretend that the act shamed him even though touching Violetta was as close to Elysium as he would ever be. This was not going to be the victory for the Romans that they thought it was.

Cassian watched as Violetta stepped out of the pool, adjusted her dress and sighed, her eyes were on the floor as her cheeks burned and her body trembled. He wondered if she had ever been the victim of Felix's 'amusements' or of she had stood with Meridius serving their masters during them. The debauchery that men like him favored was usually tainted with cruelty and violence, depending upon mood and the target of the night. Had it been terrifying for her to witness? and now that she was to be the one the acts were delivered to would be able to hold back her fear and stand strong or would she break down before their tormentors?

Stepping past him without a glance or touch he watched as Violetta made her way out to the hall and stepped away from the guards for a moment to lean against one of the cool stone columns. Cassian wanted to go to her, her breath was coming in ragged gasps that bordered on sobs and she had wrapped her arms around her torso. Wiping a hand across her face to remove any tears that may have appeared there she stared at him when the guards escorted him past her.

The look in her eyes haunting him with questions he could only guess at and the inability to answer even if he knew what ran through her mind. He wondered if she questioned as he did the cruelty of the gods, if they existed, that they would bring them so close, to show them what they might mean to each other, only to have them both tormented for their feelings.

He saw the shame flood her eyes when she stood, tears raining unchecked down her cheeks as she walked past him, and it ate at him, stabbed him like a blade in the arena. This thought brought a mind shattering moment of clarity, this was the arena though there were no sands and the crowd were much smaller, the need to survive was the same and he would be damned to Hades if he let either of them fall.

He squared his shoulders and decided then and there that the title of champion would be his again; the name of Otho would be a distant memory and defeat a thing of forgotten nightmares. They would not fall to whatever madness the drunken merchant and his evil offspring had planned but would stand in each other's glory, all else falling away.

A guard came to grip each shoulder and shoved him towards the passageway, passing her their eyes met and his heart stopped. Looking at her he saw for the first time in years a reason to keep fighting, it was not about cheating death anymore when he entered the arena sands, it was about her. He did not resist the direction of the guards even when they moved him out of her gaze, but he turned his head to call back to her with a laugh and a wink "Never fucking lose." before he was brought to the chamber filled with Romans and soft candle light.

The scene that greeted them when Violetta moved from behind Cassian to face their masters sent shivers down his spine even though the room was warm from the braziers and candles that lit the space. He was commanded to stand a few paces away at the left edge of the formation and she was gestured to stand in the center. All eyes were upon her, those of Tertius flickering to meet his for a moment before returning to the centerpiece in the room while the attendants and body slaves standing respectfully back from attention behind their masters.

There was a look of pained sadness in Meridius' eyes and he thought he saw the same in the dark eyes of Jovian that accompanied Tertius though his also held something that looked like excitement. His eyes fell to the floor and was surprised to see a carpet put down. Glancing towards Violetta he saw that the blood had drained from her face. Was this what Felix did? When he intended to amuse himself? Watch his slaves engage in intercourse for his entertainment? His mind raced at the thought that she could be in his arms again but the idea of doing so before the eyes of these Romans made him feel almost nauseous and she must have felt the same for she would not meet his eyes.

Cassian wanted to wipe the serene smile from Felix' face as he watched their discomfort grow while they waited on his command. His eyes moved from the tears stained face of Violetta to the proud bearing of the gladiator, his eyes lighting with delight to see Cassian humbled and brought low as punishment for thinking that he could have any say at all in how he treated his own slave. The champion shuddered to think what the punishment would have been if he had belonged to Felix. He was the type of man that would have made him watch as he or another man had their way with Violetta, not because he wanted her or even objected to his affections for her but simply to prove that he was the Dominus and so he could do as he liked with any slave at any time.

Standing frozen, wishing he could risk touching Violetta's hand to remind her that he was there with her, that she would not suffer alone Cassian watched the merchant put his hands on the shoulders of his daughter with a smile. "Selenia, my dear, are you prepared to enjoy a gift from your father?"

He obviously favored the daughter over Vitus, but would that work in the favor of the two slaves or would it make what was to come even worse? Though he doubted that the woman had the love of pain her brother was known for, the looks between Felix and Selenia said that he trusted that his daughter would be just as devious as he would himself. He gestured towards the pair of slaves and nodded for her to stand if she wished to direct the punishment. Cassian felt his heartbeat faster at the helplessness of the situation, there was no chance to persuade Tertius to stop this even though he doubted that would have been possible he felt as though he should have tried.

Selenia's face lit up at the words of her father. No doubt she was eager to have command over the girl that she so obviously wanted for herself. He had the feeling that Felix had never let anyone else command his private punishments and this was being treated as a special privilege though if it was to reward the daughter or punish the son Cassian was not sure, but he could see that the family dynamic between the trio was unlike anything he had seen before.

"Of course, I am dear father." She answered with a victorious grin at her brother who sat with a thunderous expression on his face, obviously displeased that he had not been selected. Rising and adjusting her gown Selenia placed a kiss of gratitude on her father's cheek and slowly walked towards the girl in the center of the room. "You mean that I am to command them both to a punishment fitting their offence against you father?" She asked, slowly circling Violetta with a look that made Cassian's skin crawl and glancing at her father as though she was not sure what to do with them yet.

"Yes, my dear. I hope that you have not lost your touch for such things." He drank deeply and gestured around the room "For if you have, I am certain that someone here could think of something that would see us entertained with these fine creatures." His eyes drifted to Vitus who everyone could see looked ready to leap out of his seat to accept the task.

Felix moved his hand to gesture his son to stillness as he stepped towards his daughter and the pair of slaves "Since this celebration was to be in your honor you may command them both to whatever you wish, within our audience of course." He was not going to risk his daughter with the savagery of a gladiator alone and he intensely desired to see what she would do to punish the slave who had defied him and how she would use the girl to do it.

Cassian could see the anger and hatred in the eyes of Vitus, he knew them for he felt the same way about the Romans in the room, but it was his words to his sister; "What a glorious gift sister. I hope you are not going to waste it foolishly." That made his heart drop to his stomach. The subtle taunt had sealed the fate of the would-be lovers for he knew that if she had been going to simply command a scene of fucking that she would think her brother saw it, and her, as weak and foolishly self-indulgent and the pride of the Roman woman could not stand it if her brother thought himself the better between them. "What will you have for us Selenia?" He chided with a laugh at her indecision.

Cassian had his suspicions of what inspired Vitus to push his sister into making a speedier decision. He could sense that the man wanted to see him commanded to take Violetta, not with the erotic passion that his family seemed to favor but with a painful brutality that he would never do, but why not just suggest it instead of playing games? While his mind spun, searching for answers he watched Vitus sip his wine and challenge his sister with his eyes.

The gladiator turned his attention, briefly, to the silent Spaniard, Meridius, it did not take much to note the tightness of his jaw or the thundering tick of his pulse. He had heard Violetta reference him as a friend like a father but had they, since she had been in his bed, become lovers? Was that why the man stared at Violetta but refused to meet his eyes? Had he taken the fullest advantage of what had been commanded by his Dominus or was that the look of a father afraid for his daughter?

CHAPTER 8

Violetta was doing the best she could not to shiver in fear, she could not believe that Selenia had been given the chance to command the punishment, to demand anything that she wished; it was as though Felix knew her deepest fears. She watched the woman as she smirked at her brother, Violetta knew him well enough to hear the jealousy he was trying to hide, and it frightened her to think that she would be in his bed in a few short hours. How could it be that minutes ago everything had seemed almost perfect and now it had changed into the perfect nightmare.

The way Selenia watched her, studied how she reacted to the nearness of Cassian had to mean something, she was not a casual person and knowing the kinds of things she would do to gain her father's favor Violetta was terrified to think about what she would do to someone who had blatantly disrespected him and had even moved against him in front of his guests. Turning her head to look at Otho Selenia smiled icily, and Violetta knew she had decided but she still flinched with some surprise when she snapped her fingers. "Otho." Her eyes lit up when he obeyed, he turned his head, attending her command. When she pointed to the floor in front of Violetta the girl did not know which of them was more surprised. The Roman woman's face lit up when the gladiator did as commanded, letting her turn him until he faced Violetta so that the girl was staring right at him, with nowhere else to look unless she wanted to deliberately turn her head and risk being disobedient.

Cassian was close enough that she could feel a heat coming off him as he stared down at her, she could almost smell the lust in the Roman though she could not deny that she felt something similar it would not be lust that would play into this punishment. Violetta felt, in the pit of her stomach, that she would be the tool used to impart the lesson that was to be taught in that small room.

Violetta did her best to hide her outraged jealousy as Selenia caressed Cassian's skin gently as she moved behind him, looking at Violetta and then around the room and gave her first command; "Gladiator, I want you to strip Violetta of her dress. Do it quickly, I would have her bared before us all. Do not be gentle for I am not inclined to see my desires delayed." It was a trap and Violetta prayed that Cassian could see it too. Selenia obviously suspected affections between them and waited to see if he would refuse to cause her humiliation or if he would even pause to consider the command.

Cassian's eyes gleamed at Violetta; she saw him bite his tongue as he winked at her. Would he dare speak? His grin became hedonistic and she watched his body tighten before he broke decorum and spoke "Domina? you command me to fulfill my own fantasies?" She was in shock at the words and yet there was truth to the statement; never had she dreamed he would have to do this with her in front of those that called themselves their masters. How many dreams had been filled with his touch? With an urgency that had demanded he strip her to nothing in moments so that they could make passionate love but never had she dreamed that it could be like this.

"Your will directs my hands." He turned his head to look down into Violetta's eyes and lifted a hand to her face so that he could trace the tips of his fingers down the line of her cheek while he brought the other hand unseen up to her shoulder. When her eyes lifted to meet his Cassian wrenched the fabric from her shoulder, not caring if it ripped and yet he made certain that it was not enough to cause it to slip from her hips and expose her completely, these perverted Roman's did not deserve the sight, he squared his shoulders and looked towards his Dominus, every inch of his face the champion she loved not the penitent slave they had brought with them that night.

When his hand touched her face Violetta's eyes flicked downwards and a soft blush rose on her cheek though she fought it. She had been about to whisper to him when he tore the fabric from her chest and the sound became a startled cry of shock. Instinctually her hand flew to her mouth the stifle the cry, her teeth digging into the back of it was the only thing that kept her from reaching to cover herself.

She did not know if she wanted to laugh or scream but either one was a risk with this audience. Composing herself a little she let her arms fall to her sides and shifted her legs apart which also served to hold the dress in place around her hips, had he done that on purpose? To give her a moment to compose herself? Her chest heaved as she fought the shame of the exposure, sucking in the air to her lungs she looked up to meet his eyes searching for a sign of his feelings in the blank mask of his face.

Selenia gasped with pleasure when the man ripped the dress away to reveal creamy white breasts that were full and round with soft pink tips. Violetta shuddered when the woman licked her lips, staring at her body with a curiosity that was no longer idle but a growing hunger that would soon demand satisfaction. A marked cough from Vitus seemed to bring her back from the edge of her daydreams and she turned her head to look at the gladiator; "Did I say you could speak, slave? Finish the task. I would have her *bare*. Now."

Her voice was like ice and her eyes matched before she turned and brought her hand hard across Violetta's face "I gave command." The hand that had struck her face fell to cup a breast, kneading and rolling it in her palm as she moved behind her to tug the long dark strands of her hair. "I will be obeyed, or you will suffer the consequences." Was her softly spoken threat, "And suffer you will my little lamb." She whispered hotly in the young woman's ear and pinched the nipple that had beaded under her attentions.

Cassian stood still as stone before her, she wondered if he was attempting to maintain his composure in the face of the abuse, he was being forced not only to witness but to play a part in. He was looking into her eyes and gave a slight shake of his head while his gaze intensified. His look cut a mark upon her soul, branding it as a part of his. His were calling on her trust, demanding strength from her that she was not sure she had. If she could follow his lead, do as he did, she would be able to make it through this with her dignity still intact but with the way the Romans were staring gleefully at them it did not seem likely.

"Feel nothing," He drew her attention back to his eyes when he whispered so quietly that no one else would be able to hear it though he did not care that Selenia was beside him, she no longer existed to them. "Nothing at all." He lowered his hand from her cheek and ripped the rest of the dress away. Letting the gauzy fabric fall to a puddle on the floor she flushed bodily as he stared at her, breathless and mesmerized as though he had never seen a naked woman before. The slight smile coupled with the gleam in his eyes made her feel like a goddess with beauty to rival Venus herself.

Her jaw trembled slightly but she mouthed the word back to him "Nothing." Staring into his eyes she barely flinched when the rest of the dress was stripped away leaving her naked and exposed before the rest of the room as she moved her legs apart to fulfill the command of Selenia. Pressing her eyes closed she repressed a shudder at the touch of the woman's hand on her flesh and then the tug of her hair. This was a nightmare come to life, not a dream of a lover's touch but the Hades of her darkest nights. Her body responded to the touch as though it were the edge of a blade instead of the touch of a woman, but her eyes locked to those of the champion which had no pleasure in them but simply anguish at the molestation before his eyes.

"You can stop now." Selenia said to Cassian and gestured him to stand back, her voice was still cold, and her hand remained deep in the dark length of Violetta's hair. She flinched when she caught Selenia locking her eyes to the gladiator who seemed far too distant and cold not to be affected by what was going on in front of him. Violetta was certain that he was holding his emotions in reserve so that he did not give further cause for violent acts and she was determined to stay strong with him but when the Roman danced her hand down from her breast to her belly and then between the legs, she had commanded to be spread she could not help but whimper in agony.

"Well now, do I excite you little lamb? Or is it the tower of masculinity before us that sends heat to your core?" She was stroking and playing between the dark curls and almost laughing at the struggle she could feel as Violetta fought her body and mind, not wanting to feel the pleasure but unable to deny the natural reaction of her senses. She hated Selenia for this and wished she were bold enough to show her displeasure, but it would only lead to more pain and she would be alone to bear it.

Cassian's reaction to this new torment was instantaneous and savage; he took Violetta's head back in his hold once again, his hands over those of Selenia in her hair, and growled deep and viciously as he covered her mouth with his. The kiss was not a seduction but a claim of his ownership of her heart, to show her the depth of his desire and remind her that there was nothing like the passion that sparked between them. Violetta tasted his outrage and protective need and knew then that nothing that the Romans did would change that. His tongue swept her mouth, tasting every inch and demanding a response. As soon as he felt her return the kiss with the press of

her lips and a darting sweep of her own tongue, he broke the kiss with a swift
wink and stepped back, lowering his head in what could only be preparation
for the wrath of the Romans that he must have intended to be focused on
him instead of her.

Vitus was the first to react, jumping to his feet and taking the gladiator by
the hair he pulled his head back as Violetta cowered physically, thinking that
he would strike her as his sister had done. "You think to lay hands upon my
sister? filthy slave!" he bellowed in Cassian's face. Violetta cringed when he
twisted the honey-colored hair in his hand and growled in the ear of the man
who had just sacrificed himself for her; "I will have your balls if you think to
lay hand upon her again." It sounded like a brother defending his sister, but
no one in the room had any doubt that the gladiator knew which 'her' he
was speaking of. Violetta trembled and bit her lip with her eyes to the floor
when he shoved Cassian roughly to the side before, he returned to his seat
and downed the rest of his wine quickly the cup out for Meridius to refill.
"Remember that, Spaniard, should you ever consider making her your next
conquest. My father may have taken your tongue, but I will remove the cock
of any man in this house that beds her outside of express command."

Cassian barely reacted to the man's wrath; his balance was not so delicate
that a shove could send him off it. He tossed his head when it was released,
and Violetta could see his eyes dancing with the urge to laugh at what would
have been a threat if there was any chance that his Dominus would have
allowed it. Cut off the balls of the man who stood his greatest asset? He
stepped back and kept his eyes locked on Violetta, inviting her to share his
strength, to lean on him and together they would soar, if she was able to
stand strong beneath the blanket of fear these Romans had her under.

Violetta was startled from her determination when her hair was pulled
even tighter than before. "You will pay for that gladiator." Selenia hissed at
Cassian "But I will not damage goods that will not stand as mine in the
morning." She thrust her finger inside the girl, sudden and cruel with her
assault. The Roman smiled at the sharp intake of breath Violetta could not
stop. It was torture for her though it was meant to torture the man who cared
for her, but her next words too the shame and agony a step farther.

"Meridius fetch me the small whip." She commanded with an evil grin
as she added a second finger between her legs. "If your lover cannot control

himself Violetta then perhaps a lesson is needed." Violetta could see that even the lanista was getting nervous now. There was no telling what madness Selenia would engage in now to prove herself to her brother She watched the older man's lips twitch for a moment and shook her head to stop him from protesting. He held her like a daughter and as any father would do, she knew if he could speak it would be to ask to take the pain of what she was about to bear.

"Hurry slave. I would not want her to quake before you return." Violetta looked to the heavens in silent prayer when Selenia's eyes met the jealousy in Vitus' glare with a daring laugh, he had not yet done what she was doing so casually, and it was sure to drive him wild with rage that she would suffer in solitude when he got his hands on her at the end of the night. She could not help but wonder if Felix could be moved to deny Vitus once again if she pleaded upon bended knee at his bedside that night once the guests had departed?

There was a deadly calm that had settled over the gladiator as the room waited with bated breath to see if he would react to the obscene act of the command for a whip. Violetta was anxious to tell him that she would be alright, they were not going to kill her before his eyes. She could find the strength to accept the abuse but only if he did not try to take it upon himself. She lowered her eyes from the heavens to look at him but before she could attempt to speak, he did it for her. "Breathe," He whispered, unsure if it was to her or himself, she replied; "Just breathe."

Violetta watched Meridius return with the whip but he would not meet her eye and so she could find no strength in the man that had stood like a father to her for years. Her body was tense, and her breath was not steady, the woman's hand not arousing her but hurting her with rough and crude motions. She saw the whip placed in Selenia's hand and bit her lip in fear of the pain to come, now that she was faced with the reality of the moment she did not know if she could stand strong and hated for Cassian to see her as weak but still she turned her eyes to his and tried to find the strength she needed in his eyes, begging with her own for him to give her a sign that he stood with her, cared for her, that what they shared was worth what was about to happen.

Tertius was on his feet in an instant and stepped behind his gladiator. He seemed surprised at such behavior from his man; gladiators were known to be fiery and passionate, but this type of bold, outright disobedience and defiance could not be entirely welcome outside the walls of the ludus. Did she drive him to this? Even to the most forgiving and indulgent Dominus his actions were unacceptable, but in this house, they were utterly dangerous. Here where the slaves were used for entertainment without thought or care for what it would do to them. He was not likely to be overly concerned with such things himself, but this was his champion, he could not have him maimed or driven mad but the likes of the daughter of the house of Census.

Violetta wondered, watching the lanista struggle to find the words that would calm his man Cassian had no idea of his true worth though, or the rumors of the battles that had been fought by Tertius to keep him years ago. Since her return from the ludus it seemed nearly every slave in the house had a tale to tell of him and she had soaked up every word just to hear of him.

"Keep your fucking hands to your sides," He finally hissed in his ear "Or find yourself damned by their removal upon return to the ludus." He could have little intention of doing so but the pride of a Roman could not allow a slave to know that. He must have still thought that Cassian stood in the shame of his loss of title, and would believe that anything was possible, even his sale to a lesser lanista or a whorehouse.

Felix stood from his seat and approached Selenia with a frown. He did not like to use the whip on his slaves; the scars it could leave were ugly and took away from their beauty when on display. He had often told her, at night when he was drunk or in mornings when she had eased the pounding in his head, that she was too beautiful to have marked like that and so Violetta was hopeful and relieved when he raised his hand in warning to his daughter.

"Do not be driven to break what you do not possess my dear. I would not have her bloodied in my bed." He sat back down when Selenia nodded, the slight pout on her lips revealing that he had guessed her intention. Just as she had begun to feel the spark of hope he spoke again with an indulgent smile, shattering the fragile feeling and sparking tears to Violetta's eyes; "Just a few strokes to make your point dear heart."

Cassian winced and nodded at the words of his Dominus as he curled his hands into fists. To live without hands was the worst punishment a Dominus could inflict upon a slave. The shame and humiliation would be relieved only by death which would come slow for no one would touch a man, slave or free, in such a state but would simply leave him to his long and painful death. If they questioned him about his actions this night, Violetta wondered if he would tell the truth or would he find an explanation other than that of his affections? Would they punish him more or less if they understood? The lanista was surely a man of business but perhaps his wife was a woman of some compassion? The thought was enough to give Violetta some hope as his eyes flicked up to meet hers and in their amber glow was a silent and tender apology for his failure.

Selenia tightened the grip on the whip in her hand, looked to her brother and then her father for permission to begin but before he could say the words, she looked at the dark-haired boy accompanying the lanista. "Good Tertius. I would beg the use of your body slave. I fear Violetta is not disciplined enough to take the lash without moving and as I would make sure that your man has the best possible view of his punishment, I need someone to hold her still." She smirked at the gladiator, while Violetta's head whipped to look at the youth in question.

He was younger than she was but there was something in his eyes that said that he was less childish than his face might suggest. The Syrian was uncommonly beautiful; he wore his dark hair past his shoulders and had exotic paints at his eyes and jewelry on his wrists. The boy looked as nervous about being called away from his master's side as she was about him laying his hands upon her but no protest, she could have thought of would have been heard and so after casting her eyes downwards to gather her composure she raised them to meet Cassian's for the last time before the added torment of waiting was finally over.

The inferno in his eyes coupled with the look on the gladiator's face that caught her breath and she stared, completely captivated by him. He like a warrior; driven, perhaps even possessed, was this what he was like as a champion? A man that could strike terror into the hearts of his opponents with a single glance and he was looking at her as though she were the prize, he would win from the sands. And a surge of strength rushed through her, she would do all she could to be worthy of such devotion.

She met the eyes of the lanista's boy with her newly forged determination shining in her eyes and a slight nod of her head when he did as commanded and put his hands upon her shoulders, partially blocking her view of Cassian but she could feel her would be lover's eyes upon her regardless of the presence of the young man holding her still for the Roman who unfurled the whip at last and began to swing it back and forth, cracking it in the air and laughing each time Violetta jumped at the sound not knowing if it was the one that would land on her flesh. She had been commanded against scarring the girl, but Violetta feared she wanted her to scream just enough to break the defiant will of her would be lover. Meeting his eyes, she watched him tighten his jaw and glare at the woman behind her with a deep hatred but Selenia answered his glare by sending the lash to connect with her back, inhaling with a pleased hiss when the motion was met with a scream of agony.

She could not help it, her back felt as though it was on fire and she cried out, tears springing to her eyes and flowing down her cheeks. She wanted to run from the room but even if she dared the boy holding her would not have let go. Her eyes widened in fear and pain as the leather strap struck again and her knees almost buckled but the boy was stronger than he looked and held her up, daring to whisper "shh" just before Selenia ran her hand over the rising welts. Nodding once to him she looked towards the man staring at her like a statue before hanging her head to wait for the next blow.

The smile that crossed Selenia's face at the sound of Violetta's cry was almost as broad as her brother's and she could not bear to look at either of them. Snapping the whip in the air again Selenia spoke coldly, her brow arching elegantly "Do you know why you are being whipped Violetta?" She leaned closer, menacing the girl with a brush of her silk dress against bare skin "Why you are suffering this pain?"

"No Domina." She said in a whimper, not daring to raise her eyes at all. She could feel the eyes on her in the room and did not think that she could hold onto her composure if she met their laughing gaze. Meridius would be raging but nothing but his eyes would give that away, Vitus would be dangerously aroused by her pain and the thought of being the one to feel the effects of it later that night was almost enough to break her spirit completely. She could feel the boy's sympathy in his touch and the way that his thumb rubbed her shoulder where he gripped her but the feelings of the rest of the audience, including Cassian, she could only guess.

His features were set in stone but inside he was in a raging turmoil. He looked tense, as though he was fighting the urge to cry out in anger when the lash struck her flesh, flesh that should be under his hands instead of Jovian's. She prayed that he did not hate the boy for it but the turned any hatred towards the woman who had commanded it and left them no choice but to fight for the eye contact that had failed when her head fell in the wake of the strike as tears streamed down her cheeks. Violetta wished that he could be the one to wipe the tears away and put a stop to the brutal act but there was nothing to be done that would not make it worse on her body and his control. When he "Stay strong." He whispered, watching her agony and fear. When his eyes met hers for the briefest moment he began to whisper, though if it was to her or himself, she could not determine but she caught the faintest hiss of "Stay strong" and pulled enough strength from it to square her shoulders for the next blow to come.

She was not sure if Selenia believed her or not, but she continued hissing in her ear, letting the length of the whip drape across her victim's shoulders and dangle down her back. "You disobeyed me child." She said with an evil smile "And that cannot be allowed, no matter who is influencing you." Her eyes flashed to Cassian and her father as she prepared for the final strike. Violetta reminded herself that Selenia had been commanded not to maim her with the whip and she could hope that she carried no ill will towards her for her own actions. While preparing her dress she had spoken to Maya, who was kind and now looked at her with pity in her eyes, she had revealed that in her time in Rome Selenia had become quite skilled in applying punishments that did not leave a mark as her hostess, Tertulla, hated for her slaves to be scarred but took a great deal of pleasure in pushing the limits of social acceptance when it was time to see them punished.

Pulling hard on the whip so it left a burning trail around her neck Selenia delivered the final blow in a perfect line down Violetta's spine. It would leave a bright red and painful mark that would last for a few days but there would be no scarring, not this time. "See that you remember this lesson my little lamb." She said, her hands dropping to grip her hips with a bruising strength as her eyes met those of the gladiator over a trembling shoulder. Violetta was blinking hard to try and hold back the onslaught of tears, but her breath was stolen when she met the gaze of Cassian watching the conclusion of her torment.

If looks could kill, then she believed that Selenia would have been dead before the first strike of the lash had landed upon her flesh. His hatred appeared on his countenance as an inferno of white-hot rage, his jaw clenched, and his pulse pounded at his temple she worried that he might give in to a sure desire to take the life of each Roman that had a hand in this hour of affliction. The muzzle that was their shared slavery trapped the words that they would have shared; hers to ease the troubles rising in his soul on her account and surely, he would have something of comfort to say, to ease the terror she still felt racing through her that would not ease until the Romans left her in peace.

Selenia had not stopped circling Violetta, her hands running across her skin, dancing back and forth so that every eye could not help but watch her, even the Syrian slave boy that had held her for the blows was mesmerized by the motion of her gestures. She watched as the woman's eyes met her father's and silently repeated the question from earlier that day; she wanted to possess her, completely and utterly, to take her back to Rome when she left. Standing behind her, breathing lightly on her shoulder she dropped a hand to cup the soft curve of her bottom, but was stopped short when Felix shook his head in reply, he would not let her have what she desired. Violetta allowed herself a sigh of relief but felt the flash of anger in the hand still touching her at the refusal of her unspoken request. Angry and denied she pinched hard before stepping away, letting the lash fall to the floor, giggling at the whimper that followed the grip.

forced to watch the Roman's hands play over the body of the woman that his soul seemed to have claimed as his own while she had the look of some secretive sexual pleasure washing over her face, pure lust shining in her eyes. He inhaled deeply and took some solace in the fact that despite the rapturous look upon her face she would never get what she truly wanted, the willing body of the woman she tortured and humiliated for pleasure.

Felix rose from the seat and places his hands on his daughter's shoulders before turning to smile at his guests, ignoring the trembling slave that had entertained them all; "I think there has been enough for tonight. Gratitude for the loan of your man, good Tertius, it will not soon be forgotten." He gestured for his son to rise as well. "Come, let us adjourn this room to say farewell to all who attended, your guards can fetch your man to your cart." He gave both his children a commanding look to remind them that they were not to linger to find more of their own pleasures but were to join him as they should to end the night united as a family and swept from the room with Meridius following in his wake though he did not notice the man's backwards glimpse towards Violetta as they left her and the gladiator behind.

Following the lead of their host Tiberius and Lycithia stood and the lanista wrapped an arm around his wife's waist and pressed a kiss to her cheek, the token act of affection allowed him to lock eyes with Cassian briefly, the smile on his face flashing into a dangerous glower that made Violetta shiver. There could be no mistaking the meaning behind the glare; if he chose to disobey, to not submit to command, the cost would be what had been promised and more. The look faded as quickly as it had come and the lanista called after their host "This night has been much enjoyed by Lycithia and myself, much gratitude to you for the invitation and it is my immense joy that you have found some pleasure in my man though not perhaps what had been anticipated it was still an enlightening experience." With a final look at his man and a snap of his fingers summoning Jovian to attend him as well the lanista and his wife followed the host family from the room, preening as though her pain had brought them some accomplishment or raise in stature.

When the collection of their Dominus' left the room Violetta finally let go of her emotions and sank to her knees, reaching for her dress that lay in a puddle of fabric on the floor. Each move pulled on the freshly marked skin and caused her to wince though she did not shed anymore tears, the blend of pain and shame had frozen the tears in her eyes though they would certainly fall later that night in whatever privacy she was able to find. She could only pray that Felix would be kind enough to order her to her own cell instead of to the bed of Vitus as previously promised. There was only so much that she could bear in a single night. She clutched the gauze of her dress to her chest as though covering her nakedness now would erase the shame of the past, make horrors unseen, unfelt and buried deep enough not to hurt or haunt. Raising her eyes from the floor they met those of Cassian as his footsteps drew nearer in the absence of their masters.

He watched her in total silence, a statue of indecision showing on his face. Violetta wondered if he was considering the threat made by his Dominus and if speaking to him was worth the risk. Whether Tertius would follow through with the act of severing his hands she did not know but she suspected that as a fallen champion he was not able to test his word. He stared at her, spellbound, making her feel as though she was beautiful, a breath stealing goddess that could stand beside him in some other life.

Their eyes met briefly, and he offered her a smile of soft encouragement, but she turned back to finish tying her dress. She thought it was a dream as he moved to step up behind her, his breath falling on her skin like water and his hands reaching to touch her but hovering just about the curve of her shoulders. "Did I not say that my affections could bring you pain?" He whispered with a note of sadness in his voice. He had told her that his touch would cause her pain, but she had not thought it could happen like this. She raised her head when she had finished with the cords and looked silently into his eyes, trying to smile.

For those brief moments that their eyes had me time stood still in the world, no seconds passed and the stars themselves stilled so that all that existed was the two of them. The nearness, the burning tension between them was like a fire that fed her soul and she needed him more than she had ever needed anyone before.

She looked up into his eyes as she turned back to face him, fastening her dress into place so that she was completely covered. It was so tempting to touch him, to lean forward just enough to press herself against him and let herself fall apart in his arms. She wanted to be strong, but it was too much to bear. The affection she had for him was shining in her eyes and gave her a strength that she did not understand. Reaching forward her hand brushed against his and Violetta shook her head sadly, certain that this would be the last time that she saw him, "Apologies... I..." The words she was about to say died on her lips as the guards of his master entered the room to take him away. He was almost out the door when she called his name "Cassian! Do not forget..."

He almost resisted the pull of his guards dragging him towards the door but that would have led to a report being made to Tertius and so he reluctantly moved with them but pulled to a stop, turned his head to look at her as she called out his name.

A genuine smile of deep affection lit her eyes when he looked back at her, the tenderness in her eyes as she lifted a finger to her lips in memory of the heated demand of his kiss. By the gods there had to be a way to see him again, to have moments alone with him again. She would gladly submit to any demand of her Dominus and his children to have that chance. Prayers would be sent every night that Venus was not so cruel as to ignite a love such as this; a thing of such consuming fire as to burn all the world, if there was to be no respite, no release or chance of satisfaction. Ignoring the presence of his guards, seeing only him Violetta lifted her chin defiantly and repeated back his words to her, an oath of their shared fight for this love "Never fucking lose."

CHAPTER 9

Opening his eyes Meridius saw the sun was high and hot as Felix Census rose from his bed. That it was Meridius and not Violetta rising from his bed to see his robes prepared did not seem to change the smile of satisfaction on his face. He was glad the Roman had decided on kindness the night before and had sent the girl to her cell instead of the bed of either of his children, both of whom had informed him of their desire for her. In his late-night ramblings to himself, in the presence of only his body slave, had revealed that he felt regret at allowing the lash to be raised to such a tender and delicate body which had prompted the rare moment of pity for her. He had sent her to her bed and commanded the impressive Spaniard to his bed instead.

Now he listened as Felix lay awake, having a single sided conversation with himself. He was considering how to best use the information he had learned the night before to his benefit. Meridius could tell that the gladiator had some feelings for Violetta, it was obvious to him if not the others, but whether it was possessive lust or more than that he could not tell for certain and it truly concerned him as a man who loved her like a father.

Felix had not gotten his mind beyond the point that he was determined to find a way to inspire the man to victory in the arena once more. That the girl seemed to be the key to the fulfillment of his desires, and the gladiator's, was obvious and so he sent word that she was to be bathed and scented for presentation that afternoon, he then sent word summoning Tertius to meet him for words regarding his man Canus, the lanista's desire for coin would ensure that he did not refuse the invitation.

"I find myself famished this morning." Felix said with a joviality that marked his delight in his own decision. "Go to the hall and bring much food to my office. There is great works to be done this day and I need sustenance after last night's more vigorous activities."

He was preparing a plate of the best cuts of meat and pieces of fruit for Felix when Selenia and Vitus met at the breakfast table. She was obviously nursing an ache in her head from the wine but otherwise seemed quite satisfied while Vitus was surly, likely from the dose of Opium he had taken the night before to curb his anger and disappointment at his father's decree that denied him Violetta. The Spaniard hid his chuckle at their attitudes regarding the girl that neither of them would possess no matter how much they desired her.

He watched the pair interacting and wished he could tell them how ridiculous their petty battle was. "Good morning dear brother." Selenia said as she lay on the lounge across from Vitus with a smirk "I trust that you... slept well and were satisfied last night?" Of course, the woman knew otherwise, and likely enjoyed pushing him to edge of his temper. The trust was that he was likely still fuming with rage that their father had denied him Violetta at the last moment before he had drawn her off to his chamber where he had informed her that she was dismissed from any service for the remainder of the night.

Popping his jaw to the side Vitus glared at his sister, the taunt was not missed, and he was clearly in no mood to meet it with anything but anger "You ruined my night with your little game with the gladiator. Father, the soft-hearted fool, took pity on her after what you did and sent her to her cell for 'rest'." Meridius knew that had Felix allowed Vitus his he would likely still have been busy tormenting her instead of eating with his smugly smiling sister. "I would not preen so much if I were you." He snipped back at her. "He will not let you take her to Rome, and I was told that even now he is having her bathed and scented for presentation, maybe he means to sell her though I doubt it, either way you will never own her and certainly not have her as I will. She was promised to me and I will have her." Drinking deeply, he watched the knowledge sink in and Meridius left them to their pointless argument to bring food to the elder Census. If he could still speak, he would have enjoyed telling Felix of his children's foolish debates over his property.

Across the city Tiberius Tertius sat at his desk considering the summons that had just arrived from Felix carefully. There had been a time not long before when more than one man had wanted words regarding the champion gladiator, which had ended in bloodshed and death; he would not hesitate to exercise the same tactics if they became needed with the merchant. Cassian was not for sale and would never be, the man would rise like a phoenix upon the sands bringing coin beyond count to his purse and honor to the ludus and the name of Tertius.

If he did not then, as any failure, he would be sent to the pits to earn what coin he could among the savages and criminals before he died at last, nameless and without glory. Standing to his feet with a deep sigh the lanista sent word that he would answer the summons, to refuse would cause offence and besides the man did serve some of the best wine in all Velletri even if it was early in the day for libations. "Come Jovian." He said to the dark-haired boy at his heel "We will go and see what kind of foolishness the merchant thinks will bring Cassian to his possession."

No one was to tell Violetta why she was being bathed in the middle of the day, or why her hair was brushed and braided as some delicate scent was applied to her neck and the crevice between her breasts. Meridius could tell, watching her as the women finished the last details of her dressing, that she was beginning to worry that she was to be used to entice another merchant to trade with her Dominus. There were other girls who had been put to the same use and more than one Roman man had stared at her when she had been laid on the table the night before. They had not been secretive about their wish to enjoy her, but she had likely missed the dismissive shake of Felix's head at each suggestion.

When she whispered to Meridius, asking if he would tell her why she had been summoned? Who stood inside the office of their Dominus? However, he could not give her an answer that he did not have, but instead offered an encouraging squeeze to her hand as the command for her to enter was heard. He nodded to her and resumed his mask of blank expression as he fell in behind her, hoping that he was not going to be forced to bear silent witness to more callous pain delivered for the pleasure of those they served.

Felix looked up with a smile as Violetta entered and after finishing his drink, he stood to walk towards her with an expression that made Meridius' skin crawl. The sun was streaming across the warm tiles and causing her freshly washed skin to practically glow in its light. Her hair glistened and eyes as blue as the Mediterranean itself stared fearfully back at him, begging for answers and for a moment he was taken back to the market eight years prior when he had seen her naked upon the auction block.

A smile spread across the Roman's lips "Very well turned out but, I think, the hint of fear is unbecoming." He circled her and pushed the back of her dress open to look at the marks on her back that were still bright red but not stitched. "Tell me, does your back still cause grievous discomfort? Enough so to make certain tasks unbearable?" He asked with a mild interest in his voice. Felix was not a man who held to the theory that the pain of others could equal pleasure for the one wielding it which was something Meridius was grateful for, for his own sake as much as Violetta's.

Violetta kept her head straight and her shoulders squared when he moved her dress, her eyes cast down to the floor as he had taught her the first week she was in the house. They both knew if she answered him the wrong way she could end up on her hands and knees before him that moment or even worse, sent that night to the bed of Vitus and so she paused a short moment before replying in a cautious voice "There is some pain still Dominus but the medicus says there will be no scar to show the act." Felix looked as though he would attempt to see how fit she was, making Meridius ready himself to step in to distract him, when they were interrupted by the voice of Selenia from the doorway.

Gliding into the office with a smooth smile Selenia regarded Violetta and Meridius with a mild amusement and sat beside her father's chair, pouring a cup of wine and studying the girl and her Felix while ignoring the Spaniard to his relief. "The celebration last night was a wonderful surprise; indeed, it exceeded any expectation I could have had upon returning home. I am sorry to say that my visit will be more limited than I had first told you, I have been invited by several to attend celebrations and as they are with Praetor's and Senator's I dare not refuse."

Like every member of her family the female Census was determined to rise into the elite of the Republic, but unlike her father and brother Meridius suspected she had no intention of bringing her family with her. "I know you would love me to stay home in the villa, but you did teach us to pursue the rise of the family at all costs did you not?" She let her eyes rake over Violetta again before asking "What is it that you are up to today father? More games?" Her bored tone did not fool Meridius, she was ready to ask to take Violetta with her to Rome again and that could not be allowed to continue.

Felix kissed his daughter's cheek gently and shook his head as he returned to his desk while Meridius nearly sighed with the relief of knowing Felix well enough to know that he and the girl that stood as a daughter to him was safe from the separation he feared. Gesturing Violetta to the wall he noted that she watched Selenia with a lingering fear in her eyes. "I am waiting on the arrival of Tiberius Tertius actually my dear. I expect him any moment so that we can have some discussion regarding his gladiator that holds some interest to me after last night."

Meridius hoped that the lanista would be less than agreeable to his plan; things would be much easier if he wasn't; they would be able to return to their lives, but Felix was, as any good merchant, prepared to make a few bargains to get what he desired and that did not sit well in the Spaniard's gut.

"Unless you too have business with the lanista I would advise for you to go about your day, I am unsure how long the negotiations will take. Do your future hosts still reside in Velletri this day? Perhaps it would be wise to seek them out, with your brother in attendance, so that your honor is not damaged of course." The pair shared a laugh at their own jokes for they all knew that Selenia was not to be a virgin bride. Meridius wondered how much the woman would compromise to gain position in Rome.

With a last lingering look at Violetta in her elegance Selenia left the room with a smug smile plastered across her face. Meridius felt the same feeling of satisfaction that she had been distracted away from asking her father once again if she could take possession of Violetta. Now if he could only stop the other Roman in the room from involving his daughter in his schemes, he would be a happier man and could get back to finding ways to ease the fear he could see in Violetta's eyes.

It did not take long after Selenia had left for Vitus to come storming into his father's office. Meridius stepped into his path to stop him, the merchant did not want to be disturbed and the anger on his son's face told that he had been predictably enraged by whatever his sister had told him about their father's meeting with the lanista. It angered him that his presence caused Violetta to shrink back against the wall, cowering in fear at the thought that he might touch her and all the while a man who loved her dearly stood nearby, helpless to aid her in the vipers chose to strike.

Felix sat at his desk, reading the scroll he held in his hands. There was no doubt among those in the room that he had seen his son enter the room and even less doubt that he knew his son was angry. "Father, your damned Spaniard will not remove himself from my path. Command him to move before I do so with force." He snarled viciously, his hands raising to rest against Meridius' chest, ready to push against the man as he towered over him. Even though he was a slave he could not help the mocking look in his eyes that would enrage Vitus even more and keep his attention away from the frightened girl.

"Meridius, step aside and let my son come to talk to me." Felix said in a voice that told of his boredom at Vitus' anger. "I'd rather have his upset dealt with now instead of it interrupting me later while I am in meeting with the lanista." He turned his head to address the now fuming heir of his name and made Meridius smile with his annoyance. "What is it that vexes you so early in the day that you must disturb me now?" He set down the scroll and reached for his cup with an air of expectation.

Vitus glared at Meridius for a breath before addressing his father. "Selenia tells me that you are going to sell Violetta to the lanista? Why would you do this when I, myself, have offered to buy her from you at more than she is worth?" He looked towards the girl cringing next to the wall. "I will not let you do this; I will not let you send her to that beast in the ludus to be ruined."

Meridius' eyes flickered back and forth between the two debating the girl as if she did not stand in the room, able to hear every word. He had never liked Vitus or Selenia, both were spoiled and all the more vicious for it, but he was determined not to let either of them have what they wanted from the girl. There was not a lot of power he could wield but what he could do he would, to make sure that she was safe from them.

"You will not let me?" Felix said with a frown, rising from his seat. "I think you forget your station in this house, son. I stand Pater Familias and the Dominus of this house. All slaves within it are my own." His voice bordered on angry "They are mine to do with as I wish and if you continue to push this... agenda of yours then I will send her back to the villa or to Rome or sell her to the damned lanista!" At the final word he slapped his hand down upon the desk so hard that Violetta jumped, and his wine spilled, causing Meridius to step forward to clean it before papers were ruined. "Today you will do as fucking commanded and see Selenia escorted as needed."

Vitus stared at his father, his face showed the surprise he felt at his father's vehement anger and Meridius could not help the snort of amusement he released at the look on the Roman's face. He had longed for the moment when the younger Census was put in his place in some regard, no matter what it was. That it was this, with Violetta, made it even better. He stood tall, glowering as the Roman wordlessly exited the room to obey his father's command to escort his sister around the city.

Felix looked first at Meridius and then Violetta. "The lanista should be here within the hour. I want this room to be spotless. Meridius, get all the papers except the contract out of sight. I do not wish for him to have anything to touch that could ease his anxiety. The game to be played is delicate." He looked back and forth between the pair of slaves "This is to go perfectly, or I will be greatly displeased." He stalked from the room telling them both that he intended to return just before the lanista was expected.

Tertius was smiling as he was ushered into Felix' chamber, obviously impressed by the rich decorations surrounding. The silk tapestries and marble statues placed to demonstrate a simplistic taste, the sparseness of the display only serving to accent the quality of his host's possessions. Meridius wondered if the man was secretly jealous of men like Census. He had heard that he sought a seat in the senate that he would never have. The note of forced politeness in the lanista's voice, the clipped tone, soon answered his question; the man was beside himself with jealousy, but he still greeted his host as though they stood upon equal ground. "Good Felix," He nodded before sinking into a chair of such softness that he had to force his face not to reveal his surprise at its comfort. "Gratitude for a second invitation to your home, I must admit it came as a surprise after the events of last night. Your note said you wished to break words regarding Cassian. What exactly is it that you seek in his regard?"

Felix smiled, "Good Tertius I hope my message did not disturb your rest so early in the day. I know it was, perhaps, rude of me to intrude only hours after your return to your villa but I have been inspired by an idea that just could not wait for a later hour." He leaned forward in his seat and met the lanista's eyes with the gleam Meridius knew meant he was ready to bargain. "A partnership that involves your man Cassian. Would such a thing be of interest to you?" He could see the thoughts floating in the eyes of the man across from him and waited with bated breath to see what he would say.

"A partnership? If you think the man is for sale, even after poor showings of late, then you are gravely mistaken. Cassian is not for sale." His eyes wandered to the girl, lingering for a moment longer than the Spaniard was comfortable with. Every one of the men could see why the Celt wanted her as he did, she was a delicate and rare beauty but how what did she have to do with the conversation regarding his man except to remind him of how she inspired fire in the returning champion of the city? "I do not think you understand the worth of the man if you think a loaned slave in my bed is an enticement then you know less of gladiators than I thought." Tertius continued with annoyance in his voice

Felix laughed at the expected and obvious response from the lanista. "Good Tertius I think all of Velletri knows that the man is not for sale and besides I have no desire to possess him or learn the skills of a lanista." A smile spread across his face and he beckoned Violetta forward to stand at Tiberius' side, causing Meridius' pulse to race slightly "I do however possess something he desires and in truth who can blame the man for his lust when the offering is so sweet."

Turning his attention back to the girl as she stood closer, Tertius began to inspect her in earnest, rising from the comfort of the seat to circle her as he would if she was to join the ludus instead of being used to inspire one of its men. "Violetta, that is your name is it not?" He asked her, smiling when she nodded without raising her eyes. Was it madness, lust or love between her and the Celtic gladiator he wondered? Either way it could be used against him and that meant so could she. "You have my interest Felix. What do you propose?"

Felix almost laughed and even Meridius could see how simple it was to manipulate the man if the ownership of his champion was not threatened. It was almost too easy, but Felix contained his laughter with a drink and nodded towards Violetta. "It is my thought to make good use of his lust, while it lasts, to inspire him towards further victory." He leaned back against the pillows as he continued "Such as; if he was the victor in a match, I would be inclined to send her to the ludus for the duration of the night."

Meridius was almost certain he saw a flutter of joy in the girl's eyes before he continued "But if he were not victorious, and yet lived, then we could give common thought to a punishment for her that suited his loss." Flexing his fingers, he watched as the Roman carefully watched them both, the tremble in Violetta's knees suggested that this gladiator was not a man she feared as Vitus seemed to hope but one whom she held close to her heart and the spark in Tertius' eyes confirmed that the merchant had found the way he needed to maneuver the lanista into being business partners. It would see them both to great profit if it worked and was a minimal loss to him if it did not.

A beam of sunlight snuck its way past the heavy drapes that had kept the brightness of the midmorning sun from blinding them all while each of them waited to hear the lanista's answer. Looking at the girl he stroked his chin in a moment of reflection before asking the wiser question; "What is it that you ask in return for her favors?" The man lived for profit; it was not possible that he would do this for nothing.

Felix smiled languidly as he leaned back with a look of complete calm and satisfaction that Meridius knew well. "I would have you make it known that Cassian is not up to form, that you fear he may have lost his fire for the arena so that when I make my wagers upon him, in what will seem a drunken folly, there will be better odds and more coin to my purse when he emerges victorious. Of course, each time it will be to your utter amazement and my complete delight." His eyes wandered the room, almost caressing each possession with a devious smile as they landed on the decorated girl who he beckoned closer to the desk so that he could caress a hand lightly down her back, his fingertips lingering on the welt marks left there from the night before. "I am sure, should you choose to agree to this bargain, that there would be some conditions you would like applied as well? To satisfy your man?"

Tiberius stood and placing his palms flat on the older man's desk he looked Felix in the eyes, his voice sweet to the point of almost taunting him, as if he were testing his desire to see this plot brought to life.

"My man fights in tomorrow's primus match at days' end. See the girl to the pulvinus, passed off as a woman of noble birth and ensure that his eyes will rest upon her the moment that he takes the sands and looks up to see the one he desires dressed not as the slave he thinks her to be but a peer of his Dominus and yourself."

Meridius could see the game that they were playing now; it would drive the Celt wild and vicious with the speculation that the girl might not be who he thought her to be. He was pushing to see if Felix was willing to take the risk to see a slave in the attire of a Roman and then the lanista would risk the man's heart and fire to see Cassian regain his title to stand champion of Velletri once more.

Felix did not flinch under the stare that would still the mightiest of gladiators but smiled and said smugly "A feat easily accomplished. I will be at the games the length of the day. Are you certain that your man will see her?" He stood and gestured for Violetta to fetch and pour the wine before he handed a glass to Tertius "Join me in a toast towards profitable endeavors?" If it was a game of wills the man thought to play, he would find his opponent to be one of unbreakable spirit even if the pawn he used to play did not possess the same. What kind of comfort would she need at the end of this? It would not matter for Meridius knew that he would be there to offer it.

Tertius nodded and reached for the wine offered by soft and trembling hands. Bringing the fine cup to his lips he took Violetta's chin in grasp with the other, forcing her to look up at him and bringing the Spaniard to an uneasy awareness. "Whether or not he sees her is better put to the one charged with the task itself, don't you think?" He replied, letting his grip become painful, almost bruising as he studied her eyes waiting for an answer.

His pulse raced when Violetta slowly raised her eyes to meet those of Tertius for a moment before turning them down to the floor as she winced in his grasp. "I will do what I can to please, Dominus." Her voice was a whisper as she stilled completely. She was the bait to be played against a warrior's affections for their coin purses. "Whatever is required of me." She bowed her head and Meridius, pitying the fear she had to be feeling, prayed that Felix would leave it at that and not demand further words from her.

"We agree then." He said with a laugh as he extended his hand, clasping it tightly over Felix's forearm.

Meridius clenched his jaw in annoyance that one he loved was to be used in such a way. Cassian would see the woman he had defended dressed in luxury and jewels and the gladiator would not be able to help but wonder if she was who she said she was. Slave or noble the question would drive him to victory so that he could have his answer. This partnership would lead to renown and coin for both Romans and when the Celt tired of Violetta it would be simple enough to see it ended, leaving her broken in heart and body.

Meridius swore that he would be there, to hold her tight enough to put the pieces back together and they would carry on as they had, forgetting this foolishness eventually.

Returning the lanista's grasp Felix grinned and handed his now emptied cup to Violetta to be refilled. "Decision warms the heart. If all goes as I expect the bounty brought to both our houses will be more than either of us can imagine right now." He turned to Violetta and took the refilled cup from her hands. How it was that he would accomplish the lanista's dare was not so certain as the merchant had made it seem; to get the slave to the pulvinus on the second day of the games and dressed as a Roman of note that no one there would know could be dangerous for all involved.

Meridius knew that Violetta would be resplendent and impossible for the gladiator to miss in the light of the evening primus, yet her features could not be disguised to hide her from the rest of those on the pulvinus. The details of her dress would surely be left to Selenia and though the conniving woman would have her fun dressing the girl as a doll he was certain Violetta herself would likely not enjoy the attention so much.

CHAPTER 10

Vitus had walked the grounds of the villa in the hopes that it would clear his head and reveal the course of action he should take in dealing with his father's meeting with the lanista. Should he get Selenia to join him? Neither of them wanted their father to sell the girl though they both had different reasons to protest the sale; Selenia lusted for her beauty and would eventually grow to hate her if more men noticed her slave than herself but Vitus could see her use beyond the pleasure of his bed.

Though the breaking of the girl to his will would be a deep pleasure he knew that there would already be talk among the elite of Velletri and there would be certain men curious to see the woman who could make a man so well known for his control lose his grasp and move against a woman of Rome. Vitus knew that he could use her fearful submission to him to further excite the nobles of the city, his friends took pleasure in instilling terror in such creatures but more than that he thought to strike while the iron of curiosity was hot, exhibiting the woman so that all who wondered could see what it took to bring the renowned champion to heel.

He paused in the door of the room where his sister still lounged, slowly savoring her morning meal as her hair was re-styled for the day. "Will you come and speak to him with me? Or is your mind too engrossed in deciding which lover to favor today as I escort you about the city like a pimp?"

Selenia stood and walked towards her brother with a blaze of anger in her eyes that made him want to laugh. "You overstep brother and know it well." She raised her hand as though she intended to slap him but instead lowered it and smiled smoothly "You are going to have to adjust that mentality for the men we will be meeting are higher in rank than our own father and would not take kindly to you thinking the woman they court is a whore." She turned on her heel to return to her seat and met his eyes with an annoying calm "I am not sure why it is that you wish to speak to him anyway. He is all but certain to be selling the girl to the lanista who attends him even now." She sipped her wine as he held back his rage at her final words; "You will never have her now Vitus. Set sights upon other prizes, she is lost to you."

Watching her smug expression as she sat opposite him, he got to his feet and snarled "He had best not, I have waited these years to have her and I will not be robbed of that moment now." Storming from the room he marched into his father's office bellowing "You cannot do it! I will not have you sell Violetta to that pathetic lanista." He had forgotten that the girl did not belong to him except in his desires but the thought that she might be given instead to that groveling flesh peddler and wasted on gladiators and their brutish lusts set him in a rage.

Vitus turned his head at a cough from the man he spoke of whose presence had been pushed from his mind by the force of his anger at his father. "I would offer apologies Tertius, but I am a man who speaks the truth, the wording of it however I do offer apologies for." He knew that his father would be enraged at him later but to his surprise in the heat of the moment the merchant was surprisingly, eerily calm. "My apologies to you as well father. I had not expected you to be at business so early in the day, but disturbing word was brought to ear, by the sweet whisperings of my sister."

He turned his head to look at Violetta with a lustful disdain he continued "She spoke of your desire to sell the girl and I wanted to ensure you knew that the first offer made for her purchase was by me." He returned his attention to the lanista with a shrug "I am sure you wish her to spread legs for your gladiator, but I have desired her possession for years instead of days."

It was a balance of aggravation and relief when Felix did not respond to him except to pointedly re-introduce him to the lanista. "Tertius, no doubt you have memory of my son Vitus from the celebration last night?" He smirked slightly, "though I am certain it is his sister and her theatrics that linger in the mind."

"Indeed..." Tiberius seemed to be fighting back his frown, societal decorum demanded that he join his host in ignoring his rudeness even if his temper screamed to put his fist through his face. Returning his attention to his host he gave a curt nod of his head and smiled "On this note I shall bid you farewell until our next meeting. I hope that you achieve the terms of our agreement to the benefit of all." With a smirk and a look in the direction of the girl he added "May the games bring all our desires for glory to fruition and success." Without further words, he turned and took his leave of father and son, leaving Vitus and his father to the harsh words that were sure to come once they were alone with the slaves.

Vitus barely waited until the lanista was outside the room before he stormed up to his father's desk and hissed at him as he set down his cup of wine with an annoying calm. "Selenia says you mean to sell Violetta to the lanista. Why would you do such a thing when you have promised her to me, and I have not yet had even a single night to use her after years of waiting?" He was whining, and he knew it, but it was just an hour ago he had all but promised not to make the sale and here was making gods knew what kind of bargain with the flinty little man.

"You continue to forget, my son, that the girl belongs to me and as her Dominus I may do as I wish with her." His father said, holding up his glass for more wine, they both watched as Violetta skirted the desk to avoid him. "I am not, in fact, selling her to anyone. My dealings with Tertius have no effect upon you yet and should the time come that they do I will inform you of the details. Until such time as that I will remind you to keep your nose out of places, and things, that do not concern you." His eyes were a cold and silent challenge for the boy to defy him when he was in the right and the girl was his and his alone until she was sold. "I remind you not to forget who is the master of this house Vitus, and I intend to stay as such for many years to come."

"Do I note tension between you father?" Selenia said as she strolled into the room, cup in hand and a smug smile on her face. Vitus realized that he had stepped right into her hand by doing just as expected and angered their father by interrupting him. "Apologies for my late rising, I fear last night's excitement was slightly too much for me, and with no gentle touch to sooth me to sleep my rest was not as it could have been." His sister cooed as her eyes ran over the girl that was practically cowering against the wall instead of meeting her gaze with the brazen attitude of the night before. "I had hoped for this one to attend me and finish the night pleasurably instead of with the chill of the moon."

"Apology unneeded but appreciated." Felix said to his daughter with a warm smile that Vitus never seemed to receive. The bond between father and daughter had always been one that had been soothed easily with a few words or even a look though that with his only son was always a strain to see to peace. "I myself may have over indulged last night or else I would never have let you raise the lash to a slave not your own and so much in demand. Your little game with the gladiator made it so that no one could have enjoyed her last night no matter how light the touch or," He looked at Vitus "how much they enjoy the pain of others." He shook his head "Had it been any other than Tertius I would have stopped you by force, but I wanted the man to see how much his gladiator was willing to sacrifice to save her."

Selenia nodded, accepting her father's gentle admonishment with a graceful smile that irked her brother with its insincerity. "Of course, father. I would never seek to displease you or abuse your generosity with your slaves." She held out her hand for Violetta to bring her a cup of wine and watched the anger rise on her brother's face when she caressed the girl's face with a smile, the tip of her finger lingering on her lip before she turned her attention to their father once again. "Are you truly selling this little one father? I would like the chance to see if she takes pleasure as well as she takes pain." Her eyes lingered on the girls back when she walked away, the bright red welts standing out in stark contrast to the pale skin.

The room was filled with silence and then Vitus smirked "You will be pleased, my dear sister, to learn that father is not planning on selling her away from our midst. She is merely to be loaned... much like one of your dresses or a mask." His eyes flashed dangerously as he moved to stand behind Violetta, running a fingertip down the length of one of the welts. Her shiver excited him, and he knew that night it would be his pleasure to be the one to make her scream. "Is this not joyous news, Selenia?" He asked, stepping away from the girl towards the door "It seems that not only do we keep our household decorated with the most beautiful slaves in Velletri, but we are entering a new business of renting out whores?" He laughed darkly when Violetta cringed in shame "Now we can make enough coin to buy you the villa in Rome so that you can continue to master the new trade of the house of Census in the Capitol where I am certain you will bring honor to our father hmm?"

Selenia was better at hiding her rage than Vitus had ever been, but his words were more than she could stand. "It is indeed joyous my brother, but I think perhaps the coin would be put to better use buying you a bride since it seems that you lack the skill to obtain one for yourself and it would be a shame if our father's noble house was not continued simply because you cannot find a woman fool enough to marry you." He watched their father sputter, holding back his laughter as he drank his wine and Vitus' face flushed to match its rich red color. She had always been able to get beneath his skin like this and he never seemed to find the nerve to return the dig and make her lose her temper.

Aware that his father was laughing at him Vitus forced a smile to his face and stood "I think I would be better off in the company of my peers than here or escorting my sister to her... appointments." He sneered at her then rose, nodding his head to his father then looking at Violetta. "I expect her in my bed tonight father, as you promised days ago." When the old man nodded, he took his leave of the room with a satisfied smile, noting that the girl had paled to the point of near tears at the thought of him. Her fear would be easily manipulated when he had her alone and if she was soon to bed the gladiator again, he would make sure that the time she spent in his bed would be put to the best uses possible and every drop of pleasure he could wring from the time would be savored.

Selenia giggled behind her hand and looked at her father with complete delight in her eyes "He still cannot stand to lose can he father?" The raise in his eyebrow told her that though he agreed with her he did not approve of her constant taunting of her brother. With a sigh she rose to her feet and replaced the cup on the desk before straightening her gown "With your leave I will make my way to my appointments for today." They both knew what she was going to be doing during these 'appointments' but both pretended that it was something else that would not dishonor the house of Census. "Unless there is something else you need of me before that, dear father?" Her tone was warmly adoring but she was eager to be gone to begin her own business of pleasure for the day.

"There is a favor that I would ask of you before you continue your day, one to be executed with the greatest discretion." When her brows arched with elegant curiosity he continued with a vague gesture towards Violetta "I need for you to stop in the market to make purchase of a dress for her, one that you yourself would wear. I am taking her to the pulvinus tomorrow and she must appear to be as Roman as you or me when she attracts the attention of the gladiator. There is a great deal of importance that rides upon his fascination with her and I would have you ensure that she meets the desired expectation." He smiled and held up a purse of coins that jingled when shook "Spare no expense and see yourself treated as well." The smile that came to her lips was expected so when she took the bag from his hand and kissed his cheek, he returned it with a wink "See this done and earn your father's gratitude and affection thrice over my beloved daughter."

With a delighted laugh Selenia left the study and summoning a pair of her fathers' larger male house slaves and her own attendant body slave, Maya, left the villa to make her way to the marketplace of Velletri. Though her father marketed silks of the finest quality there was no one in the house that could make a dress of finery in such a short time, so she would have to find something premade and glorious. The gown she would purchase for herself would cast the other into shadow with its finery and how it would draw all eyes to her but she would make sure that her father's little toy looked the part of the Roman woman she was meant to, even if she did not understand the game she was happy to play a part and earn her father's favor while her brother protested, raged and looked like a child who did not get his way.

The market was buzzing and full of life; merchants trying to outdo each other by yelling louder with greater compliments to those passing them by. She made her way through the stalls easily, remarking to herself how much smaller it was than the market of Rome and how her father expected her to find garments of the same degree of finery as her own was beyond her but after some time she did discover, by chance, a man who she had dealt with in the capital. They smiled and laughed, commenting on how the rural cities had so little appreciation for the true finery he had to offer. It took some moments and haggling for him to show her better than what he was offering the simpler eyes of Velletri, but he eventually produced a silk dress of soft pink, pale but warm like the sunrise that would complement her rosy complexion perfectly. For Violetta she decided upon a deep turquoise with cream detailing to accent her youth but still exhibit her beauty.

"This should satisfy my father and leave me more time to attend to my own affairs and perhaps leave this city with brighter prospect with which to greet you upon your return." She said to the merchant with a knowing smile before she handed the wrapped material to one of the slaves and made her way to the villa of a man expecting her with wine and an empty bed.

Back at the villa of Census, Felix sat pondering the interactions of the morning; his angry and demanding son off placing wagers with his father's money, his conniving daughter who was determined to squeeze as much from him as possible and the lanista with his outrageous dare to have Violetta seen on the pulvinus as a Roman by his gladiator as he was about to fight. The man would either regain his title with startling force or be dead within moments, with hope for the former he turned his attention on the girl patiently waiting for his next command with a blank expression on her face as though her body had not just been bartered once again to increase the wealth of her master and perhaps even that of another Roman. Only a few weeks had passed since he had first sent the girl to the ludus but already it was proving to be one of his better decisions. She had been purchased on a whim for her pleasing face and innocence but never had the merchant thought that the sacrifice of her virginity would bring such exciting profit to his house. "I hope you play your part well tomorrow Violetta." He said, holding his cup out for more wine. "Much rides upon the fascination you seem to inspire in men."

CHAPTER 11

"See him to the Medicus." Cassian heard Tertius called from the balcony as soon as the former champion winced after being struck by a weaker opponent. "When he is cleared to fight see him back to the sands and training until sunset."

This was the way of the ludus and lanistas.

If the gladiator was to win, he had to earn it and there was no easy restful night before the games. He would train until he was ready to fall over from exhaustion then eat and rest until the next day when he would be bathed and dressed before riding a cart down the steep hill to the arena. When he had reigned as champion, weeks ago, the crowds of men and women had screamed with lustful delight at the sight of him. Flowers had fallen from windows, dresses had fallen from shoulders to expose breasts from every window and he had been paraded as a prized stallion through the streets on the way to the arena. Not this time. As a fallen champion returning to the fight there would be no such jubilation this day. Unless his title was reclaimed he would still be forced to answer to a false name. In such an event Cassian was prepared for a long delay in returning to the ludus while the Romans celebrated as if the achievement was their own, but if he fell, he would be left to be burned with the rest of the corpses, one more legend falling short of expected glory.

With an annoyed toss of his head he threw his training swords to the boy, Cicero, who cleaned and cared for such things until he reached an age where he might train to use them.

"What fucking madness is in his mind now?" He muttered to himself as he made his way down the sunlit hall to the infirmary carved into the rock of the ground beneath the villa. "Well, Arturo, it seems your gods grant you the inspection like you wished when I returned last night." The gladiator grinned, leaning against the door and watching the man inside putter with his herbs and potions.

They had been friends far longer than Cassian had been a gladiator and Arturo a slave medicus. The 'Heathen Priest' as Tertius and the Romans named him had been captured in a battle, sacrificing his own freedom to save that of his king, who was rumored to have been his lover. That was something that no one, even Cassian, could confirm.

"Tertius wishes me cleared before taking to the sands in the Primus of tomorrow's games concluding the Saturnalia celebrations. I need to be ready for that fight, old friend."

Straightening Arturo laughed and pushed his long hair from his face with the back of a hand painted with the blue markings of his faith. His deep blue eyes sparkled teasingly as he nodded for the Celt to enter "If you had allowed it then you would not, perhaps, be in the discomfort you are now hmm?"

Few men in the ludus would have dared to tease the fallen champion but there was little that could not be spoken between these two. When Cassian had taken a seat on the table the medicus removed the bandage slowly from around his patient's wound, being careful not to risk the tear of any stitches. He surveyed the injury that had brought the man almost to his knees and thus his death only a few weeks before.

"It is none the worse for the strain of last night or weeks training." He said with a smirk as he dusted his fingertips over the wound.

The Celt knew stitches were intact, and the edges were well approximated and healing with no visible sign or symptom of infection.

"You are the man most favored by the gods above any I have met. A lesser man would have been incapacitated for weeks after such an injury. You, however, train and gain position in the primus even after a night put upon display that saw you return flushed and agitated. Who was it that saw you to that state?" Arturo asked softly, not noticing the guarded look in his friend's eye.

Cassian shook his head with a dark grin and moved his friend's hand from his thigh to the almost healed wound on his side. "You and I are both aware of the true cause of my pain. Arturo. You know what I need to do, or the title will stand forever outside my reach, tomorrow is the last chance to reclaim it and all it means."

"You know that what you are asking for could compromise you more than the wound?" Arturo said quietly with a sigh. It was a dangerous game he played, and his request made it even more so, for them both, if it was granted.

"And yet absent the aid, the risk of failure is far greater." The gladiator locked eyes with his friend and waited for his decision; he knew it was not an easy thing to ask of him and he hated his own weakness for needing it but if he was to rise to the title of champion once again there was no risk he could not take to get there.

Shaking his head with a smirk, Cassian knew he would have his way when the medicus turned to the locked cabinet against the wall, retrieved a bottle, an empty vial and several green, oval leaves. Adding some dust from the bottle to the vial he then finished filling it with the juice that stood in a jug on the table that held his loaf of bread for the day. Arturo extended both hands, the vial in one and the leaves in the other.

"You have two options if you are determined to do this, which is against my advice. The opium is likely to bring you hallucinations along with the pain relief and burst of adrenaline. It will be sweet on your tongue, thanks to the juice. The coca leaf will be bitter and take longer to work. It will not bring you the visions that the other will, but your heart will race faster. It could cause a skip in rhythm or an episode of failure. Both are a great risk and if you do this you may find yourself wanting more of them. You will hate me when I deny you that which you want most, and you could want it even more than you want her." Arturo said, waiting for Cassian to meet his eyes before he set the drugs down on the table.

"I am not a man given to addiction, Arturo." Cassian said. "I am stronger than the drug and after this, either by death or victory, I will never require the detestable drug again."

"Remember, take it just before taking to the sands. It is not the strongest blend, but it will still do what you wish it to though its effects will not last for long. The aftereffects, should you live to feel them, will last much longer I promise you."

With a grin and a nod, the gladiator tucked the vial into his balteus, rejoining his guards he immediately made his way back to the sands. Though the heat of the day was rising his spirits joined the climb as his foot hit the training ground once again. He had a purpose, a goal, and had obtained the means to achieve it even though it was one that he loathed as much as he hated to grovel before the Romans. The vial contained opium, though not pure or even strong compared to what most who partook of it would use, it would suffice to dull his pain the next day and allow him to fight as though in primed physical condition.

Tomorrow night would see him to either a shameful death or a glorious victory, though the thought of victory's spoils were tainted slightly by the lack of his right to voice his choice for his prize his life would mean there would be a chance to lay eyes upon 'her' again even though they could not break words with each other. Just to see her face would cause his heart to soar. He accepted his practice swords once again from the boy with a grin and with a nod from the Doctore cleared his mind of all things except victory. "Who among you is ready to face me?" He called to his brethren with the laugh of a man certain of his ability to win.

Tarcarus of Thrace stepped forward to meet the challenge of the one-time champion with a serious expression on his face and his weapons at the ready. "Your time is passed Cassian. I will take the title from the man that took it from you. Step down, accept this and relinquish this primus to a man that will actually bring honor to the house of Tertius." The Celt shook his head, the braids at his temple falling over his shoulder as he laughed "You think to take it from me, Tarcarus? Come and see yourself to ground in the attempt with wood and stand grateful that I do not hold steel to send you to the afterlife."

The two men paired off and Cassian met the Thracian's eyes with a chuckle but when Doctore called for them to begin all signs of laughter disappeared and were replaced by the dangerous assessment of a trained killer. Muscles tensed with the astounding power of revenge unleashed against a man that had nothing to do with his anger. There would be no quarter or mercy. He would see this fight to its end even if it meant that he was in danger of meeting his own upon the arena sands the next day.

The Thracian struck the first blow, but the Celt blocked with an ease that would have made him laugh any other day but today it was just another lesson to take to heart and to the sands. Within seconds he had matched blows that would have sent many of the other men on the sands to the ground, but the man stood his ground and returned each strike. It took only moments before Cassian had him, he learned more in those first few minutes of combat than he would have learned in weeks of conversation. When he took a knee to the back it set him off balance for only a moment before the instinct of years on the sands took over. He moved with the momentum of the blow instead of fighting it and turned to use it to rain a hard blow to Tarcarus' shoulder.

They began to spar, trading blows of sword against sword with a melodious drumbeat of wood upon wood. The other man hit hard, but the Celt hit harder, moved faster by a fraction and thought just a second quicker and so they danced the training ground until for the fifth time the former champion sent his opponent into the sands on his face. "Doctore, I grow tired of these foolish attempts." He laughed, tossing his weapons to the ground. "Take up arms yourself so that at least I may train against the only man here who stands my equal or better."

The dark-skinned man laughed and looped his whip to his belt, the good-natured ribbing between them was a thing they were long used to. As he held out his hand for his own training swords he was paused by the sound of a wagon on the hill and the opening of the gates. "Jupiter spares you once again, Cassian, for new stock arrives and they need my lessons more than you need to be humbled."

Slowly each man on the sands stopped their training and made their way to the floor of the dining hall to watch the arrival of the recruits. Every man among them remembered their own arrival and were prepared to give as good as they had gotten themselves; the hazing and teasing would continue until each man either earned the branded mark of Tertius or they died on the sands. The worst would be carted off to the mines having been deemed not worth the continued training to be a gladiator.

The wagon was narrow and crowded with bulky men who had not bathed for days, perhaps weeks and Proximus was the largest of them and so felt the most crowded. He had never thought to find himself in a slave wagon ever again, but the circumstances of his life had changed and not for the better. Once the most renowned gladiator in Rome he had been sold to Tiberius Tertius and therefore sentenced to fight in the provincial city of Velletri where he would have to battle his way though the ranks of their gladiators before anyone even took notice of him, his titles and laurels would be ignored or even used against him.

He sighed and rested his head back against the walls of the wagon, the sounds of the muttering men and even the brief noise from the city were nothing when compared to the roar of the crowd of the Circus Maximus in Rome where his name had been on every lip roaring like thunder from the heavens. They had not told him the reason he was sold but what else was to be expected of Romans? Perhaps his Dominus had discovered that his wife had been summoning the champion for 'private' audiences? Or maybe this man Tertius had made him an offer impossible to refuse, either way he was now back at the bottom of the ranks and would have to fight his way to the top once more.

"Get out of the fucking wagon!" The driver bellowed and looked up at Tertius who had arrived to survey the new men, including the once champion of Rome. He barely locked eyes with the Doctore though he had seen the man fight and in more recent years, train the best gladiators in the Republic. It irked Cassian that his friend was no longer afforded the respect that he was due for his blood shed.

"Cirandon. I have brought you a new shit of recruits. One of them has even seen the inside of the arena." The driver pointed towards Proximus "That one fought to entertain the Emperor himself in recent games celebrating his birthday. Maybe you can make a decent champion out of him if Cassian fails again." He laughed until he caught the offended look on Cassian's face and turned to see that the look on Tertius' face matched that of the Celt.

Cassian looked up to see Tertius hand his cup to Jovian who was eagerly peering over his shoulder at the men on the sand. Looking back at the recruits there was only one that seemed to stand out. If the new man was lucky and he felt merciful, then the former champion might last a few days before they attempted to kill each other. Two fallen champions vying for the same title, though one would have to prove himself worthy of 'the mark' first, was sure to result in bloodshed between them at some point he simply hoped that killing the man did not anger the lanista to the point where he denied him his primus and the chance he hoped for upon those sands.

Cassian stepped from the sands to join his brothers in watching the arrival of the new men, curiosity and tradition taking the place of his desire for steel in his hands. With a frown he assessed each man; was there not more than enough men scratching to earn the mark and trying to achieve the title? HIS title? Carefully watching each man as their feet hit the sands for the first time, he saw how most of them struggled with the restraint of the shackles and some seemed to fear to even meet the eyes of the marked men but there was one who held himself differently. He was a head taller than the rest and he moved with a proud bearing that was not bold but almost indifferent, as though he knew that he more than belonged on the sands but that he knew the thrill of them as well as the anguish. There was no doubt that this was the man the driver spoke of. Who would win if the day came when they met upon the sands? He had never fought a man from the arenas of Rome before but, he thought with a smirk, they likely died just the same as any other man.

The big man at last met Cassian's eyes and the Celt could see the bafflement in his expression when the men around him deferred to him with the respect his title demanded. It was easy for any man who had been in a ludus before to see that he was their leader though many wondered how a man of less than six feet tall could be the champion that even those in the capital whispered about. His thoughts about the former champion were put aside when Doctore stepped forward, his whip in hand, ready to address the recruits that would live or die under his tutelage.

"Do you pathetic excuses for men know where you are?" He called with a severe frown and a loud voice that carried over the sand and out into the wildness of the countryside around the ludus walls. The attention of everyone, Cassian included, in sight was now on the newly arrived recruits, dozens of eyes lingered on each one, weighing their worth and attempting to burn holes through to their souls. If they survived to earn the mark, they would each be welcomed as brothers but until then they were less men than the dogs that skulked around the edge of the grounds. It was the big man that he had been watching that Doctore had his eyes locked on, expecting the answer and much more as he read set down the list of names left behind by the driver.

The giant looked to the men on either side of him, he seemed to be expecting that at least one of them would venture an answer but when they remained silent, he met the expectant gaze calmly "We are upon the sands of a ludus, a school for gladiators, a house of death." Cassian laughed when a few of the men cursed and shuddered their fear. They would not last the first week and certainly not the months of training it would take before any of them except him would be ready to take the sands of the arena even this small city had to offer, but what of the man from Rome?

"Behold the Germanium Wolf: Proximus." Doctore pointed the butt of the whip at the towering giant and paced the line of men. "This man fought in the games honoring the Emperor's birthday in Rome. This is a man who once stood champion, that has been sent to the underworld and fought his way back to the land of the living. Study him and learn from him but remember..." He paused to meet the man's eyes as he squared his shoulders proudly as the champion Cassian knew he had once been and still had the heart of. "Whatever glories he may have earned outside this house he is still merely a recruit in the house of Tertius and like all of you he will have to prove his worth before receiving the mark of the brotherhood and the right to call himself a gladiator once again."

He paced before the men, meeting the eyes of each of them though some did not have the nerve to meet his steely gaze. Cassian smirked, remembering the day he first stood upon the sands to train. "He does however stand correct in his words. You are indeed within the walls of a ludus, the fabled house of Tertius has seen fit to welcome you into its deadly embrace. Here, upon this sacred ground you will sweat, you will bleed and some of you will die for the honor of this house. Failing your ability to prove yourself worthy you will be re-sold to lesser houses or to the mines. Some of you may even prove yourself worthy of death in the pits if you fail to earn the mark but be warned, there is no mercy here, only your suffering will show your worth."

Proximus nodded with a deep frown and as the instructor was about to step away, he called to him "Doctore. When I stood champ... in another life I too fought as Dimachaerus." He swallowed almost nervously when the man simply raised a brow "Will I be afforded that chance here as a gladiator?" He had noted the dual blades in the hands of the smaller man and knew that some lanista's liked for their champion to be the only men of their chosen discipline, but he was too good not to be able to use the same dual blades. He had to show them what he was worth and not matter what came with the training and the dawn he would not stop until he showed them that he was a gladiator.

Cassian groaned inwardly, to have another man at the ludus who not only had once stood a champion but used the same weapon's technique as he did was enough to give even the most confident of men pause. The man's stature would have been enough of a challenge to overcome, the crowds loved for the giants of their imaginations to be brought to life on the sands and he was not a comparable size though he knew that his presence on the sands was beyond what any could expect but now he had to contend with this man and it did not sit well with him. Letting his weapons slide to the ground he approached Doctore. Once he stood next to him the pair of men locked eyes, there was no need for words between two men that saw things the same way and had for many years; they both knew his concern and its validity.

"Have no care Cassian." The dark man said with a smile, white teeth glowing in contrast to his skin. "He is not one, not yet. There is much for him to prove and learn before he can even hope to stand against you even in training." He clasped a hand over his shoulder and Cassian shook his head, baffled by the lanista's decision to have a former champion of Rome brought to train with the man who was to fight to regain that title for the honor of his house.

"I would but have explanation Doctore." He said in a low voice "Was the man trained in the pits? Is that what is meant by the underworld or do you simply embellish for the sake of his fellow recruits?" It was a common enough thing to do especially when the trainer was attempting to make a point about how much a man was lacking in skill or discipline.

"Break words with the man yourself Cassian," Cirandon replied with a grin "See if his legend exceeds your own." He stepped away to go and see to the beginning of the new men's training, calling for the logs to be brought forth while Cassian held back the laughter that always came when he saw their faces as each one was laid at the foot of a man. "May your gods aid you in discovering which of these men think they have what it takes to join the brotherhood with honor."

The branded gladiator laughed and gave his friend a look of mock offence "Break words with a recruit? By the gods no." He shook his head and winked "Words with a champion are earned, not given the first day one's foot touches the sands. Let him come to me if he dares." He would not be the one to approach and show that he was concerned for the ability to regain his title.

"You mean former champion yet to reclaim his title?" Cirandon said over his shoulder. The reminder was well meant even if it was badly received by the one he said it to. As much as Cassian disliked it part of his job as Doctore was to keep even the most justified of ego's in check. "Come, you who would be men! Prove to me and to your Dominus Tiberius Tertius that you stand worthy of his time to see you trained for the arena. Pick up these logs that lay at your feet and walk until commanded to stop. Any man who fails or falls before command to cease is given will be deemed unworthy of this house."

His whip sliced through the air, cutting the sounds of their protesting moans. "Begin." He called in a voice that left no room for complaint as the men shouldered the logs that were twelve inches thick and began to walk in a circle around the pallus. Two men could not even lift them and so were pulled immediately from the sands to be sent to auction the next morning, the laughter of the marked gladiators flooding them with shame, but Cassian did not join the laughter, instead he studied the intensity in his friend's face, wondering how he had found the will to live after the loss that took him from the arena.

Cassian continued to watch for a few moments before turning away to resume his own training, this time against a Carthagian by the name of Baxus. The spear he wielded was no match for the power of the champion's dual blades which moved as though inspired by the gods' themselves. "You offer no contest Baxus." He laughed the third time that he sent the taller man to the ground unarmed. "Change tactic or see a better man to your place." The other man simply shook his head with a grin and called for another to replace him. It appeared every man among them was eager to see it they had what it took to take on the champion of Velletri. "I will beat you all to a man if you insist. It will be my pleasure to school you while Doctore oversees men who are less worthy of his time than you." One after another he sent them to their backs, some took more effort than others and some were easier than he thought they would be, but they all ended the same; defeated.

When the last of the men had fallen, and even Tertius himself stood upon the balcony cheering with enthusiasm, Cassian finally tossed the blades to the ground and strode from the sands where the recruits paced in their endless circle around the pallus. He sat and ate, deep in thought as he hid the pain from his face. The wound was not yet healed in his gut from where the Murmillo, Altacus, had almost sent his guts spread across the blazing sand of the arena but tomorrow he would be able to fight as though the blade had never touched him, with the help of a drug he hated almost as much as he hated the Roman's who exacted their will with little or no thought to the suffering of others.

It had not been easy to convince Arturo to give him the Opium but in the end the bond of brothers beat out the caution of a medicus. It would be dangerous, Arturo warned him of the visions the drug could bring to his eyes and told him not to trust what did not seem natural or right because it could be the drug and to focus on those hallucinations would get him killed.

He did not care about illusions or haunting visions brought by the liquid, he cared about victory and the prize he hoped to secure by achieving it. Always Tertius granted him a woman upon victory, coupled by wine in copious amounts and though in times past he had been satisfied with the whores or willing house slaves he would be no longer. All he wanted was her, the woman who calmed the fires of rage in his chest and brought him to think that it was possible for him to feel, to care and perhaps love again after the betrayal and death of the woman he had loved before.

He would demand Violetta be brought from the house of Census as soon as he left the sands and the lanista would find a way to see it done or face the reality of a champion who would not fight. In the few moments of quiet afforded him in a day she was what he thought of and after the night before and seeing her as he had dreamed, fully bared before him, his thoughts sent lust thundering through his veins with a fire that would only be sated by her in his arms as he buried himself in her.

"You lose yourself in thought champion." A familiar voice interrupted his internal musing and he glanced up to see the towering hulk of the young gladiator Agrus. Looking up at the man and out across the sands to the Doctore as he instructed the new men, he shook his head "That is not my title, yet, but this time tomorrow you can call me that or a dead man." He grinned and gestured to the seat across the table from him. Watching the young man sit he smiled a little "Do not tell me that you too seek to possess my title Agrus?"

The German shook his head and took a bite of the flat bread "No. You know that I have no such goals Cassian. I may be good, but I will never be good enough to take down a champion, especially if that champion is you."

There was admiration in his voice that made Cassian smile slightly. "I merely wish to rise in the ranks as far as I may and we both know the best way for that to happen is for me to train more with you. If you would?"

The young man's voice was uncertain as he watched his house champion weigh the thought but when the Celt nodded Agrus almost leaped from his seat. "Gratitude brother, you will not regret it." He lingered for a few moments longer before rising to go and join the others who still trained upon the sands though the heat of the day was rising and soon all except the recruits would be dismissed from the sands for the hottest hours of the day, he knew like the other men did, not to intrude too much upon the champion when he was deep in thought.

CHAPTER 12

Cassian watch Agrus go with a shake of his head, the boy was known for his hot head and strong arm but how would he fare under his tutelage? Was he worthy of teaching him after his fall from grace? They would soon find out and when they did, he hoped that he did not fail a man who put his trust in him. He watched the man who stood as Doctore and remembering being the young gladiator in need of guidance and how long it had taken him to build the nerve to speak to the man who had reigned for years as the champion, who had fought and lived against men thought unbeatable.

Cirandon , as he had then been called by all, had cast a terrifying shadow upon the sands and at the tender age of sixteen Cassian had been certain that he would be laughed at even if he was not thrown to the ground for the impudence of speaking to the champion without invitation but instead he had been invited to sit and had even been given an extra portion of bread at the command of the man that would one day become his dearest friend. They had talked for hours that day; about Cassian and his fighting, the battle against the druid, how he had come to be a slave and why he wanted to be trained by the champion. In those hours a lifelong friendship had been forged and the next day the young Celt began his journey to the title he now sought to reclaim.

So much had happened since then and there were things that he could never tell the man that was like a blood brother to him; that he had thought himself in love with his wife, that they had found chances to lay together in passionate embrace before her ultimate betrayal that led to her death by the poisoned cup or that he still mourned her in his way even though he had found reason to love again in Violetta. He was not certain what would happen but if he let himself feel deeply again and lost another woman he loved there was no doubt in his mind that it would destroy him and send him to his death at last where he would face the wrath of Hades for the things he had done, for the betrayal of the bond of brotherly love was one that the fates would never forgive.

While he sat lost in thoughts of rights and wrongs in his life, weighing his self worth against his wrongs he did not notice the changing of the sun or that Cirandon had left the recruits to their mindless circles to come and sit beside him, studying his face as a warrior studies his opponent before a match. "Your face speaks of a troubled mind old friend." He said at last with an encouraging smile. The student had long ago surpassed his teacher in skill upon the sands but there were still times when the younger champion still needed guidance in other matters, this was just such a time. "Find tongue to voice thought and find my ears open to hear, and to aid you in the discovery of a solution."

Cassian shook his head and returned his thoughts to the present to offer a half smile to his old friend. "The solution is presented but it is the consequence of its discovery that leads to dark thoughts." He knew what would be said if he dared to mention the drug or the pain that made it necessary but still there was some comfort to be found in the easy comradery "Other thoughts turn to a matter of deeper problem; the woman. I want no other than her but does voicing such desire to Tertius bring her to my arms or place her in danger of his manipulations?"

The fear that his words might bring her to specific attentions from the lanista had been troubling him since the wagon ride back when he had listened to the Roman's discuss their surprise at his reactions to her and his actions in her defence. It was not until he had heard Tertius describe her as a 'delicate flower that would tempt any man' that the thought of her danger from the man had entered his mind.

It was bad enough that she faced the horrors of her own Dominus and his sadistic offspring but to put her in the path of his own who took no pause before using slaves for any and every use that would bring him either pleasure or power was a thing he could not risk, not for his own desires. "I fear I may have lost my heart to her Cirandon and cannot find the strength to regret the loss." He smiled suddenly, picturing her face and wondering what her laughter would sound like if ever he heard it. "What do I do? Ask for my heart's desire or simply leave it to the gods to bring her to my arms once again?"

He knew Cirandon could see the fear that he was trying to hide but it was there in his eyes for those that knew him well to see, it was strange to think that he cared for this girl after such brief encounters when none had ever held meaning before but then it had been a similar way with his own wife. She had been the body slave of their Domina gifted to the arms of the freshly crowned champion all those years ago.

"I think that it is a difficult thing you are faced with, but I would not advise going to Dominus and trying to demand that she is brought to you, that will anger him and endanger your woman." He shook his head and paused a minute in thought "When asked if you want a woman brought to your cell then it is the time to ask for her or when he mentions such a thing to you but do not think to make demands, it would not serve you or her well." He paused and looked Cassian in the eyes "Her safety rides on the least amount of people knowing that she holds meaning to you, remember that." He smiled and squeezed his shoulder firmly.

It was the same thoughts that he had been afraid to speak aloud, his affection, his love, could be the greatest threat to Violetta if the depth and strength of it were known to the Romans but how could he not feel? How could he stop caring for the one woman who had set his heart burning after five years of ice-cold deflection and mockery of intimacy. "I care more for her safety than my own desires Cirandon, but I have to see her again, to hold her is like feeling the peace of Elysium itself." He paused and looked at his friend before shaking his head, he had forgot for a moment who it was that he spoke to. "Apologies. I forget it is a thing you have known and have had denied for some years. It hurts still?" His lips twisted in a frown and he added the words 'Because of me.' in his mind.

Cirandon shook his head and patted the younger man on the shoulder, a smile hiding the true depth of his feelings "It is no longer the sharp sting that it was, but the ache will never fully fade until I hold her in my arms again in the afterlife." He stood and smiled "I pray that it is a pain you never know brother but in regards to your Violetta I feel that you are indeed meant to hold her again, and all I can say is that I hope that you are wiser than I and treasure every touch, smile and moment as though it could be your last for in this life of blood, sands and death it could be your final moment at any time."

No one, not even the man he held to heart like a brother would ever know that the last words between a husband and wife had been before that fateful night that had seen her ripped from this world. Cassian doubted that he dared to think of them himself, but he hoped that the knowledge that she had loved him until the end gave him some peace and made him think, as he was hoping, that perhaps his beloved Nala guided the girl to the arms of a man who needed love more than he had known possible. This was the once in a lifetime chance at love that not every man got but each man craved like air in his lungs.

"I hope you are right my friend." He said looking out at the heat rising off the sands "But if I am to earn the chance then it is time that I return to the sands that call to me almost as loudly as her arms." Cassian stood and stretched, pulling each of the muscles of his back as he arched backwards like a cat, every move precise and planned to ready him for battle.

At the nod of his trainer Cassian took to the sands, retrieving his weapons from the awestruck Cicero. He attacked the pallus as though it was an opponent in the arena, he ducked and rolled, blocked and jabbed with his blades. Every thought and action went together to create a tapestry of deadly art that would be the death of his opponent on the sands the next day. The heat of the day had sweat pouring down his face and arms, leaving lines in the dust that coated his chest. He could see Agrus watching him from the sidelines, eager to join in and show the others that he was the preferred training partner of the champion, a thing that would raise him in the eyes of the other gladiators. "Come on then German pup," He called with a dark grin "Show me what it is you can do against me." He laughed aloud when the young man paled for a moment then picked up his sword and shield before stepping cautiously onto the sands to face the man before the eyes of the rest of the ludus and their Dominus who had his Syrian body slave close to his side.

The young man's face was full of surprise, it was obvious he could not believe that this was happening, right now, when everyone could see. He swung his sword, stretching his wrist and approaching from the Celt's left. Crouching behind the shield he circled slowly, feigning a few strikes before moving in earnest towards his chest.

Cassian watched him like a lion watched a cub attempting its first hunt. There was no laughter in his eyes as he blocked the blow and pushed back. The man was strong, but he could not rely on strength alone to earn victories in the arena. "You lower guard when you swing like that Agrus." He said as he mimicked the move but used his other sword to block a return strike against his exposed side. "If you use the shield like this you will do better and be less likely to end upon your back bleeding from your lungs."

They sparred back and forth the rest of the day, each match ending with Agrus on his back, but it was obvious that he would soon land more than just a few chance blows against his opponent and perhaps even see him to his back soon. "One day Cassian I will see you to your back and see how you like the view while I enjoy the laurels of victory." He grinned "Upon that day you will owe me a cup of the wine that Dominus seems to keep you supplied with."

Cassian laughed and held out a hand to help him up after sending him down once more "Agrus if such day arrives, I will gladly give you the jug itself in celebration of the fact that something got through that thick skull of yours." The younger man was doing well, better than he thought he would but there was still lots for him to learn. "Try again and this time go with your instinct, don't try to outthink me just be natural." He noted a small smile on Cirandon's lips and realized that these were the same words he had once said to him. "Begin."

The wooden blades clashed under the heat of the sun until both men were bathed in their own sweat and coated in sand kicked up by the motion of their feet. Both men were pushing themselves to the brink of exhaustion, Cassian more so due to the pain in his side than from the German's blows but Agrus was trying as hard as he could to best him and it showed, every ounce of energy he had was being used and it showed on his face. The bigger man charged once more, and Cassian swept his left arm low to catch him at the ankle and send him sprawling face first into the sand but as he rolled to get up the sound of Doctore's whip cut through the air and he bellowed for them to stop while the other carried on their training. "Cassian, Agrus, eat and then bathe. Your training for the day is ended." When both men were on their feet he continued "Champion you are to your cell until summoned for tomorrow's games. Agrus you have done well today but will rest and rejoin the others tomorrow. If our champion returns to us, then you may continue your training with him."

Cassian chuckled and pushed the hair from his eyes before handing his training weapons to Cicero, and when Agrus had done the same they left the sands together to sit and eat the first portions of the evening meal and so they had the best of what there was and a bigger portion than the rest of the men might get that night. "You did well Agrus." He said over the edge of his cup "Do not think that you failed. You have a lot to learn about control, but you have the strength and determination to go farther than you think." He watched a slow smiled creep across the man's face as he continued "Those upon the balcony noted your work as well." He wondered if it was only the lanista that he wanted to impress or if it was the boy as well? He had often seen young Jovian linger near the rail when Agrus was upon the sand but surely, they both had to know how futile such interest would be. Tertius kept the boy and his cock on a leash tighter than a gladiator's grip on his weapon. "That was your intent was it not?" He asked knowingly.

"Well... I..." Agrus stuttered and flushed a little as he looked down at the food still on his plate "Since my brother and the fire seven years ago, I have been trying to be seen as anything other than what I was then and not to be 'just another German'. I want to be seen and I want to see the inside of the arena Cassian, in the afternoon heat I want to fight and stand over the body of an opponent that I have gifted with an honorable death. I want the crowd to roar my name at my victory and I want the rewards that go with such a performance." He grinned and grew more confidant as the other man nodded his understanding. "You have it, even now when you take the sands men and women scream your name, but do you remember a time when none knew you? When they cheered more for the man you faced than for you? It is a sting I can bear no longer."

Cassian looked at the other man for a moment before speaking, how did he tell him that the odds told that it was much more likely that he would die beneath another's blade before he ever heard the fickle crowd of Velletri roaring his name. He had no idea how long it took and how hard the work was, how many men had to die before they thought a man's name worthy of remembering even for a month. "Are you prepared for the sacrifices that you will have to make to even begin to come close to earning what it is you seek? The hours, the blood and the pain?" He would not paint a fantasy for him of easy paths to glory. If he wanted it, then Agrus would have to fight for it and he would have to fight hard and be willing to sacrifice everything he had ever held dear and endure things beyond the training and the arena to win the renown of the elite of the city.

"Do you have any concept of what you will have to do?" He stood before Agrus could answer and shook his head, sending his hair flying over his shoulders. "Think about all that you have seen me go through in the last few years and know that there was so much more you did not see. If you think that you have what it takes to go through that then this is the path for you but if you are not certain, completely certain, go back to the sands now and tell Doctore that you are not ready." He did not wait but walked away from the table into the halls of the ludus to find a bath and begin to prepare himself to face death once again the next day and pray that it brought his heart's desire to his arms one more time.

CHAPTER 13

Dawn broke over the skyline of the city and Violetta started to rise from her master's bed. Her body ached from the use Vitus had made of her, though he had followed his father's command that no mark be left upon her that any eye could see, he seemed to know just how much pain could be inflicted before it was evidenced by a bruise. She had thought his father a thoughtless brute when it came to laying with women but Vitus reveled in the tears and the small whimpers of pain that she could not hold back under his hands. When he shifted on the bed as she left it, she paused, afraid he would pull her back down to satisfy his morning lust, but he continued to sleep as she made her way out of the room.

Pausing to lean against the wall Violetta took a deep breath to calm herself and steady her hands from their shaking. It would not last forever, he would tire of her eventually and move on to some other poor woman to torment though her experience would bring her to pity the next poor soul to have to suffer as she was now. She could not help but hope that it was sooner rather than later that his attention shifted. When she felt as though she could react calmly to meeting anyone in the halls, she moved quickly to return to her own bed to put on her only other dress, setting aside the one that she wore to be mended later, Vitus had ripped the side open in his eagerness to terrify her. She was just about to pull her dress over her head when a voice stopped her completely.

"Do not bother with that dress Violetta." Felix said from the doorway. He must have seen her return from his son's quarters and wanted the chance to see her before she could hide any marks he had put on her skin. Stepping into the room when she stilled, he smiled when he saw that there did not appear to be any bruises or other marks, even the red marks from Selenia whipping the girl had faded so that they would be easily hidden. "You are to be bathed and prepared for the day at the arena." He was standing a breath behind her and let his hands slide to her slender hips, as he pushed her slowly towards her pallet by walking behind her. It would not take much if he wanted to sate his lust for a few hours, all he need do was push a little more and see her to her hands and knees, raise his robe and thrust deep into her.

She knew what he wanted and had even begun to move into the desired position when there was a sound from the doorway. Turning he saw Meridius standing in the frame and with a nod and a gesture he let the merchant know that the bath and other things were prepared as he had commanded.

"Tell them to make sure she does not smell like a slave but is scented as a proper Roman woman." He muttered and stepped away down the hall, pausing to call over his shoulder to the Spaniard "Selenia will join you soon to oversee the details of her dress and then Violetta is to come to me for the final instructions for the remainder of the day. If this venture ends in failure due to her actions, there will be pain to remember it by."

Although he likely knew that the two held each other with deep affection it was more of a fatherly bond than of lovers and would still ensure that the slave made sure that Violetta did as was expected; arriving at the baths and preparing her as was needed to complete the charade.

Violetta looked at Meridius with complete gratitude in her eyes, she did not think she would have been able to tolerate the invasions of the father after her night in the arms of his son. "Gratitude." She whispered, choking back tears, when he simply pulled her into his arms heedless of her state of undress. His hand on her back was soothing but the expression in his eyes was more troubled than her own. She wondered if it hurt him to see her abused in such a way after years of the protection he had provided. She knew that later he would tell her, in his silent way, what he felt, and he would listen to her talk about her fears and pains but right now all he could do was lead her gently to the room filled with a steaming bath where some of the older women waited to clean her and scent her properly. She looked around the room for the dress that she would wear "What am I to be dressed in? They cannot mean for me to be naked... can they?"

The women shook their heads at her fear and shooed Meridius away with appreciative smiles on their faces, the man was handsome and well favored among the women for his silent charm and his skills in beds or shadowed corners, but this was not the time or place for him. "Domina Selenia is to bring the dress you are to wear. She will make sure that we prepare you to look 'Roman' enough." One of them said with an obvious sneer in her voice. "Is it true you are to be on the pulvinus of the games?" The other asked, shushing her partner with a stern look.

"That is what I was told." Violetta said quietly as she stepped into the water. The heat of the bath was a luxury and at this hour of the morning was almost unheard of for a slave in the house of Census. Savoring the warmth, she was reminded that this was a day unlike any before it and so much was depending on her ability to behave like their masters. The thought of failure terrified her as much as the idea of Cassian falling in the arena but if he won and the farce deemed a success then it was possible that she would have her hearts desire to be in his arms again, without the eyes of others on them. The thought brought a smile to her lips and a flush to her cheeks. That is what she had to focus on; the reward of the venture instead of the pain of its failure. Soon enough Selenia would arrive with her groping touches and devious eyes but until then Violetta let herself revel in the warmth of the bath and the administrations of her fellow slaves commanded to attend her care.

Selenia applied the finished touches to her makeup herself, there did not seem to be a single slave in the Republic that could add the kohl to her eyes the way that she liked it to be. Straightening she practiced the smile she would give to her father when she saw him, he would certainly be impressed by the selection of dresses purchased and whichever ones were not selected for the girl to wear would end up added to her own wardrobe as well. There was no flaw to her plan to get as much from her father as possible before leaving to return to Rome, she simply had to convince him that she was perfectly capable of choosing her own husband so that he would not feel the need to come to the city to do the job himself.

With a snap of her finger to summon her attending slave to follow her she glided her way down the hall to stand in the doorway of her father's office "I have arrived father, as you wished for me to attend you this morning." Her smile was smooth and glassy, her eyes expectant of the praise she was certain he would heap upon her work the day before. She could see from the way he had arranged her purchases what decisions he had made, the exact one she had predicted and so the rest of the dresses would become hers. "Your choice is made then?"

Felix looked up with a smirk "Yes, I see you have arrived... since you are standing in my doorway." He chuckled then continued speaking; "and yes I have decided upon the dark blue though I may keep the others for future use." He looked up at her, his eyes holding back laughter at the outrage she knew was on her face. They knew each other's games better than most and he had guessed correctly that the expanded selection had been made with herself in mind. "Unless of course you could find some use for them?" He smiled, and she relaxed slightly, nodding to him but before she could speak further, he held up his hand "I need for you to oversee the girl's preparation for the day. There can be no doubt in anyone's mind that she is in fact a woman of Rome here as a potential bride for your brother. Is that understood?"

Not only had he sent her shopping for the slave but now she was to oversee her dress as well? This was beyond ridiculous and to have the little chit pose as a bride to Vitus was to invite disaster but if he commanded it then what was she to do. "If that is your wish father it is a small thing to do for such lovely dresses as I picked out for your little toy." She took a seat and watched him. "She is a toy, is she not father? There is no special affection for her that you treat her with such regard?" Her questions served more that just to remind her father that however lovely the girl was she was just a slave and had to be kept in her place. She also wanted to know his answer what the chance was that she or Vitus would ever truly get to have her the way they desired. She would have taken her to Rome if she had been allowed. A lovely innocent slave was the perfect tool for the seduction of a senator and the one she had her eye on had an interesting preference for girls of just Violetta's type, having her could tip the scales that already leaned towards her for a perfect victory against her rivals.

Felix took a sip of his morning wine and laughed aloud at her question. Yes, it had been years since her mother had gone to the afterlife after a swift and deadly fever, but he had never remarried and never taken any slave to his arms in favor over the others apart from Meridius. She could not blame him, the man was a god, trained in the giving of pleasure better than any she had ever known.

"Selenia, the girl is used to satisfy my lust in bed when the mood strikes, and I used her to ally my house with that of the man that owns the greatest gladiator I have ever seen, the biggest asset of this city in regard to attracting the attention of Titus Claudius." She knew he held hopes of being introduced to the inner circle of Rome but was beginning to wonder if that famed Senator held some special meaning. Forcing a look of interest on her face Selenia returned her attention to her father as he spoke. "But enough talk of things that hold no meaning. I have asked you to come here to see to it that the girl is properly dressed, and it must be done quickly, no more attempt at manipulations. See it done, now."

With a sigh and a nod Selenia left her father's office and made her way to the bath where Violetta was just being aided out of the water, beads of it dripped down her thighs and the thought of that soft skin made Selenia lick her lips with the temptation. If her father had not commanded her to hurry, she would have enjoyed this moment and drawn it out with a few beautiful lessons between her and the girl she desired.

Violetta stood still; her eyes cast down to the ground when Selenia entered the room. She knew of her attraction to her but prayed there would be no time to pursue it so that the day went as planned by Felix. "Come. See her dried and dressed. My father awaits his showpiece and he is not in a patient mood this morning." Selenia circled the slaves as they dressed one of their own and spoke only to instruct them in the ways to make sure the gown was perfectly fitted to her frame as if it was bought for her alone.

"No. The breast should sit higher." She said with a shake of her head she pushed the woman adjusting the dress out of the way and abruptly reached into the silk to cup the softness of her ripe breasts in each hand. "Draw it tighter so that her assets are on prime display as a woman of Rome would do." While the ribbon was retied about her ribs the older woman let her thumbs circle and caress the tightening bud of her nipples before settling them back in the dress, the lace barely covering her. "That is how Roman women wear this type of gown, you ought to have known." She said with a vicious smile as she put jewels around her neck and wrists, before putting a sparkling comb in her hair. "There my little flower, now you look the part of my brother's bride and temptress to the champion."

She shuddered as the woman manipulated her body and fought back the urge to cringe but managed to stay still until all was done. She looked down at the finery that was beyond her thought of ever wearing with dread. The plan would not work, Cassian would not recognize her in this beautiful false finery, they had done too much, and it was going to be for nothing. She shook her head sadly until a glass was brought and Selenia commanded her to "Look up and see my masterpiece" A gasp tore from her lips. The daughter was the artist that her father claimed to be.

Lifting a hand to touch her face Violetta could not believe that the woman reflected was herself and yet it was impossible to deny. Her cheeks had been painted to a pretty flush that was not overwhelming nor obvious and the Kohl around her eyes made them stand out and seem larger, brighter, than before and her body beneath the silken dress looked as though she had stepped down from the heavens and she blushed in earnest at the sight of her breasts put on display as though they would fall from the lace holding them back if she bent over or moved suddenly. "Domina, I..." She was lost for words "I am ready to attend Dominus, if you approve."

There was so much in the woman's eyes that it looked like she wanted to say. It was likely that the socialite of Rome had no interest in the small provincial arena where the common folk were close enough to nobility that they could be smelled. Violetta wondered what promise or threat had been made to bring her out for the day, but these were not things to say to a slave and so Selenia stayed silent, whatever her opinion.

"I think you will do what my father commands and do it well or suffer the consequences." With a quick snap of her fingers she dismissed those that had dressed the girl and led her out into the hallway. Stopping suddenly, she pulled Violetta to stand beside her instead of just behind. "This is where you are to walk today." She said with a dark smile "Pretending that you are my friend, visiting from Rome to meet Vitus." He would love the idea of the girl being his 'bride-to-be' but almost as much Selenia would enjoy having her play the part of a dear friend that no one would think anything of her being physically affectionate with. As they walked, she linked their arms and leaned close to whisper "You must play along with the guidelines I set out for you or the others will know, and you will be punished, and your gladiator will know of it and his spirit will break." The woman smiled when she saw the fear flash in her eyes and they both knew that she had found her means of manipulation. "If he is a broken man then you know the next time he sets foot on the sands he will be dead before the sun sets." She straightened as they neared the office "Now come, smile and prepare yourself. Much depends upon it."

Felix looked up with a broad smile at Violetta's appearance and stood to inspect her, circling like a wild dog circles helpless prey before it attacks. "She is lovely, better than expected." He said to Selenia as if he were inspecting a statue and not a living person "You have outdone yourself daughter. Has she not Vitus?" All heads in the room turned to see the man standing in the doorway, staring at her as though he would eat her alive. Violetta's eyes widened and she felt her heart begin to race when her tormentor stepped into the room.

"Yes father." He said, his voice almost a growl "There stands before me a vision of grace instead of a mouse's shadow which snuck from my bed this morning." He must have been fuming with rage to find her gone when he woke, but the way he looked at her, coupled with the fact that she would be within his reach all day long and his to touch and toy with until night saw them back to the villa, had him practically panting with desire. "Are we ready then, to depart? I for one am eager to see what joy the day brings us upon the sands of the arena."

Walking the hall between the siblings and behind their father Violetta felt as though she was well and truly trapped. She might appear to the eye of any observer to be a free woman but dressed as she was, with the intention of her masters, she was more a slave than ever before; one wrong word or move could see her identity discovered and painful tragedy brought to her life and that of the man she cared for. The hand of Vitus upon her backside and Selenia linking their arms might as well have been chains for the way they held her securely in place until they mounted into the carriage that would take them to the arena. She prayed that wherever he was Cassian fared better than she did on that ride through the city.

The ride to the arena was strange and uncomfortable for Violetta. She had made the ride many times before with Felix and there were times that Vitus had accompanied his father, but she had never felt so visible and exposed before. People were looking at her sitting with them where before she had been nothing but a faceless slave. The attention was unnerving but not as much as the conversation in the wagon; she was to make eye contact with those speaking to her and to laugh at the appropriate moments, she was not to be alone at any time, especially with other Romans and she was to respond to Vitus' attentions as though she was looking to him as her future husband. The final command had put a broad grin on the younger man's face

"I promise to be an attentive lover. Have no fear of that." Vitus laughed when she lowered her head, but the joy fell from his face when his father continued speaking but to his children as if his son had not spoken her nightmare aloud "As for the two of you it is just as important that you do not terrorize her into making a mistake that would be costly to all of us." She knew the rules of the arena well enough to know that he would face a fine from the magistrate and the trio of them would face a time fallen from social graces which could not be afforded with the much-esteemed Titus Claudius coming to the city to be a guest at the villa. "Violetta." He called her name so that she would look him in the eye. "For this day, and this day only, you will address me as Felix or Census, and Vitus and Selenia by their given names. You must not let anyone have cause to doubt that you are who we say you are. Understood?"

She nodded and forced a smile because she knew he expected it. To them this was just a game and she was a piece in play, a means to the end they desired with no thought towards her. She was filled with fear and excitement but the uncertainty of what she was going to face had her sweating though the day was not yet hot and there was a breeze blowing from the speed of the wagon that should have cooled her. As they got closer to the arena, she began to pay attention to the other carts, looking for the one that would bring him to fight. He was not meant to see her until she was on the pulvinus but that did not mean that she could not see him. She craned her neck and turned to look but she could not see him, on the verge of standing in the cart to look Vitus slid an arm around her shoulders and leaned to whisper in her ear with a smile on his face "Still yourself and behave as a proper Roman woman not a child." Though his face was cheerful and to the unfamiliar eyes might have even appeared to be flirtation his hand was like a vice that would almost surely leave a bruise the next day. She did as commanded, without pause and when her eyes fell, he continued "Smile or are you so stupid as to not remember command given but moments ago." She raised her head and forced a bright smile and even managed to laugh at the appropriate moment when they arrived, and a guard made a comment about the house of Census attracting all things of beauty.

CHAPTER 14

The returning champion strode from the ludus, his eyes filled with a singular purpose; victory. He would win this day and see his woman back to his arms and the safety of his position's protection. Lucius stopped him from heading directly to the wagon that would take him to the arena, directing him instead towards the infirmary where his friend awaited with the new armor that had been hastily ordered to see his lingering injury protected. Brushing his hair, still damp from his morning bath, out of his eyes Cassian grinned at Arturo "Well old friend, the day of my victory has arrived, and I stand ready to meet glory or death upon the sands."

He had a broad grin across his handsome face, freshly shaved of a few days growth but still shadowed enough to remind any that looked upon him that the man was not a tamed and broken dog but a wolf. Powerful and rough but not a mindless brute, his eyes shone too brightly with quick and clever thought for any but the biggest of fools to think that he was a mindless animal. "You will attend the games as well?" He asked with a grin though they both knew that he would not be needed as the Celt would either rise to glorious heights without injury requiring the skills of the medicus or he would take such an injury that there would be no point in having the man wash his hands in preparation.

"I see no reason to attend this day Cassian." The medicus said with a slow shake of his head, his hands moving swiftly to fasten the armor as though he had done so hundreds if not thousands of times before coming to the ludus "You will fight as you have always done though if you do as you suggested yesterday when we broke words your prowess will be compromised the moment liquid touches that laughing tongue of yours." Though they both knew he suffered addiction to the substance himself Cassian knew the once holy man would not let himself stand by and watch a man he loved as a brother fall to its painful withdrawal or risk his addiction to the same opiate. "You would improve the odds of your victory if you reconsidered its use."

Cassian shook his head as his friend wrapped his torso with thick quilted padding before buckling a leather tunic in place. Though he would still fight as Dimachaerus his movement had not been restricted like this in years. The

133

vulnerability of the still healing wound made it necessary but as the leggings, grieves, bracers and finally the broad balteus adorned with a wolf head were buckled around him he found himself feeling more like a Roman centurion than a gladiator. "I cannot recall the last time I faced such a hindrance to motion upon the sands." He said with a sigh as he tied his hair at the nape of his neck with a leather cord. "May your gods see me to victory regardless, so that I may reclaim what is my own." At his nod of understanding the champion rejoined his guards who escorted him to the wagon that would take him to the arena and once inside he allowed his mind a few final moments of distraction as he recalled the pleasure of her embrace and the honey sweet taste of her lips as their bodies joined in a fevered heat.

Tertius nodded to Cassian as he joined the rest of the gladiators in the wagon. Looking at the medicus he nodded, not seeing the Celt roll his eyes in annoyance at the delay. "Be prepared for our later return. Wounds will be tended before the victorious receive wine and women." There was a collective groan from the men in the wagon but the lanista settled them with his hand while the champion laughed robustly. "You all know the glories that await you upon victory but to savor it fully, you will need tending by the skill hands of Arturo before that of others." He did not notice that the champion of his house did not join in the eagerness of the others and Cassian wondered again if he should speak now and inform him that it would only be the one woman who stirred his soul and ignited in him the fire that he had displayed at the house of Census?

The wagon left the ludus yard before he could break words, so Cassian was left sitting, deep in thought, as they journeyed down the hill to the city, he wondered how he could manipulate the lanista into securing the woman for him. His mind drifted to the object of his desire and wondered what she would think if she stood upon the balcony to see him fight. Would she be thrilled? Appalled by the blood and violence? Would his tender little priestess be frightened by the world that he reigned over? If there was a way for her to become of the house of Tertius he knew that the lanista would not bring her to the games, but he hoped that, even just once, she could see him in his full glory as the city's champion with the crowd roaring his name loud enough to shake the heavens.

Cassian leapt from the wagon as soon as the door was opened, his feet hitting the familiar sands just outside the arena yard as he looked up at the structure with a resigned grin; today he would either return to his former state of prestige or finally greet the afterlife and all those he had sent there over his years fighting for his life. His personal assigned guards, Auctus and Lucius, escorted him towards the gate of the arena tunnels with one in front and one behind him to fend off anyone fool enough to attack the gladiator, but they did nothing to stop the throng of hands reaching out to touch him. There was no threat in the touch of the women and children outstretched to caress the arm or shoulder of the once champion only their small personal pride in their bold achievement, so he smiled as he walked through them, his mind upon much more urgent things than this. He was so intent upon strategy and avoiding death at the hand of his opponent that he almost did not hear the voice of Tertius calling for him over the crowd as he stepped through the gate.

"Cassian hold a moment. I would have words." The lanista grinned when the man stopped suddenly and turned to face him with his head bowed.

"Dominus." He said, his voice deep and guttural in his mindset of primitive violence. The man had used his true name in public and not the false mocking 'Otho'. "My time is yours of course. As my name is now my own again?"

"Yes, yes. Of course." Tertius nodded to the guards who took a few steps away before he continued "All eyes are upon you tonight in the primus, including those you most wish to see." He paused a moment as the knowledge sank in. "Live and you will see her delivered to your arms but if you die then she is to face the cross." It had to be a lie but only barely for who knew what kind of madness Felix might put the girl to in his anger at his favorite gladiator's death. "Her life is tied to yours Cassian, do not see her to death because of your loss."

The lanista kept speaking, going on about how he had been told about the circumstance by Felix himself, but the gladiator was no longer listening. His only thought was the threat to the life of the woman, his woman, he had planned to live but to know that if he failed it would cost her everything was something that sparked a deadly rage inside him. When the Roman dismissed him, he walked away between his guards, murmuring assurances that he would indeed reign victorious champion once again at the days end. He did not hear the Roman's answers but as soon as he was out of sight, he removed the vial given by Arturo and downed its bitter contents in a single gulp, paying little attention to a slight difference in taste and praying to any gods that would listen to aid him and see her spared.

The hours in the cells of the arena had waged war upon his senses and by the time the sun had set the drug had been in full effect for hours and his head was swimming in the sounds and colors. He was supposed to be standing behind the gates to the sands, waiting to be called to fight but that did not seem to be where he really was. He could hear voices that did not belong and wanted to turn his head to see if the voices had bodies to go with them. He was relaxed which was good before a fight but when one of his swords dropped from his hand into the sand of the ramp. "Hades help me what was added to that? This is not the effect of Opium." He whispered to himself, crouching to retrieve his weapon. His pulse raced and then slowed to a crawl and the world spun once again as he stood, the roar of the crowd like that of some distant animal having sighted it prey.

"Cassian, you have been summoned. Go." The words came from a familiar voice, but he could not place the name that went with it, but he still gave a nod as the hand gave a firm shove towards the opened gates. He found himself in the center of the arena with no idea how his feet carried him there, his name was roaring around him on the voice of every Roman in the stands. He smiled as was expected, it was reflex not a conscious thought, but when his eyes landed on the pulvinus and caught the mythic blue gaze of a young woman standing at the edge of the balcony his world stopped and it was all he could do to stare at her. It could not be her could it? Where was the frightened and vulnerable girl he had held in his arms? Who was the silk clad, polished Roman that met his eyes with such longing that it pierced the opium's fog?

It was harder than she had thought it would be to not look down as they made their way through the crowds to the stairs leading to the pulvinus where Felix was the first to mount the stairs and announce their arrival, placing the blame up her supposed late sleep for their delay. She could hear him greet the lanista and his wife but before she could follow Selenia she felt Vitus grab her arm again to hiss "Whatever game it is that my father plays at you still serve the house of Census and tomorrow, or tonight if the gladiator falls, you will be mine again. You will serve my every need when not at my father's side and you will know your place. Do not give me cause this day to be... unkind to you. I treated you with care last night but if I am displeased then you will know true pain beneath my cock." When she nodded fearfully, he took her hand and said loud enough for the few that were watching her with some degree of pity to hear "Allow me to assist you dear lady. I would not have beauty such as yours marred by a stumble upon the rickety stairs of our humble arena when you are used to the marble splendor of Rome itself."

Violetta allowed him to help her and it took all her will not to cower when the Romans moved to greet her and spoke to her as though she was one of them and not the slave who had served them all food or drink at some time or another. Strangely enough it was the wife of the lanista that came to her aid, guiding her to a seat and speaking to her in an almost motherly tone as she explained the games. She could not help but wonder if it was genuine friendliness or if it was just to maneuver her closer to the front of the pulvinus. Felix and Vitus both watched her like hawks but did not move to join them, even when the magistrate himself sat down beside the two women and began to casually join the conversation of educating the young woman about the traditions of the games. Violetta nodded and smiled along but she could not help but scan the windows that let those in the cells preparing to fight see the sands. Was he there? Could he see her already? What would he think of the finery she wore? So many questions swirled in her mind but most of all she wondered; could he win?

Smiling and chatting awkwardly to the noble Romans Violetta watched the fights that seemed to grow with brutality and gruesomeness as the day progressed. Selenia and Vitus were her near constant companions and it seemed that even Lycithia found them to be stifling. Sipping the wine handed to her by the magistrate Violetta drank carefully, the idea of becoming drunk in the company of all the elite was terrifying even without the threat of Vitus lingering about to make her even more uncomfortable. The sound of Cassian's name being called to the arena pushed all other thoughts from her mind.

Their eyes met across the distance and in that moment, they knew each other but there was something different in his eyes; was it shock at seeing her in finery at the sides of the Romans that had tormented them both only days before or was it that Vitus was near at hand, practically breathing her breath since the lanista's wife had moved to join her husband while their champion took to the sands? Her breath caught in her chest, her attention so focused on the man upon the sands that she did not notice the Roman lean over to whisper as he grasped her shoulder.

"Now I see that the lanista's game is better played than even I had thought." Vitus obviously saw that the gladiator's eyes were riveted upon her and the monster had thought of a way to raise the gladiator's rage to a deadly and disastrous level. He angled himself so that he blocked the others view of he and Violetta and that entire corner of the pulvinus before locking his own gaze with that of Cassian. Leaning forward he lathed his tongue over the curve of her shoulder as he had the night when she had sat at his knee and juice had spilled upon her flesh.

He was making his own twisted statement that, win or lose, there was nothing Cassian could do that would see her from Vitus's grasp for long. Felix Census might loan her to any of his choosing, but she would always return to his house and Vitus would be there waiting when she was returned. Lingering remnants of any other man's touch would soon be erased from memory and replaced with his own. He saw the light of understanding in his foes eyes and laughed before turning to face the magistrate for his address and forcing the girl to do the same.

"Violetta?" She watched the man upon the sands whisper her name and yet it did not seem that he knew that he had said it. He had to wonder how it came to be that she stood with the nobility dressed in finery and with jewelry sparkling in her dark hair and upon her wrists? It was utterly impossible and yet here she stood, staring him right in the face unless this was some trick of the mind or a dream then it was truly real. He narrowed his eyes as Vitus moved to touch her, his hands tightening instinctively on his blades as she watched him with terror in her eyes. Was he just as much a pawn in this game as she was?

She could not know that Tiberius had promised that he would hold her in his arms at the days end if he stood alive and victorious, but that she would face the cross if he failed. She saw his face as Vitus licked her flesh and red flashed in his eyes. He would not lose now, if nothing else he would fight to see the Roman to payment for the insult in his actions.

Trying hard to hide the disgust and fear she felt at Vitus' touch Violetta read her name once again on the lips of the man standing upon the sands and her heart sank as she understood the true depth of the game played by their masters. She prayed that Hades would claim them all for this cruelty. She forced a smile to her lips though it would not take a fool to see that it was pained and that she was uncomfortable as she shifted slightly to be out of physical contact with Vitus. She could tell her move displeased him, but she could bear his touch no longer, especially when Cassian looked as though he was in agony from the sight of it.

There had to be a way to convey to him the truth of what was happening. But how without allowing the secret of her identity and the truth of their affections to be revealed and pain inflicted upon herself or the one she cared for? Hoping that her quick action would show him that she despised the touch of Vitus and had no desire to be near him she made her way to the side of the magistrate and asked him boldly "Do you favor the Celt sir? I have heard that he is a titan of blood upon the sands." She stared down at him with a deep longing in her eyes that she hoped he could see. "I pray that if he stands victorious at fights end there might be some chance to look closer upon his glorious savagery. In the country provinces I did not find the chance to behold one such as he, and the champion of Rome was not deemed safe enough to be near. I would not wish to let such a chance slip by."

The magistrate, a pompous and self-important man took the attentions of the young woman in stride. He likely though it was not surprising that she preferred the company of a sophisticated man to that of the younger Census who was a fool at best and a sadist if the worst was to be believed, he patted her hand gently, easing her closer to him in the process. She hid her revulsion well as he began to speak. "My dear girl I assure you that such an animal would hold no interest to such a gentle creature as yourself." He smirked down at the gladiator with disdain in his voice "You see they are mindless savages and they fuck as brutally as they fight. A delicate lady such as yourself would, I am certain, be terrified of any man if you were subject to such brutality."

The Romans, including Felix laughed but Violetta turned her head to meet the eyes of the man upon the sands and whispered towards him though he could not possibly hear her "I think him a god, not a beast." They paid no attention to her as the lanista stepped forward to address the crowd. Tiberius Tertius was dressed in his finest robes, gold thread embroidered upon the dark blue that shone in the torch light illuminating the early evening. His hair slicked back with the most expensive scented wax and as Violetta watched him approach the front of the pulvinus she thought he looked foolish, as though he would do anything to appear as one of the elites. He and his wife seemed not to know that the nobility of Velletri would never accept him as one of them no matter what he did or how eloquently he spoke in moments like this.

CHAPTER 15

Cassian stood utterly still, captured by the sight of her beauty upon the pulvinus dressed in fine fabric and jewels. Watching her, a part of him swore that if she was ever his and under the house of Tertius instead of Census that he would find a way to ensure that she possessed such things if only to wear them for him so that he could marvel at the pure beauty of her in them. The question formed in his mind as she moved among the elite; was she a noble or the slave she had told him that she was? Was it love blooming between them or just a game played with his heart and mind? He saw Tertius step to the balcony's edge and speak words of praise for the Celt teetering upon the sands that were lost on the ears of the man himself for all he saw was the woman he desired at the side of those he hated and even the sand beneath his feet seemed unsteady. Violetta had turned away from one Roman to stand at the side of another and yet she looked at him with a longing he could almost feel. Watching her be subjected to the touch of a man that she was so afraid of sent all the pain of his past wounds to the back of his mind and in its place an agony he had never thought he could feel.

No matter what lies had her standing with those he despised he could not stand the thought of her anguish. Not when it might be within his power to see her spared that, even if it was just for the one night and then they went back to their lives that would seem to be more separate than he had imagined they could be. Nothing was as it should be but when he turned his head to face his opponent, he found the one thing that made sense in a world turned upside down. He would fight, blood would see this madness ended at least for that night and then he would be able to step free of the drug's haze that clouded thought and action.

At the moment of the lanista's distraction Violetta moved to the far edge of the platform, the contact with the magistrate had worried the gladiator for the man was of a singular mind in his experience. His eyes had not left her face as she moved, even if she had not been a woman, he knew intimately he would have been fascinated by her delicate features and graceful movement. He was ready now but the man taking stance to fight him was no less prepared. He could not fall, he was the champion, the title was rightfully his and today had to see it restored to him.

Felix made a brief eye contact with Tertius and nodded to him before returning his attention to the man standing upon the sands. They glared at each other, the Celt a murderous look in his eyes that was not for his opponent, but for his oppressors and the merchant one of intense greed, he was here to make money off the blood of other men. The purse from this victory would be substantial since many had been more than eager to wager against the fallen champion who had not won his last match but had been spared due to the favor of the magistrate. They had all laughed in the cells when he had been announced as a champion returning but if he had not bet against his own man and Cassian stood victorious at the days end, Tertius would have more than enough coin on hand to see his woman to his arms if it was required. The question on his mind was what did the merchant want? Why was he so intently staring at him and why had he brought Violetta to the pulvinus? Who was she and what was their relationship really? Master and slave or something else?

He was uncertain of what was reality and what was the result of the drug coursing through his veins masking his ability to fight the confusion and concentrate. Was that Violetta with the Romans or was he dreaming? He had never felt like this before and he swore that if he lived, he never would again. Opium would never touch his lips before a fight or of his free will again. He could not afford it's clouding of his mind, not when he stood here. He watched his opponent step back at the instruction of the man who would command the fight to start in just moments and yet he could not find his focus to fight. When they were the required steps away from each other the third man nodded to a trumpeter who offered the crowd three short blasts before the battle began with the roar of the crowd joining its song.

It was that roar that brought him out of the daze to fight. The adrenaline that surged through him pushed him from the clouded thoughts as an antidote to the poison and he gripped his weapons tight as he shook his head to clear the last remaining vapours before they got him killed. The clearing of the drug did not prepare him for the other man's speed and skill. After less than half a dozen steps he broke into a run and darted forward as though he were a wolf attacking a deer frozen with fear. When he thrust his sica straight towards Cassian's face he did not have time to raise arms to block the strike but instead had to wrench his head hard to the side, the blade missed his cheek by the breadth of a whisker.

The champion roared with rage, half at his own foolishness and half at the other man's near ability to wound him, but his opponent was already gone, having used his own momentum to spin himself out of harms way. The move brought him to Cassian's back and when he spun so that they faced each other once again he was ready for the second vicious stab to his face and parried the blow with his blades crossed before his face. He swung his own blade down then lunged it upwards in a move that would have seen the other man spitted upon his blade, but he was just off his mark and the two men disengaged, panting with the shared effort.

In the back of Cassian's mind, he knew that Tertius was worried about his performance. It was as though the gladiators played a game of cat and mouse, but he was the mouse instead of the cat. This was a role he had not stood in for years and if he had been less driven to win it would have frightened him but there was not time for that now, there was only the fight.

Upon the sands the two men fought, at least one oblivious to the sound of the crowd as they warily circled each other with weapons at the ready. Suddenly without even a feigned warning Cassian attacked savagely. Punching towards him, one sword wielding fist at a time, he was able to drive the man backwards across the arena with a quick pace that made the him almost stumble in hasty retreat. The precision and timing of his strikes would have been all but impossible for even the strongest of men to stand against and this man, though he had been able to surprise the champion, was not the strongest man he had ever faced.

He could see her in the corner of his gaze. Violetta did not move, not even when Selenia came up behind her and placed both her hands on her hips. Was she even breathing? All her focus seemed to be on the men fighting upon the sands. He could almost hear her heart thundering in her chest and when the Roman woman's lips touched her ear, he could only imagine what she whispered.

"If he falls, you will be mine. Father will let me take you to Rome to my deep delight." She nearly jumped from the balcony, surprise in her eyes as well as a deep fear. "No." Was all she could say, her lips moved in a hushed whisper while her eyes stayed locked upon the sands not leaving the men engrossed in their battle. He knew she did not believe that he would fall, he was too good to die like this to a man who was not worthy of remembering even his name.

His dual gladiuses were drawn back in preparation of running the man through, he had no thought in his mind for Tertius or Census but instead all his focus was upon three things; the regaining of his title that would come with his victory, his life that would come with the same and on Violetta. He had to know who she truly was and why she appeared as both slave and Roman. That question would have to wait for its answer because the fight was not over, not yet. In desperation from his knees the other man swung his shield like a discus to smash the metal edge into Cassian's kneecap, grinning when he staggered from the impact of the blow.

Roaring in pain the Celt let the tips of his swords fall just a bit and that gave his opponent the opening he had been looking for. The other gladiator rolled away and jumped to his feet, launching a counterattack with a relentless furry of slashes aimed at the Celt's unprotected face but his moves had become predictable. Blocking the blow to his face was easier this time but Cassian could not have predicted that his opponent would spin and let the blade of his sica slice across his arm with flashing strike. Blood sprayed across the sands and the champion bellowed his outrage at the assault. The fool had just signed his ticket to the afterlife in blood.

Cassian threw himself forward, thrusting his swords over and over towards the gladiator who though trying desperately to defend himself was failing miserably even with his shield and the advantage of drawing first blood between them. His sword struck the wood of his shield and stuck for a moment before he pulled it out and embedded it again and again until the shield cracked and the man holding it had no other option except to drop and face the dual blades of the Champion, holding only his single sica. In that breath they knew which of them would be standing the victor in mere moments.

Pausing to take a deep breath, the pain from the wound was lancing its way up his arm and shoulder into his soul. There was no choice but victory, she needed it from him more than he needed it from himself. Tightening his jaw, he let loose an attack that was more savage that skilled. The speed and intensity that he used gave his opponent no chance to retaliate and if the man had been less skilled, he would not have even been able to defend himself.

The blade of the gladius in his right hand cut though the taut muscle of the other fighter's stomach, the line of bright red blood showing through the black hair of his belly. The sound as he pulled his weapon free was wet and seemed to echo though he was certain that was just in his mind for the crowd was on their feet roaring for their hero's return to glory. The shriek of agony that ripped from the opposition was real though and their eyes met with understanding.

Blood pouring from the wound he let the sica slip from slackened fingers to fall to the ground. Towering over him Cassian knew that there would be no resistance when he smashed the pommel of a gladius into his shoulder to knock his weapon to the ground where he swiftly kicked it far from desperate grasp. Staring down into the dying eyes he nodded once, some men might toy with a dying enemy, but it was not in his nature to play with such cruelty. This fight had gone on long enough and the numbness of his arm told him that care would be needed before long. This was over, and he had won.

He stabbed the warrior's right thigh with a strength that sent him crashing to the sands. He could not and did not make any attempt to rise, he knew that his time had come and that he would greet his brothers that had died before upon the sands in the afterlife that night. The man at his feet was defenseless and slowly bleeding to death, Cassian looked up to the pulvinus and locked eyes with Tertius. He received the nod allowing him to end the man's suffering and took a quick breath to center his aim before driving the blade in his left through the center of his chest.

Even though he had known that it was coming there was still a pained look of shock in the dying eyes when the steel cut through skin and tissue, the force of the thrust soon reaching his heart and ripping it in two so that it beat no more. He looked around him and he could tell that the crowd loved him once again, he was their champion and now, perhaps, he could be hers. His eyes met Violetta's and he was surprised to see tears on her cheeks, "The Roman woman weeps for the slave? Or the slave weeps for the victory that keeps her as a pawn?" He said to himself as he offered the public the grin that they adored him for.

He released the swords from his grasp and raised his hands high to the heavens, the crowd roaring with shared delight. He had won many victories upon the sands, but none had tasted so sweet as this, the first won for her. He could see, as could all Velletri, that the loss that had cost him his title had nothing to do with a lacking his skill but more of a faltering of will from him and the lucky chance stolen by another man. It had only been his years as champion that had saved him that day and it was unfortunate that the man at his feet did not have the same as it could have spared his life. He had proven his own worth to the crowd in response to their mercy and now not only was he once again Velletri's champion, but he had seen the life of Violetta spared if it had ever been in the peril it had been made to seem.

Letting his arms fall back to his side Cassian could not help but notice the blood streams trickling down the curve of his bicep, he shook his head with a smirk. Arturo would have words to say as he stitched the flesh back together, but they would have to wait for his focus was still upon those standing on the pulvinus. His lip curled to see the hands of the siblings upon Violetta when it should be his hands touching her, his body she was pulled close to. Would he ever have the chance again or would he now be left wondering what, if anything, he had meant to her? Shifting his gaze to meet that of Tertius it was not hard to read the unending greed that flashed in his mind, this would not be the last time that he was manipulated for the lanista's gain but how many more times would his heart be put on the line to make a few more coins for the man who would control his fate?

The man who claimed to possess Violetta was no longer with the others on the platform, but he did not need to be with his viperous offspring there to do his bidding. He could see the tears on her cheek but was it because she might now be forced to please the 'barbaric slave' once again or was she afraid of those she stood beside? He did not dare to hope that her tears were ones of relief for his safety in victory. He gave the slightest nod to her but then the gates opened and the guards beckoned him to depart the field of his return to glory and see the wounds of his body tended while he held a faint hope close in his heart that she would come to him, even if it was to bid farewell. He would be able to ask for explanation then though he feared what she would say more than he had feared the blade of the body left behind him on the sands.

Instead of being led to the infirmary as he expected upon his return the reinstated champion was surprised and more than pleased to find himself taken to the bath which had been prepared with fresh water, it was even scented with the sandalwood usually saved for occasions when the gladiators would be presented to the Roman's for display or other uses. He did not linger in the water long though it was soothing, there was more pressing matters upon his mind, the chief being would Tertius summon her or was he to spend his days wondering at what he saw?

Rising from the water Cassian retied his subligaria and entered the hallway only to find that even now he was not escorted to the infirmary but the cell he had not occupied in months on the far side of the sands, removed from the rest of the gladiators. The light of lanterns poured out of the door and he held his breath as the entered, hoping that as he raised his head 'she' would be there but instead he was greeted by Arturo's teasing smile before the man moved to inspect and stitch the wound on his arm. "Do not speak a fucking word of drug's use or I swear to the heavens I will fight the energy to kill you this night."

The medicus chuckled softly as he tended the wound and cleaned it. "Pain is always preferable to hallucination when the alternative is death. At least that is what I have found." They both laughed, friendly banter between the two of them was common but tonight the medic could sense something else, an impatience that was not usually there when they spent time together. "I would tell you to sleep but I am guessing that you have a deeper hunger for a woman than for that. Sleep when you can and when you wake you will feel less of the drug and more of yourself." With a laugh he shook his head, patted his shoulder in a brotherly gesture of affection and saw himself out of the room, closing the door tight behind him.

The bed creaked beneath his weight and he sighed, at least it was not the cot only inches off the ground like he had slept on for the months since losing his title, but what about Violetta? Where was the lanista's promise now? "Wound throbs more than cock." He muttered "Head more than that." He put his head in his palms that rested upon his knees unable to even speak the words that his heart was throbbing more. He closed his eyes trying to find some rest or at least the determination to try and rest without knowing what had happened to the girl he had felt his heart ache for. "Fucking opium." He growled as the image of her in luxurious fabric on the pulvinus with Vitus's tongue upon her skin played itself across his mind with a more vivid clarity than he could stand. The wicked look in his eyes had told him that the show was for him but what was her part? Her eyes had said... he couldn't even be sure dammit. He was lost in the ever-circling thoughts of was she slave or was she Roman when there was a knock at the door. "It is late. Too late for breaking words."

CHAPTER 16

Violetta joined the rest of the crowd in the cheers that rose to the heavens like thunder at the fall of the challenger, and the rise of the city's champion once more. She had not noticed the tears of relief that were cascading down her cheeks until Vitus leaned over to growl venomously "Wipe face before notice is taken." As quick as she moved it was too late for the magistrate had already seen them and moved to speak to her, calling loudly with a smile she did not like "Good lady why do you weep? Surely not for the death of a slave?" He smirked when he turned his attention to Vitus and remarked "Your bride to be is of tender heart, poor lady." He knew full well the acid tongue and free hand of the younger Census and shook his head at the thought of such a soft heart married to the monstrous man. Putting the matter behind him he turned to have his cup refilled and rose to speak with a few of the other nobility before they departed.

Violetta tried to find words to explain herself as she watched Felix grip the arm of Tiberius with a satisfied grin "Your man saw bargain fulfilled with glorious finish. The prize is his until the morrow when my man will fetch her." He said as he stood and grinned broadly at the others upon the pulvinus "If you will excuse me, I believe I now have some debts to collect." He quickly departed and left his unhappy children to see that the deal with the lanista was met, even though neither of them wished it. She could barely contain her joy at the thought that she would soon be in his arms. They had all been taught what would happen if they made it appear as though he did not honor his word and that alone would ensure that she was at the gates of the ludus within the hour.

She could see that Vitus was fuming at the Celt's victory and how it would cause his plans to go awry for the night. She knew how he had intended to spend it and offered another silent prayer of gratitude to go with the one thanking the gods for the victory of the man she desired. He cast a glare at the man down upon the sands who should have been basking of the glory of his title returned but instead stood still with his eyes locked upon her. With a smirk Vitus put his hand upon her shoulder and drew her to his side, completing the charade that placed her as his bride to be. "If you would forgive us a quick departure, I feel the need to get my intended back to the villa as quickly as is possible."

His arm around her waist brought an understanding smile from the men and a look of genuine pity from the few women upon the balcony. They knew what he was like, his appetites were well known and the cause of their avoidance of him. Violetta could not help but wonder if they would pity her more or less if they knew the truth of her position. Her eyes stayed fastened on Cassian as the Roman drew her away, but it was only a moment before Selenia placed herself between the eyes of the lovers and placed her hand on her hair as she whispered, "Come little one, we must prepare you to meet your lover." Fighting to repress the shudder she nodded but still craned her neck, looking over her shoulder to catch a final glimpse of Cassian before they descended the stairs and he was lost to her sight. "Yes. I would be ready to meet him as swiftly as possible."

While Selenia moved her through the crowds Vitus moved to speak with Tertius, his face full of the rage he could not contain and his voice, though hushed, was full of contempt for what he obviously saw as foolishness on the side of his father. "Your man has won the day and my father has left me to see that his side of the agreement is kept." He pointed to the bottom of the stairs where Violetta stood at Selenia's side as she flirted with some of the more affluent men who had not held a place on the pulvinus. His was in a worse mood than usual as he spoke to the lanista, Violetta could hear it in his voice. "Would you have her return with you now or have her brought in her proper attire to your ludus within the hour?" He crossed his arms and sneered "Since this farce is between the two of you and he has gone to collect his winnings, the decision falls to you alone."

Violetta felt like such a fool in the silks and jewels beside Selenia as she flirted and teased with most of the men that came close. Some of them attempted to flirt with her as well but she kept her head down and the older woman was quick to deflect them "Lest my brother's wrath fall upon you for flirting with his intended bride." She wanted so badly to correct her and to run through the halls until she found the cells holding the gladiators so that she could throw herself into the arms of the only man that made her feel safe.

He may have been the champion of the city, but it did not matter, he was the champion of her heart and he meant more to her than a title. The look in his eyes when he had seen her standing with the Romans was haunting her. She wanted more than anything to be able to explain herself to him, but would he listen or reject her? Making this day full of pain to go with the humiliation she felt in the knowledge that the wrong word or glance could lead to the discovery of her identity and see her punished before those that she had just spent the day with. All she wanted was for this day of stress and torment to end so she could dream of him if nothing else.

The lanista eyed the son of the merchant with an indecisive expression. Cassian had elevated his house once again, because of him coin would cover his palms in even greater abundance than before. Everyone would want to see if he had truly recovered or if it was mere chance that had seen the title returned to him. There would be rewards all around, a sacrifice to Jupiter, incense for the medicus of his ludus and she would service the needs of his champion since, at least now, she was what he might desire.

"Let the champion be pleasured by splendor. See her to the ludus dressed as she is within the hour. It will give time for my medicus to inspect him and tend to any wounds after he bathes." He looked down the stairs at Violetta and grinned with a strange look in his eyes that sent a shiver through her. "Let us see what lays at the root of their desire shall we?" He grinned, nodded and moved himself down the stairs, pausing only to drop a kiss to the cheek of the girl responsible for at least some of the champion's return to form.

Vitus nodded and took a deep breath before following him down the stairs to meet the women. "Father will want the jewels removed in the cart but otherwise his little whore is to be sent as she is to the ludus. It looks as though that one at least will not be yours when tomorrow comes Selenia." He almost laughed at the angry flash in his sister's eyes. He gripped Violetta's arm tightly and led her towards the wagon, almost shoving her up into the cabined space in his hurry to be gone. "You will take off all the metal and jewels, now. They will not be risked in the presence of savages."

She nodded and began to unfasten each piece as his sister climbed inside to sit next to him as though it would lower her to sit next to Violetta now that the day was over. "It is not as if that dress would be up to my standards in Rome, brother." She said with a snide roll of her eyes as Violetta struggled to remove the adornments that had been piled onto her to make her look the part of the Roman.

With a savage growl of frustration that his dig at his sister did not have its desired effect Vitus reached out and ripped the comb from the shining chestnut locks which pulled Violetta to the floor of the cart as she stifled a cry of shock and fear more than of pain. When he had removed all the finery but the dress, he gripped her wrist and shoved her back to the bench. "You'll be his whore and when he is finished with you then I will have you to myself and no one, not even father, will dare to disrupt my plans for you." When she nodded fearfully, he leaned back to the cushions. His face was full of smug satisfaction that fear of him would taint all the time between now and when he was able to make good on his words.

The rest of the short drive passed in silence; Violetta was able to hold back her tears from the rough removal of jewelry that had left scratches but luckily not drawn blood. The sight of it would have sent Vitus into a gleeful frenzy and his mood was volatile enough as it was. When they stopped in front of the ludus it was with a sigh of relief that she stepped down from the wagon behind him, leaving a decidedly pouting Selenia behind them.

Vitus' pounding on the door saw it opened by a woman with smooth soft brown skin and wide eyes that seemed kind when she was shoved through the door "Tell your Dominus to send word if he wishes her retrieved tonight, if not I will return for her in the morning." With a parting glare that made her shudder he slammed the door and was gone back to the wagon, the last sound from it that she heard was Selenia's laughter as they drove off leaving her face to face with the quiet but somehow soothing woman.

Upon entering the house of Tertius, Violetta felt a tremor of fear even though the woman from the door was walking with her, guiding her towards a set of stairs that she assumed would take her to the ludus. Anything could happen to her here and there would be no one to help her, Meridius was not going to come around a corner like the guardian or father and stop a man, any man, from touching her as he had done for years.

When they reached the top of the stairs cut into the cold stone of the hill, they were met by a tall man with skin darker than the woman beside her but his glistened in the flickering light of the oil lanterns. She caught herself staring at the scars upon his chest only to be interrupted by his soft voice asking her "You are Violetta?" When she nodded wordlessly, he smiled, a gentle and calming flash of white teeth "Come, he is waiting for you." He beckoned her with a nod and held out his hand to help her down the stairs. She looked to the other woman who smiled, somewhat sadly she thought, then took the calloused hand and moved down the stairs trying not to let her fear show in her eyes.

The warmth of the sand was still on her feet when the dark man opened the door and she saw him in the soft light. She could not help the gasp that fell from her lips. He was glorious, even with the fresh stitches upon his arm and without the armor. Skin like polished bronze and muscles like chipped marble that she ached to touch but did not dare even move towards. She felt a gentle hand push her inside and close the door as she found her voice to speak. "Victory is yours, champion."

He looked up at the sound of the door opening and the look on his face said he was prepared to rebuff whoever it was that disturbed him, but when he saw, her his heart raced. She stood before him in the blue richness that she had worn that day though slightly crushed as she had been dragged to the floor and minus the jewels and adornments. She stood fidgeting shyly, the confidence she had displayed on the pulvinus was lacking also. Her footsteps were halting and timid as the door was closed behind her.

Slowly Cassian rose to his feet and stepped to meet her. "It is, but are you? What brings you to my cell?" Looking at him she wanted him to pull her into his arms, strip the evidence of Rome from her body and show her that they belonged together, that their souls whispered to each other in the night. "Why have you come to me?" He whispered, brushing the back of his knuckles down her arm.

A cautious smiled crossed her lips "I did not think to meet you again, especially in this..." She gestured to the dress "Ridiculous falseness." Her eyes searched his for some understanding but looked down as his fingers touched her so tenderly her breath caught. "I am here for you, to be with you as a reward for your victory today if such is your desire." Suddenly she felt the weight of uncertainty in her shoulders, looking to the ground in preparation for his rejection of her presence and her heartfelt desire to be in his arms.

Tipping her head upwards to look him in they eye, so she had no other option but to reveal herself to him. "And yet you bring the glory of it to me? Why, Violetta?" Everything in his eyes said he wanted to kiss and taste her mouth but if he thought she stood a Roman and he did more than he had already dared then it could mean his life before he would have a chance to explain himself to even his own guards that trusted him.

Staring into the amber sanctuary of his eyes when he tilted her head to meet his gaze, she placed a hand to his chest as though to steady herself. The touch of his skin beneath her fingertips was like the softest of velvet and yet he was hard as stone though warm. "The choice was not given. I have done only as commanded by those that dictate our lives, out there." She flicked her eyes towards the door but then returned her eyes to his. "I would be dressed in your arms alone but instead wear what your Dominus ordered that I should. Though to what end it was intended I can only guess for you would know the man better than I." She searched his expression for answers, had her fear been realized? Had the day placed doubt where before there had been only affection?

Covering the hand on his chest with his own he stared into her eyes with a piercing discernment and asked the question that burned in his throat "What was your place upon the pulvinus this day that saw you to finery, and words with the magistrate himself?" They were standing so close all he would have to do is bend his head and he would be kissing her. The inches could be closed in the time it took to draw a breath, but she felt as though her dress and days position was pulling him in opposing directions. Roman or slave? The answer would dictate not just this moment but so much more in their lives. the rise of a champion or the fall of a god could be determined by how much he believed of her answer. More than anything she wanted him to trust in her, to believe in what lay between them but his touch said something held him back

"I held the place of a pawn played at the whim of my Dominus and yours." Finally seeing the battle in his eyes for what it was she sighed "I was not there on any merit or value of my own but merely as a piece to be played between them to achieve the result they desired to further their own gain." With a deep sigh she leaned forward, her forehead resting against his chin as she was unable to look him in the eyes. How could she make him understand that she had not lied to him, would not, and that though she was with him now because of the bargain between the men who owned them both it was her desire to be there freely. "I was told to play a part or see myself to pain, so

I did what I had to do to survive but in truth there is much more that I would have done to have the chance to be here with you like this."

Perhaps his head was still foggy from the fight but there was something that he seemed to be missing in her words. He took her hands in his and stared down into her eyes and he whispered his question, as he was afraid to say it loudly in case this was just a dream and the gods heard him raise his voice to question it. "And why are you here, exactly?" His heart was racing beneath her palm in anticipation of her answer.

"Why?" She tilted her head confused that he did not already understand. "Because by some design of fate, and both our Dominus, I have been blessed. Given this chance again to be in the arms of the man who possesses my heart and soul. Other's may command my body, but they cannot command my heart. You, only you, have my heart and all the love that I can bear. There is no other that holds such a place in my heart." Rising to her toes Violetta closed the distance between them, her body pressed against his; soft curves to the firm unyielding chest of the champion and her trembling lips only a brush away from his own should he wish to move to accept her kiss.

The tension in his body was fading, the desire in his eyes building to match her own. No matter what else, whether he believed her or not, she knew he wanted her and the evidence of that was rising between them. The air between crackled and sparked as though in the height of a thunderstorm. She could see in his bearing that the temptation to mindlessly take what she offered, and he wanted beckoned to him from the depths of his soul. Everything but the truth of who and what they were, two slaves that felt a passionate desire for each other, a connection that was intensified by the dangers they had both faced that day, was stripped away and bared down to nothing but the moment. His eyes bored through her like a blade and he inhaled the scent of her before he paused, holding her completely still as he clenched his jaw tight, tightening every muscle before he whispered "Love? Did my ears just hear you break words of love?"

A red flush rose on her cheeks as her eyes darted down to the ground. "I... I did not mean to, yet I cannot take back words already uttered." She eased herself back down to her feet and bowed her head in anticipation of his laughter which would be well deserved. That she should love this man, a gladiator whom she barely knew seemed as unlikely and unreal as the silks she wore but just as undeniable. It was truly laughable, their circumstance until this night they had touched and broken words with each other only twice before. What in the heavens had been in her mind to bring utterance to such emotion that she could never hope to be returned by a man such as this? The gods themselves had to be laughing upon their thrones to see such foolishness.

He stared at her intently, searching for the truth in her words and perhaps finding it in the innocent blush upon her cheek. He drew a sharp breath as though the depth of emotion in her eyes stole the breath from his lungs. There was desire there but something deeper than that shone out only for him, something that made her heart leap in her chest, that she wanted him to believe completely with everything that he was as she did.

"You did not mean to?" Cassian chuckled; his voice thick with a smoldering passion as he wrapped an arm about her waist while the other reached to tilt her chin back up to face him "Let me taste the truth of your words." He brought his mouth to hers in a kiss as brutal with need as it was yearning for her response. His mouth was hard, plundering as his tongue parted her lips and lathed the lining of her mouth as he tasted her soul.

She could not help but give in to the demands of his kiss, putting everything into it that she wanted to say but could not find the words for. Her hands smoothed over his chest, taking in every ripple of muscle when he tightened his arm around her waist and looped the second one there too. She could feel the scars on his flesh and caressed them, memorizing each one. There was something about him that possessed her utterly in a way that could not be bought or sold in a market but burned from the core of her being. She was lost in him and to the moment of this kiss that was everything she had hoped for, she could feel it from him and simply wanted more of it, more of him. The roughness of his unshaven face scraped against her face, but she did not care that it was rough, it simply meant that she would still feel him in the morning.

He pulled her closer as he intensified the force of his kiss, the sweetness of her surrender only fueling his fire more. He let his hands trace an unseen line down her side, his thumbs slipping naturally over the curve of her breasts, cupping them as he lowered his hands to her hips, taking a possessive hold there. His entire body felt hot, flushed with pleasure that seemed just out of reach. His tongue swept and probed her mouth, drinking her in while she was vaguely aware of the fact that his fingers had moved up the curve of her spine and were working the laces that tied the gown at her shoulders. The ribbons gave way and he was at last able to tug the rich fabric down and away, slowly revealing precious inches of her ivory white skin.

In a fevered passion Violetta pushed the loosened fabric of the dress to the side, letting it fall unheeded to the floor as her arms reached to wrap around his neck, pulling him lower to press against her now naked body against the chiseled chest and his thundering heart. A sigh of forgotten pleasure escaped her lips, all other thoughts but him and his kiss, his burning heat, fell from her mind. All that mattered was this moment they were in, this kiss, this night. Daring to lower her hands her fingers danced at the edge of his subligaria but did not dare to dip beneath the fabric, not yet.

He held her captive, the urgency of his kiss proved his intent. Lips and tongue trailing a path down her neck his callused fingers swept her naked flesh, committing every curve to his memory. "By the heavens you are beautiful." His voice was rough with passion held back but carried a note of complete and total reverence when he looked down at her body, finally bared to him completely, without audience, as never before. Outlining the rounded swell of her breasts with the tips of his fingers he forced his touch to be soft as a feather instead of the urgent desperation that she saw in him. It took the strength of a champion to hold back the ferocity that he was capable of. "So perfect." He murmured in her ear, his voice deepening to a flaming fluidity like molten lava. He moved his hand to cup her, lifting her closer to his mouth, allowing the heat of his breath to brush across the sensitive bud and arch her back towards him before she even knew what was happening.

Closing her eyes as his fingers and lips danced across her skin, causing the flame of desire to spark even brighter. "I pale in the presence of your glory." She whispered in his ear as she marked the cords of his neck with her lips. Her voice was deeper than normal, like it had been that first time they laid together in a different cell than this. Her hips pressed against his as he raised her, her own hands at last gliding over the firm curve of his backside.

Through the blood-stained linen of his subligaria there was no disguising the raw power of his need for the woman in his arms. Cassian teased the tight buds, rubbing the pads of his fingers over the sensitive tips he squeezed gently as he coaxed pleasure through her body with the silent demand of his own, but the soft moans were not enough, not now when he had her to himself. They needed more and by the gods they would have it. If there was never this chance again, she knew that she would have no regret about this night. Finally, he took what he desired, dropping his hand to firmly cup the curve of her backside, watching for a flinch of fear or hesitation before lowering his head to nudge her breasts with his mouth, his teeth erotically grazing where his fingers had just been before sucking her into the heat of his mouth with a ferocity that managed to be gentle in its demand.

His name escaped her lips in a moan of pleasure. "Cassian..." First his fingers and then his mouth sending her into a spiral of desire. Her hand smoothed down his back, tracing the line of his spine then teasing her fingers around the top edge of his subligaria. Unable to help herself she slid her hand over the tight linen covering his hardened shaft. When his pulse quickened at his throat she laughed slightly "You have me at a disadvantage champion, this fight is not fair."

When her fingers and then the heel of her palm pressed against him eagerly, a stab of pleasure went straight to his heart. Releasing her breast, he moved his mouth to take possession of hers with a feral growl that declared his growing lust. Slowly he locked strong fingers over the slender, trembling ones that teased him, taunting him with their nearness to his throbbing cock. Silently staring into her eyes, he guided her in the deliberate motions of removing what she had named his advantage, holding her wrist when the linen fell unheeded to the ground so that she felt the firmness of him pulsing against her palm. "Do I frighten you?" He growled softly.

His fingers guided hers and at first, she had taken the opportunity to explore him with the other hand but when he wrapped her fingers around him, she paused and took a swift intake of breath. Hoping to hide the sound, Violetta kissed him suddenly and hard before lowering her head to press hot kisses in a line across his chest. His question gave her a moment's pause before she shook her head and dared to flick her tongue out to taste his nipples. The fire she felt for him was threatening to consume all reason while their naked bodies pressed together in the soft light and their shadows combined into one upon the wall behind them. "I am not afraid." She whispered and looked back up to meet his eyes, her hand resting over the beating of his heart. "Not this time."

CHAPTER 17

Cassian stilled in her hand, the muscles of his stomach clenching hard as the heel of her hand met his tip. Groaning with pleasure he thrust himself fully into her grasp, showing her the rhythm that pleased him most and left him throbbing on the edge of reason within the embrace of her tiny hand. His breath was coming hard, and fast, small drops of sweat had formed on his brow and he realized that he felt as though he were a young boy again, inexperienced with women instead of one of the most sought-after lovers in Velletri. He shook his head and stared down at her in wonderment of how someone so small, so innocent had the power to set off the combustion as powerful as flames in a dried field that transformed him from a rational man who did nothing without thought into a man filled with primal urges, caring only for his desire and the one who brought it to him. He wanted her, wanted to claim her and mark her as his own, to protect her against the evils brought to them by the fate that made them both slaves.

One hand slid between them and his fingers met the dampness of her arousal, bringing a smile to his lips. He probed a little more, circling and teasing the swollen flesh under his touch. He wanted to taste her again, to inhale the sweet feminine scent of her before burying his lips and tongue between her thighs to devour her until she came apart in his arms, shattering in her ecstasy before he would sheath himself deeply inside her. Her breath caught and hitched, and he knew that she was thinking the same thing, feeling the deep need that was growing between them. He returned the kiss she offered, trying to hide her feelings of arousal that were still so new and overpowering though he could see and feel it in her touch. He was about to lay her down upon the floor and take her with his mouth when she rested her head on his chin and smiled up at him before making a move that stopped everything in his world; she slid to her knees.

He wondered how she knew what to do, had the lesson been pleasant? This was not a thing a Roman noble to would offer a slave and he wondered if she did this to show the truth in words, he found himself already believing? Her hands traced up his thighs until they reached his base then as she lowered her mouth towards him, her tongue flicking out quickly to lap the bead of moisture at his tip. There was some nervousness at first but when he drew a swift breath it seemed all that she needed to hear. As much as he wanted to take her to the ground and use his mouth and wicked tongue to pleasure her until she could no longer think he had to let her do what she intended, showing that her desire was of her own and not something ordered by the Romans. With a slight nod he let her slowly wrapped her lips around him, letting him slide deep into her throat.

The reaction he felt was instant, the wet heat of her tongue and then her lips sent a surge of lust straight to his core that was as hot and heavy as molten steel. He could not remember the last time he had felt pleasure so pure, so consuming that it touched every part of him. When she closed the soft pillows of her lips around the head of his cock his knees nearly buckled, and a hand moved to rest on the top of her head to steady himself. His whole body seized with restraint and the effort it took to hold back from his baser desires for if he gave in the ferocity of his lust would frighten her and he felt as though if those eyes ever looked at him in fear that his world would end.

Blood pounded in his ears and he dared to look down once more though his eyes were all but closed as he savored each plunge and pull of her lips. His breath caught in his chest when he drank in the sight of the dark feathers of her lashes spread across her cheeks while the most sensual lips, he had ever seen stroked him with a tenderness that would have stolen his heart if she did not already possess it.

His mind went blank and he let his senses go as he drowned in the wet heat of her mouth that took him in deep and then deeper still. It felt as though she would swallow the essence of him if he let her and by all that might be holy, he wanted to let her do as she wished, to give her what her actions asked for even if she did not know what it was. He wanted this release and for it to come from her, the woman who had haunted his thoughts, was a greater pleasure than he had hoped for. "Violetta." He growled her name through a tightly clenched jaw, the only sign he could give her of what he felt in that moment.

As her tongue lathed him inside her mouth her hands were not idle, they roamed and caressed up his legs that were forced to the stillness of resolute granite. She seemed determined to give as much pleasure as he would allow her before he could bear no more. That she was willing to give to him even a small amount of the fire and pleasure that she had brought to him with only a single gaze, brought new enthusiasm to her movements and a delighted groan at the thought that he would take his relief in her. Moving her eyes and hands upwards in unison she rested her palms on the top curve of his backside she locked her eyes with his in a look of silent surrender to his will and the passion between them.

He buried his fingers in the dark silk of her hair, surrendering completely to the erotic satisfaction that she was giving to him. The soft pull of her mouth was as close to paradise as he would ever be allowed to come. It was the bliss of Elysium and the fire of Hades in the same breath. He could not focus on any one thing for they were all staggering at once; the way her lips stretched around him, the eagerness that she took him into her mouth or the way that her hands grabbed him to pull him closer, they all seemed to work together in ways that no one had ever been able to do to him before and brought him to the edge of his sanity. The pressure was building and the need for release more than he would be able to stand for much longer, his body went rigid and he knew that he was about to lose what control he was still holding on to. He had to step back, withdrawing himself from her lips reluctantly before drawing her to her feet to stare into the deep blue of her eyes.

"You... are perfection come to life." He said softly before taking her lips in a passionate kiss and letting his hand fall between her creamy thighs to brush his fingers against her heat. She was hot and wet, eager for him but more than that he could see everything she felt. Everything she wanted from him was in her eyes. The purity of her emotions, feelings that matched what he was feeling deep in his heart. This was not a heated fling or just a spark that would fade, this was real, and it was more than he deserved but he would be ever grateful to the gods for giving him a second chance to love and be loved.

Pressing her lips to his gently she inhaled deeply as he touched her, glowing in each contact of his lips and hands as though when he touched her it was like satin itself. When he slipped his hand between her thighs, she moaned her need against his chest, her teeth finding contact with his skin and nipping him slightly, just enough to make him hiss. The night was theirs and passion was like a smoke billowing between them. The emotion in her eyes made him smile and as she kissed him again, pressing her body to his it was as if she could not get close enough. Her fingers threaded through his sweat dampened hair as she pulled him near to taste his mouth again while his fingers stroked and circled and teased. "Cassian." She pleaded his name and prayed that he knew all that she put into the word; her heart, her desire and all her most honest emotions. "Show me Elysium."

If the gods never saw them together again at least he could have this night, this one perfect night with her in his arms. His breath sounded ragged as he inhaled the scent of her, and the beating of his heart was like the thunder of horses. Everything in his world narrowed to the focus on only a solitary thing; Violetta and the way she felt in his arms. When she opened her eyes to look at him, he could not wait a moment longer, he rained kisses down her neck and shoulders, over the rounded curve of her breasts as he dragged the edges of his teeth back and forth across the berry coloured buds of her nipples.

Slowly he eased them both to the ground, there was no time to take her to his bed though he would later, after this, but now the need to be with her outweighed everything else. Positioning himself between her thighs Cassian looked down at her with a hungry grin but instead of taking her with the primal need he felt he leaned down to kiss her thoroughly, demanding her response to his dominion of her and her acknowledgment of his possession. Raising his head from the kiss to catch his breath he gently slipped her legs over his shoulder Cassian angled himself to slide into her, the movement was as slow and deliberate as if she were still a virgin and this her first time with a man. His eyes closed with a groan of complete satisfaction as he sank deep into her.

She bit her lip to stifle a moan but gasped as he sank home at last. Her eyes fluttered before focusing on his face while he filled her slowly, completely. Her hips raised on their own to angle him in deeper, welcoming him to her heated core until he could go no further. When she reached a hand to brush his cheek, they began to move together, her breath hitching each time he returned home in the complete contact of their bodies. She clasped her hands behind his neck and rolled her body to move with him like a wave of growing revelry. It felt better than good, so perfectly right, to be here with her like this as though there was a need greater than themselves that had pulled them together. The urgency of the moment was as though nothing else in all the world mattered but the chance for them to make love at least this one more time.

He gave himself to her, in a way he had not thought to give since the death of Nala, burying himself so deep that he was certain he could touch her soul before he withdrew and returned, each thrust claiming more than the last. His entire world, every thought, breath and beat of his heart, was focused on the woman beneath him and how her breath caught, the flush on her cheeks and the thundering pulse at her throat. He lowered his lips to press against them against the fluttering skin before moving lower to suckle the ripe berries at the peaks of her bosom as he thrust his hips into her, his teeth grazing them as she tightened around him.

His pace soon increased with renewed energy, his lust rising with the ardor crackling between them, he was taking her harder and deeper than he had intended but he was out of his mind with need. His voice was husky and primal but blending with the sweetness of her passionate cries it was like the choir of the heavens was singing with them as the battle became overwhelming and he had to give in. Surging once, twice, a third time he crashed over the edge of ecstasy and called her name as his body stiffened in its release.

Crying his name Violetta arched her back as his body brought hers with him over the edge of glorious climax, each of his final thrusts sending new waves of pleasure across her face until he thought she would burst into shattered fragments before his eyes. She gathered him to her chest as her legs slid from his shoulders to rest on the cold ground. Her breath was coming in ragged pants, but her lips were spread in a lazy smile focused only on him. The lust between them was satisfied and receding like the tide but trust and rising affection remained and swelled in her eyes as she tried to speak but was as lost for words and breath as he was. He knew she had not misspoken before, she loved him, more than she should in current circumstances but by all the gods he could not deny he felt something similar.

When at last he had relaxed, the spasm of his release ebbing from his loins, he collapsed on top of her utterly spent but completely satisfied beyond what he believed to be possible. Every ounce of his body was spent in a way beyond the exhaustion of the arena, he felt it to his soul, and it brought a smile to his lips until he realized that his weight must be crushing to her and so he found enough strength to roll to his side. Never had he felt like this after being with a woman, so sated that all he wanted was to hold her and sleep.

He pushed himself up on his elbow to brush a strand of hair from where it had fallen over her eyes and smiled down at her. His fingers lingered on her cheek, turning her head so that their eyes met before he leaned over to kiss her lips; soft and lazy he was pure tenderness, something that he did not know he had in him to give. When she smiled at him his own grin broadened and he pulled her to his chest, wishing he could hold her there forever that the gods of this country would be good enough, kind enough, to let her truly be his.

Raising her head to look him in they eye she whispered "The night is ours. They'll not come for me until dawn." She pushed herself up to sit with her back to his chest as he traced kisses up her arm before easing himself to his feet with a groan at the effort. She looked up, for a moment she looked scared and vulnerable, worried that he would send her back but then he held out his hand and winked at her as she took it and rose to her feet with a smile.

Her words sent a bolt through him, this bliss did not have to end right now? There were no guards outside the door waiting to take her back the monsters that the law had made her masters. Looking at the joy in her eyes when he drew her close and led her towards the bed, that would be 'theirs' for tonight he suddenly felt as though he could make love to her again but more than that he wanted something more, something incredibly intimate. "Let me hold you tonight. I do not know if there is more to give than that but tonight, let it be as if they do not exist." Cassian gestured to the door and searched her eyes until she nodded.

Laying down with her close against his flesh was a test of restraint as he pulled the thin blanket up around them both and blew out the candle that had been close to sputtering into darkness. The moonlight lit her face in a beautiful glow, he could not help but take her lips again in a deep, probing kiss before cradling her against his chest. Their shared warmth would make the chill of the night a thing of trivial difference to them but as he watched her eyelids slip closed, he could not help but wish that every night could be like this. The thought brought a smile to his face as he closed his eyes and let himself slip into the warm oblivion that only comes in the aftermath of love's embrace. Tonight, he would truly know rest for the first time in years.

The morning arrived like the light of the heavens in golden splendor illuminating the sands and the room beyond; Cassian woke to the realization that love and title were once more his own and though pained by the separation of different houses there would be chances to see each other, with the return of his title he could request her without fear and the nights that he could not hold her in his arms would find her in his dreams, days filled with the image of her face and the memory of her body pressed against his in erotic suggestion just as it was at this moment. These were the things that brought the smile to his lips along with the determination to petition the gods to smile upon them enough to bring them back to each others arms once more. Leaning over to press a soft kiss to her cheek he let his lips say what he was not ready to bring to voice; an unspoken "I love you."

Violetta startled awake at the touch of his lips to her skin but the panic of waking in an unfamiliar bed was gone the moment she turned to see his face smiling at her. Her eyes flashed with the joy of realizing that the night before had not been a dream but a blessed reality. They had not spoken the words that were mirrored in each other's eyes but somehow, they both knew that he felt as she did and as their lips met the passionate longing solidified that knowledge. "Morning breaks upon us and yet my mind is still reliving the night." It was time that she should dress but she seemed reluctant to return to the blue satin she had arrived in.

Looking towards the door her face grew pensive, perhaps worried who it would be that would retrieve her; house guards with Meridius, Vitus, or Felix himself. The former and the latter did not worry him nearly as much as the idea that the son of her Dominus could be the one to take her away from his arms "They are coming for me, soon." She whispered against his chest while he held her close.

Cassian stood from the bed with more reluctance than he could believe, his arms seemed to linger around her like his body battled his mind to be with her still, but he knew that even if he stayed that they would still come for her. No matter what he wished or prayed for, she was to be returned to her Dominus that morning and he was to return to training as though his life had not been forever changed.

He stepped to the dress and crouched down to gather it in his arms while she still lay on the bed looking as though she had been thoroughly ravished the night before and needed the same again this morning. He raked a hand through his hair only to curse when it struck the tangled braids that he had forgotten were there. He frowned at the material in his arms as he stood and turned to return it to her arms "You will be missed. Every moment spent keeping memory of you alive within my mind."

He stepped away to let her dress, unable to stand next to her not knowing when the chance would come again to claim her as his own. She had taken him to new heights and now was a part of every thought and dream, his senses screamed for traces of her and she stood before him still, how would the respond to when she was beyond not only touch but sight as well. He picked up the discarded linen subligaria and tied it in place with a deep sigh that resigned him to their parting, at least for now.

He could feel her hand reaching after him as he rose, prolonging the contact as long as possible. She sighed when he handed her the dress, he hated the feel of the rich material as it meant she had to return to the reality of her position. As her fingers fastened the ribbons of the dress, she looked at him and smiled softly "My every thought will be touched by memories of your touch." She stood and he took in the full silhouette of her surrounded by the full light of dawn. She was glorious and seemed as though she glowed with the light of the heavens themselves; each curve was defined by the light and shadow. He was breathless with awe that such a woman wanted him and might care for him. Just as the tips of her fingers touched him there was a voice that began to make itself heard across the sand, their time had ended.

Violetta shuddered in his arms at the sound of the voice calling for her swift removal from the sanctuary they had dreamed for each other. "I cannot tell who it is that has come but it does not matter. I do not wish to leave your arms to go back to that place." She leaned her forehead against his chest in a last savored moment before moving towards the door which opened, light pouring in to expose the training yard and reveal her to all those upon it. She bit her lip in a way he found sweetly innocent, the idea of circling the sands while his brothers in arms trained upon it was obviously a terrifying thought, even though she would be accompanied by a guard. Not all men that bore the title of gladiator had the honor that he did. "Until the gods see fit to bring us back together you shall be a constant thought upon my mind." He said.

How could he even bring the words to his lips that described the feeling of loss that he felt knowing that she was to be taken from him? What lie could he tell himself that would make this easier to bear? His hand had lowered to the latch just as it was undone from the outside, his personal guards Auctus and Lucius stood there to allow Violetta's exit while denying him the chance to follow her at least until the gate. Before he could break words demanding explanation, he found his wrists shackled and Auctus' firm hand gripping his shoulder and his refined voice whispering words of caution since the eyes of his Dominus and the man that served were upon them both. "You have been summoned but this must be done so that spying eyes bring desired report back to waiting ears."

When she looked back at him and saw that shackles were placed upon his wrists Violetta looked as though she would cry out in protest. It was the quick shake of his head and her eyes lifting to the balcony to see Meridius staring down at them both that stopped him from breaking words that might have eased her. His gaze was locked to hers; he saw nothing else but her, but there was no joy in his eyes only an anger that burned deep in his soul. There might have been fear in her eyes, but he was glaring at the guards and the man with them, so he did not see her before they led her up the stairs to the villa and he was gone from her sight.

CHAPTER 18

The guards accompanying the silent Spaniard were in heated argument with Tertius regarding the retrieval of the girl from the arms of his champion "My employer does not care if you have to pull the girl from his throbbing cock, he would have her returned immediately." Despite the senior slave's look of disapproval, the man continued with a smirk "I don't care if she is naked, that would make the journey home just a little more entertaining." He peered out the doorway to the sands "So unless fucking is a new method of training, send your men to bring her now. Vitus will not wait, and you do not want him to come and fetch her, his temper is known to you I am sure."

Tiberius was insulted that a few house guards and Felix' body slave had been sent to fetch the girl when he had expected the merchant himself so that they might discuss the next round in the game that they played. "You can hardly expect me to interrupt the man as he enjoys the spoils of a hard-earned victory? It is tradition and he is a thorough man." The silent slave was darkly glaring at him, his upset at the words describing the girl had him wishing for just one moment to school these men in the way to discuss a girl of such beauty. "I will send a man to fetch her IF he is finished with her." He was not favoring the gladiator as much as he was protesting the fact that the guard of the merchant made demands like this of him.

The guard smirked and nodded to Meridius who arched a brow at the lanista, fighting a smirk. "This one is here to ensure your man has not damaged the girl too much." He pointed to the Spaniard as Meridius moved to the balcony to watch and make sure lanista kept his word to send a guard across the sands, the guard was not so foolish as to insist upon it himself as gladiators could be unpredictable and violent. One of guards joined him on the balcony but their conversation caused Tiberius to listen to their words before turning his eyes to lock on the door. "She is never going to be yours, Spaniard." The guard said though there could be no response "By the time they are done with her, there will be nothing left of what you desire." The lanista bristled when he raised his voice to call to his guard "I do not have all day. See her brought, now."

Tertius could not help the smile of satisfaction when she reached the top of the stairs. That she had to be dragged from the cell of the Celt was an obvious sign that he was pleased with his reward. The guard was getting anxious and the other slave that seemed to care for her seemed ready to snap with the slightest provocation after watching the woman handled as roughly as she was.

His fists clenched when the guard pulled her tight against him, fear showing in her eyes she flinched when the guard gripped her hard, pulling her until she lost her footing while struggling against him as he growled. "Did you enjoy yourself, whore? Did he beat you again or just use that sweet little body until you lost consciousness?" She kept her head down murmuring "Apologies Dominus, apologies" until the lanista reached out to take her arm in a gentle grip to draw her away from the guard.

"I see you serve your master well." Tertius said to the silent slave as he handed him the girl with a smirk at the offending guard. "I will be certain to speak of it when I see him next." The lanista wanted them gone before the gladiator was brought up from the sands. "I would not cause further delay to the return of borrowed goods, but I trust that you will relay my gratitude to good Felix, and I pray that our business can continue." As they stepped towards the door Tertius noted how the girl kept glancing over her shoulder as though in hopes that Cassian would soon appear for one last glimpse before the door shut between them.

Cassian noted her glance upwards but whether it was the leer of the guard or the frown of the other man, he could only assume was a slave that made her shudder, he did not know. Was either of them the one behind the newly learned skill that had all but brought him to his knees? Had they laid hand upon her or forced her to their bed? A flood of hatred surged through him but by the time he stood upon the floor of the villa awaiting the attention of his Dominus all that remained of her was the sweet intoxicating scent of her and the sound of the door closing behind her exit. He lifted his head to face Tertius, wondering at the shackles and if they meant that somehow title had been removed. He let the memory of the night linger upon his mind for a moment longer but then brushed it aside as the lanista approached. "Dominus, what cause is there to see me shackled and removed from training before I have even to begin it this day? Have I caused offence somehow in the night?"

The lanista was about to answer with the smug grin that every man and woman of his household had learned meant something devious was about to be announced when there was a roar from the sands that demanded his attention. Running to the balcony he left his champion shackled with his two guards to stand with him while the others returned to the training sand to calm the fight having sprung up there between Proximus and Agrus. "See them parted. Doctore maintain control or I will order the guards to see it done." He shook his head and pointed to the two men "Agrus to the pallus and Proximus, if you wish to live to earn the mark, attend your Doctore and do not cross words with men proven to be your better in this house."

The German was beginning to finally show signs of the promise he had seen in him years ago at the time of his purchase and the separation from his brother five years ago had seen more improvement than anticipated. When he had received the report that he had begun to train with Cassian Tiberius had begun to plot new uses for the man and new ventures in the unexpected pairing. Reminded by his own train of thought that the champion still stood waiting he returned his attention to the shackled man waiting with angst masked by indifference.

Stepping towards the Celt with a grin he commanded the guard next to him "Remove shackles from the wrists of the man who honors this house with his victory." As the chains were unlocked the lanista waved away the look of irritation and confusion in Cassian's eyes "Give those no further thought it was done only to make it seem as though delay was being punished though I do not fault you for savoring every moment in sweet embrace." He sat down at his desk and looked up at the man who still seemed surly "Pay heed to words about to be broken and put all else from your mind if you wish to benefit from them."

Waiting until the gladiator took a breath to calm his rage the lanista sipped his wine before continuing. "Your victory inspired the nobility of Velletri towards seeing more gladiators from this house and so there is to be a feast of celebration in your honor within days." He grinned and drank deeply before gesturing to the sands "You will fight Proximus in the man's test to earn the mark. I would set a former champion against the current one with steel in hand to thrill those that will put coin in hand to bring glory to these walls. What say you to this?"

Cassian looked surprised he had been shackled merely so that a guard in the pay of Census could report that he had been punished for an act that held no disobedience if the merchant asked about it. His annoyance was valid for who was Felix Census that the champion of Velletri should be humiliated on the chance that he would ask about the delay of his rising?

"My hands are yours to command, Dominus." Was the appropriate response to the command though his eyes said that he had so many more things upon the edge of his tongue. Nodding his acceptance of the words, as Tiberius turned to look out the window the Celt boldly gave voice to the question that must have been plaguing him about the man he had just been told to test "Was he brought here to take my place if I had not been victorious yesterday? The man claims to have been a champion of Rome itself and yet I am to administer the test bringing him to the fold of the brotherhood?"

The lanista turned to look at him as though he had lost his mind and then smiled broadly "Do you worry for your position Cassian? The man was indeed a champion and is undefeated there, but his sale was the result of his master's displeasure in him." He let the words sit between them for a few moments before continuing "Yes. He was bought with the thought that you might never recover enough to take to the arena sands again. There had been offers made for your purchase but none that were seriously entertained. I know a man like you could never live the quiet life of a showpiece or body slave to any man or woman, no matter their wealth or beauty."

The disgust that washed across the man's face told more than he might think, and he knew now was the moment to sink in the dagger of the true intent behind the match between titans. "When the test comes, I want you to remember that the cost to Proximus should he lose would be great and the weight of that loss would be felt most in my purse, yet the cost of your loss would be only the fleeting loss of pride. Consider the value of your actions when faced with steel before the eyes of the elite."

The lanista smiled inwardly as he saw the realization of trap that had been set for Cassian sink in. The day would come when they would have to fight each other in truth and then there would be an unnecessary death. He would have no choice when the time of the test came but to let the other man win for the champion's honor would not allow him to be a thoughtless man or one so cruel as to deny Proximus his own chance for glory. He would not damn another man who was worthy of the brotherhood to the mines just to save his pride.

"You will have your man, Dominus." He said with a bowed head that hid the rage that surely boiled just beneath the surface. For the second time in as many days Tertius was destroying the reputation of his own champion with his manipulations. "Am I permitted to return to training or is there more you wish of me this morning?" Was all he had to say as he stood, soaking in the reality of his instructions.

"After the medicus clears you for training you can return to the sands." His lips spread in a lecherous grin as he added "We must be certain that your night did not aggravate any wound." To the guards on either side of him he commanded "See him to Arturo before his feet touch the sands and tonight a cell in the ludus instead of that across the sands, let the brotherhood welcome him back to position tonight." He turned his back on the trio so as not to see the champion's outrage at being removed from the quarters that were his due as champion.

He had to keep the man hungry and if his anger was the way to do it then anger it would be. After the room had been cleared of all but his Syrian boy Jovian, he sat at his desk to pen a letter to be delivered to the hand of Felix Census inviting him to join in the celebration the night of the test, and to bring the girl with him so that the gladiator's conflict could be even greater. Sealing the letter with red wax and his ring, he then handed it to the boy who would see it to a runner slave that would bolt to the villa and arrive, hopefully, before the returning party.

"Why would he play at such games Arturo?" Cassian asked in frustration while the medic performed the inspection require by their Dominus. "It makes no sense. I have done as he asked and more, but he would deny me the rights of a champion that he has enjoyed telling are part of the traditions of the house set down by his father's father. Did my fall offend him so deeply or cost him so much that he would continue to punish me?" He got up to pace the small confines of the infirmary, the warm stone walls seeming to cage him in instead of offering the quiet comfort of intimate quarters with his dearest friend. "If he did not intend to treat me as champion then why allow me the night with the woman I desire? Why taunt with possibility then snatch it away like a jest? Have I more to prove to him?" With the last statement, he sat down on the sole chair in the room with such force that he thought it might give way beneath him, but he was beyond caring as he looked to his friend for answers.

The medicus shook his head with a sigh when his patient started to pace halfway through the inspection commanded without need, the man's passion was almost as powerful as his desire for victory in the arena. "You know that I am not in his counsel. The pair of Syrians would have more answers than I do. I can simply advise based on what I know of the man and what you know of him as well if you were thinking clearer." He stood and began to organize his tools for the day. "He wants you to fight to not only be champion but to be better than you were before your loss. It is not enough for him that you regained title, he will want to ensure that your doubters are forever silenced by the glory of your returned rise. If I wagered, I would lay coin to the thought that Tertius wants the eyes of Rome itself to hunger for your presence within its marvelous arena." He turned back to meet the frustrated eyes of the man that was like a brother to him. "You must do as commanded without question or protest, for now. Let him think that you are of a similar mind about your journey to reclaimed glory and I think you will see him share words to increase understanding."

He smiled at the look of frustration in the champion's eyes "Cassian, you must trick and bait his strategy from him just as you would an opponent in the arena. Only once it is revealed to you do you show that you were not of the mind that he thought you to be but until then you must feign compliance, especially if you wish to see the woman again. She was all you had hoped for was she not?" It was not the subtlest way to divert the angry thoughts, but it was the one most likely to bring a genuine smile to his lips and Cassian appreciated the effort the man made.

Cassian closed his eyes and pictured her face as it had looked illuminated by the moon as she had slept in his arms and nodded as he met Arturo's gaze "All and more. I have never known peace like that." He took a deep breath and stood "Do I pass your inspection? I wish to return to the sands if I cannot do anything else." His body ached for action and if he could not have it with his woman then he would continue to prove to his brothers and the man who would face him in the test that he was the true champion of the house and the required outcome of Proximus' test would not change that and if any man doubted then he would be quick to set them to the ground in answer.

"Yes. Go. As if any words I say could stop you." He said with a friendly slap to his shoulder, partially in farewell and partially to see if he reacted to being struck so close to the stitched wound from the sword. As the gladiator headed to the door, he called over his shoulder at him "Cassian, do not give him cause to doubt you, send some of your brothers to me. I stand bored in here since your fall from glory." Their shared laughter echoed down the hall following the champion of the house to the sands where he was met with the roar of welcome from his brothers in arms at his return to their ranks. The rest of the day was spent in combat against men that he held as brothers and pushing himself to the limits of what his body could tolerate for pain and endurance but after a short meal, he was taken back to the cell within the ludus and his anger returned.

His hands gripped the bars as his forehead leaned against the cold iron that held him back from the feeling of glorious victory. His achievements meant nothing when they were being used against him by the fates. They laughed at him even as he spoke of love, knowing he would be reduced to nothing even after he had fought and trained to come back to where he stood now. There were so many things that he had closed his eyes to in recent months but with these new dealings with Census it was harder than ever before to do so. He would play the part recommended by Arturo but how much longer would he let Tertius abuse his heart for personal gain? He could not stand idly by why the pair of Romans used the woman he loved as bait for his hunger for victory. Just as he would not let them use his newly regained title as the excuse for a celebration feigning to be in his honor only to be commanded to a loss that would justify the marking of a man that had been bought to replace him. Had he not seen enough of defeat in recent months upon the sands of the arena? If this was an attempt by the lanista to see his spirit crushed and broken, then by the gods he would show the man that there was more to him than they guessed. Never would he let it show how close he was to giving up, there was more for him to fight for now than ever before. "Damn you to Hades for this. I will never bend a knee as a broken man before a master of Rome, not while I still possess my heart." He cursed before laying down on the dirty pallet to dream of the previous night not only spent upon a bed but in sweeter arms than he could have hoped for. "Rest well my priestess and know my words were true and that you alone occupy pleasurable thoughts."

CHAPTER 19

After leaving the villa and her heart behind her, it took Violetta a few moments to realize that the guard did not seem in a hurry to move them back to their master's villa and even more strange was the fact that Meridius deliberately lingered back from the guards and kept her at his side by the grip on her arm that had not lessened as they walked. "Padre? What is it?" She asked the man who had in many ways taken the place of the father left behind long years ago when she had been taken as a slave in his stead. Turning his face to look at her completely Violetta was stunned once again at how handsome he was: bright eyes, a blue like the morning sky and a classically handsome face with a nose that might be considered large if it was not outshone by the broad grin so often upon his lips. He tapped a finger to the center of her chest and then pointed it back towards the villa as though to demand more information as to what happened. The arch of his brow posed the question as to her safety while there and her well being now that she was free of any ears that might hear the truth of her thoughts.

"I have never been happier in all my days than I was last night in his arms. He was tender, caring, gentle and..." She smiled to herself "most loving towards me." When he frowned and curled his lips, she shook her head "Do not fuss. It is my heart to give and I fear it is already well beyond my power to have it back." She flushed and looked down as the man beside her straightened with an air of annoyance that she did not understand. "Meridius? Padre? I believe he loves me as I love him, and all I desire and dream of is being returned to his arms once again. Cannot you not share the joy with me that I have something so special at last? That they cannot take away from me?" She took a step away from him before she realized he had stopped and the grip on her arm stopped her too. Raising her eyes to meet his she was surprised at the vehement rage in his eyes, it took her breath away in a gasp.

Meridius moved his hand in a rapid sequence of gestures that look like nothing to any casual observer but each one had meaning in the language he had created with her. The speed of the gestures told of his upset. "Men like him love no one woman, Violetta. They love any and every woman that is willing to open their legs or mouths to them." He regarded her with a passionate rage in his eyes though whether it was from a desire to protect her heart or a fit of jealousy she wasn't sure.

"The man has fucked half the nobility of Velletri, men and women, I would think he knows how to convince an innocent virgin that his actions are sincere but trust when I tell you that they are not. They couldn't be, not from a man like that." She knew that he himself had been with many lovers within the walls of the villa, some with more meaning than others but none had touched his soul since the first and he had not looked to find the pain of that loss again. "He does not love you, Violetta. Forget him and turn to arms that would give you more than he ever could." The final gesture was his hands folded over his heart and a pleading look in his eyes that she consider his words of warning even if she still thought she held the gladiator's heart.

Violetta stared at him as though she had never seen him before, what had come over him to speak like this. "Padre, you could not know the affections between us, but it is real." Her whispering voice cracked slightly, and she shook her head "I do not know what other arms you speak of for there is no one who cares like that for me but him." Taking a step back she shook her head and stepped away to catch up with the guards who had stopped to speak to a man at the mouth of an alley.

He would not understand that she had never looked for love or seen a man like this, she had never looked at a man and felt alive just at the sight of him. She shook her head again as if to shake the thought in her mind of anyone else, even her incredibly handsome father figure that had spoken as though he were an option as a lover when nothing else could be further from the truth. He had taken the position of protector the first day she had met him and had stayed that way since. He was a wonderful fatherly influence in her life, and she was grateful to him and loved him in that way but to share a bed? To share the kind of intimate touches with Meridius that she did with Cassian seemed to be utterly ridiculous.

The senior guard scoffed at her confused look as she walked past, his companion and the man he spoke to leered at her while muttering about the things either of them would do to change the expression on her face. Jerking his head and calling for Meridius to catch up he continued to lead them through the streets of the city that was already bustling with life, but it was not until they passed the brothels that Violetta paused to give any attention to her surroundings.

She remembered the kind of thing that went on in those places from the night she had spent bound in one on her way to the slave market and wondered if all the women hated it so much? Did liking what Cassian had done to her, what they did together, make her like them? A whore? Would Felix now use her as such to gain favor from his fellow Romans? She did not realize that they had reached the villa until the guard swatted her backside with unnerving familiarity and said, "Go wash yourself before you attend your master." But it was when Meridius followed her that she became truly unnerved and once they were alone in the hallways beneath the villa, she turned to him and asked "What is it? Why do you follow me now?"

He should have gone to Felix and they both knew it. Knowing that the others living in the cells of these halls would be upstairs at their tasks she was surprised when he took the chance and stepped up to her, pulling her tight to his chest before capturing her mouth with his, probing the heat of her mouth with the tongue the Romans thought had been removed years ago. He let go a small moan of pleasure at the contact, but when his hand smoothed over her hip, he finally noticed that she did not return the kiss and was frozen against him without the melting into him that she had seen with other women in his arms.

Staring down at her he seemed horrified to see the fear she could not hide in her eyes and even worse was the betrayal reflected at him where there had been only love before. He shook his head and stepped back though she was still trapped against the wall with nowhere to go. "Apologies." His hands flew in signs again, trying to stop her fear from taking hold. "I do not know what came over me. I did not mean to frighten you." His hands fell to his side and he tilted his head to try and catch her eye as he forced a grin, trying to be playful. "Now we know the truth of your feelings, do we not?" His hands faltered when she did not share the teasing smile.

She shook her head violently and considered, just for a moment, slapping the smile from his face. "I already knew. It is you who doubted, who held affections secret." Taking a step backwards down the hall from him, anger all over her face. "I love you dearly as a father but not like this, never this." Knowing he would not follow her again that day she straightened her shoulders and turned to make her way to the slave's baths to make herself ready to face her Dominus, and the angry Vitus that would be at his side.

The room was empty as she stripped away the silk and laid it carefully aside in the hopes that perhaps she would be allowed to keep it since Selenia would no longer desire to wear it. Stepping into the water a relaxed smile rose on her lips as the warmth of it began to work on aching muscles that had been worked more than she could have imagine in the combined efforts of the passionate love making the night before.

She could not help but wonder if it had been love, or just sex. Was Meridius right in that he was simply making her feel as though she were special to get what he wanted? Did she mean to him what he meant to her? Rinsing the last of the soap from her hair she stood and chided herself aloud "Do not doubt what your heart knows, Violetta." That was what she remembered her mother saying that to her as a child and it was the only thing that she had clung to through the years, the only thing that had stuck with her for the long years since her mother had died.

Making her way back into the villa Violetta was informed by one of the kitchen boys that Vitus was more than displeased that his father had sent Meridius with the guards to fetch Violetta from the ludus when he had made it clear upon their return from delivering her that he had wanted to be the one to do so. He had been seen stalking the villa in search of the old man and his sister who were all but certainly together. He, and she, would find them laughing together on the balcony overlooking the exotic gardens that had been his mother's pride and joy when her children had failed to live up to her expectations.

He was arriving as she entered the hall and she shuddered at the rage in his voice as he spoke loudly to Felix "I see you are both in a celebratory mood this morning. Would either of you care to share its cause, or shall I guess?" He was fuming but when his father gestured for him to sit and eat with them, he had no choice by to control himself, at least externally.

Felix looked at his angry son with some amusement and a growing irritation. It was whispered among the slaves that he was becoming more tempted each day to send him with his sister to Rome to be put at last into his place by the true men of the Republic. One day he would likely see it done but until then they had to try to keep out of his bad graces where

Violetta knew she stood, even though she had done nothing except refuse his affections. Risking the wrath of them all Violetta lingered near the door to listen further before she would present herself.

"We were just remarking upon the speed with which Meridius and the guards were able to retrieve the girl and yet a runner from the house of Tertius still managed to arrive before they did." He tossed the parchment down upon the table and wiped honey from his plate with a piece of bread "The man invites us to join the elite of Velletri to bear witness to his champion facing the man he bought from Rome. I think Cassian is going to be commanded to let the other win and so it would be interesting to bear witness to such a thing, would you not agree?" He took a bite of the bread and flicked his eyes towards Selenia to see her reaction to his answer.

"I do not understand this game between you and the lanista father. To trade Violetta for the chance at a few coins seems foolish and even worse, it is childish." He took a bite of the bread on his plate and shook his head "What is the point of it beyond a few coins that you do not need in your purse? What is the gain for I know you do nothing without thought of profit, but I fail to see it here?" He downed half of the wine in his cup in a single draught and glared at his father and sister, who was tittering and stroking her groomed hair as though she were the queen of all the world.

"My son it is good that you have never had to do merchant negotiations, your lack of vision would be costly." He shook his head and nodded for more wine to be poured in all their cups. He looked at Selenia and smiled wistfully. It was well known that he had wished she were a boy since her brother was so difficult to manage. "If you took a moment to think with something beside your cock, which always seems to desire what is mine, you would see that there is gain to be found in every association. Even if it means that one must look harder to see potential where others see only failure." He looked at Vitus as if to infer that the same philosophy applied to his relationship with his son.

"I have vision enough, father." He said snidely as he continued to eat "Mine simply does not involve tying myself to a preening shit of a lanista." He rolled his eyes as Meridius appeared "So did you bring her back? Was she in tears? Bruised?" He licked his lips in anticipation but of course the man could not actually speak and soon enough she would be present to answer his questions for herself but the desire to know was shining in his dark eyes. "Tell me again why it is that you cut out your man's tongue? I heard he was quite talented with it. Where was your 'vision' then?" The house knew how the old man had favored the Spaniard, often calling him to his bed to the pain of his wife who had, in the last years of her life found herself not only replaced in her husband's bed by a slave but replaced by a man. "Tell me father," He continued with a smirk "After you had his tongue cut out to please my mother what real use do you have for the man?" He casually reached a hand to cup the other man's backside "Is his ass really that good? Or is it you who takes the pounding from this 'god of a man'?"

Felix set his cup down and glared at his son, Violetta knew that had they been standing he would have struck the arrogance from his face. "I find him as useful as I ever did and the severing of his tongue to please your mother has made him even more valuable. If you could see beyond yourself, you would realize the merit that a mute slave who cannot write is a most precious thing indeed when a man deals in secrets." He curled his finger to summon the man they were discussing to stand at his side, trailing his touch from his elbow down to his fingertips. "What pleasures I take with him are no more your concern than they were your mother's. Unlike you I do not seek to impress with discussions upon such things." He met his son's glare unflinchingly "A man who knows his worth has no need to tell the world for he is the one who has to know it, not them."

Trying to stop the words before things were said that could not be undone, Selenia put up a hand with a smile at them both. "Enough. Father why not tell Vitus about the invitation that has come from good Tertius. It might improve upon the sour mood." She handed her brother the scroll from the table as Violetta held her breath, worried that it might be some admonishment against her or Cassian. "It seems we have been invited to the lanista's ludus to witness the returned champion give the 'test' to the former champion of Rome that was sold in a fit of rage by Titus Claudius when he found his daughter and his favored slave in the man's arms. It was quite the scandal of the season though I have never laid eyes upon the man myself I have heard he is handsome... in the beastly way of gladiators." The last comment would not improve his mood, but it might get his attention away from arguments with Felix and back on the topic of the lanista's house.

Vitus scanned the invitation then tossed it back to the table and picked up his bread instead "I do not see why we would bother with such a thing. It is beneath our station really to associate with the man. He is vile, pretentious and as disgusting as the beasts he trains for the amusement of the vulgar crowd." He sniffed and looked over his shoulder to see if Violetta had returned yet. She knew she could not hide much longer as he was obviously anxious to inspect her for new marks, to see if her eyes were red from tears or not.

"Where is the little carrot you dangle before the man's nose father? I have not yet laid eyes upon the savage results of his attentions and it holds interest to me." He wet his lips with his tongue when he finally saw the small figure approaching, stepping out from the doorway dressed once again in the proper attire of a slave. "Here comes your little whore father, freshly cleansed for the pleasure of all here. I would not take well to the smell of goat from a ludus." His laughter made her cringe which seemed to please him even more than the mark he saw upon her arm.

"Dominus." Violetta said softly with a bowed head, unable to look at Meridius and feeling incredibly vulnerable among the trio of Romans. Felix was the least evil of the three and thankfully the only one she had to obey without thought of questioning. "You summoned me, and I answered as swiftly as I was able, for as your son pointed out I had the smell of last night upon me and I would not wish to bring you offence." She hoped that whatever it was that had inspired the man to send her to her gladiator would not be undone by the late return and Vitus' angry taunts. Instinctively she poured his wine and offered him the cup with a smile and another bow of her head.

"You did well, Violetta." He said with a smile, raking her body with the same deep interest as before which was as disturbing as it was reassuring. "That will be all. Go see to food for yourself and then see that my room is tidied, and my best attire prepared for two nights from now when Selenia and I will be joining the celebration at the house you have just come from. I am afraid that Vitus will be ill and unable to attend this fascinating event with us, though I should require you and Meridius both at my side."

When she looked up with innocent curiosity, he smiled "The champion is to test the newest recruit, the former champion of Rome to see if he is worthy to be a gladiator of the ludus. It is a match with steel and the loser could be missing more than pride but his life if the match does not go in his favor." The tremble in her lip told more than she would have been able to if he had allowed her to speak. Whatever feelings Cassian had for her, she knew she was in love with him and though this game was now being played by all the Romans involved all she wanted was for him to live another day, survive to hold her in his arms again. She did not care for the life of the other man though she felt a twinge of guilt that she wished for his death instead of her lover.

"Yes, Dominus." She turned to go as he had commanded, finally letting her pleasure at the fact that Vitus would not accompany them show on her face when there was no chance that they would see it. She sighed and leaned against the cool marble wall of the hall as the reality of what could happen settled in her mind. She was still contemplating it when the familiar snap of fingers brought her to attention. "I do not need help, Padre." She said to Meridius as he looked down at her with a kind smile. "This is a task I have done many times while you were otherwise engaged." He did not seem to care but followed her as she made her way to Felix's quarters, retrieving his own garments from the floor as she tidied. He would not dare to communicate more with her here where someone might overhear her replies and inform Felix or Vitus or even worse, use the knowledge to hold against either of them later that would cost them more to keep their secrets kept.

He watched and helped in small ways that she really did not need but she felt he was trying to regain the sense of family they had held dear only hours before. The cost of his actions was becoming more and more evident as the time passed and she could not look at him or speak of her thoughts. When the night came, he would likely ask for a moment if she gave him the chance, but her heart was troubled by his surprising affections and did not yet speak of forgiveness. The look in his eyes when they met briefly concerned her more when she saw him fighting with himself not to pull her into his arms and force her to acknowledge him, his presence or his perceived right to have feelings for the woman he had watched grow from frightened girl into a woman he thought in need of sheltering care. Standing near the door he kept a smile on his face in case she looked up to meet his eyes again but as the time past he realized that she would not, so with a deep sigh he turned and left.

She had felt his eyes on her the entire time that she had attended the command of Felix but there were no words she could say to him to explain how she felt; her newly blossomed love or the way he had chosen to violate the trust she had in him. There was no way to describe how strange it was that he had kissed her, not like a father should but as though he wished her to be his lover. There were so many worse men in the employ of Felix who desired her, even among the slaves, and she knew that he would take care of her no matter what, but she felt nothing like that for him. Was it that he shared their Dominus' bed as often as she did herself or was it that her heart was now the possession of another that made her recoil from his attempted affections? She couldn't tell and decided to try to avoid him as much as possible until she knew and could understand what she felt. As soon as he left the room she sighed and sat on the bed, letting her mind process all that had happened. She felt her heart lift at the idea that she might be able to see Cassian the next day even though it was unlikely that she would be allowed to break words at all. Just to lay eyes upon him could be enough to sustain her if their eyes could meet and smile at each other.

It was hours later, after Violetta had assisted Meridius in attending Felix to bed, and she had waited without reward to see if her padre would come to her again in attempt to mend things between them, that she was awoken from the soft dreams of her own slumber. Her dreams had been filled with kisses that claimed her soul, bodies entwined in ecstasy and soft words in her ear as calloused hands caressed her skin, but they faded quickly away with the touch of a friendly hand to her shoulder shaking her to wake. "Violetta rise quickly. Dominus calls for you." Sitting upright quickly as her hands reached for her dress "Shall I wake Meridius as well? He is better at soothing his fits than I am." The other girl shook her head "It is Vitus who calls for you I am afraid. I fear he has taken too much wine. I tried to dissuade him, but he insists upon your attendance alone." The two girls shared a regretful look as they both knew what kind of man Vitus was and the actions, he was capable of especially if he had been drinking.

Resigned to the task of the night she moved silently down the hall towards the sound of Vitus barking curses and shouting at whoever was attempting to see to his needs. Taking a deep breath, she stepped into the room with her head bowed "Dominus? You called for me?" She asked quietly, wishing that he would send her back to her cell but knowing that she was in for a night of pain though whether physical or mental remained to be seen. She could feel the weight of his eyes on her as she stepped closer and the other slave that had been in the room scrambled to be gone.

"Here at last stands my father's little trophy." Vitus sneered. He was dressed from only the waist down and was drinking deeply from the cup in his hand but when he took an unsteady step the contents spilled across his bare chest "Do not stand idle, attend!" He beckoned her to clean what was spilled and when, with a lowered gaze, she wiped the wine away he reached to grab her wrist, twisting it in a vice like grip until she released the cloth and he pulled her closer "How does it feel to not only stand a slave but to be a whore for my father as well? He sets you upon a pedestal as a prize and then makes coin from the work done on your back." He wet his lips and glared into her eyes before his gaze fell lower to the curve of her breasts touching the top of her dress.

She bit her lip to stop herself from crying out but did not give voice to an answer, she had no wish to antagonize him with the wrong words, but her silence had the opposite effect. He snarled and wrenched her to the ground in a vicious throw to his feet. "Dominus, please?" She pleaded but he had already raised his hand to bring down in a vicious blow across her body that struck her back instead of her face. She had seen it coming and turned, even though it would anger him she could not stand still and let him bruise her face which would force her to answer his father in the morning, and perhaps end up being blamed for his rage.

The skin where he had struck turned red and she cried out in pain which brought a sadistic smile to his face as he gripped her hair and tipped her head back to look at him. "Tell me Violetta does he make you scream? Do you weep? Answer the question my father put to him that remains unanswered." His eyes shone with an evil that went deep to the soul as if he relished the chance to show her the darkness that lay within. He whispered in her ear that first he would see to her purchase from his father and then he would unleash himself on her completely until she was submissive in body and spirit.

Looking up at the monster that wanted to break her spirit entirely a fire flashed briefly in her eyes as she answered quietly but with an unbreakable conviction. "Yes. He brings me to tears. I scream beneath him." A quick smile lifted her lips "With unmeasurable pleasure." She regretted her boldness as soon as the words left her lips, but she would not deny what there was between them simply to pacify the ego of another man.

Vitus' nostrils flared, and he brought his foot to her ribs in a vicious kick as he straightened, when she screamed, he delivered a second blow before staring down at her, rigid with disdain and near hatred. "Consider yourself fortunate that it is not yet I who owns you." He hissed down at her while she fought back tears. "The head of this house deems it fit to dabble in fool's pleasures and games for jest while having you play part in them. I would not be so kind." With a parting sweep of his foot he knocked her hands from holding up her slight weight and sent her to the floor. Stepping away from her he tripped on her outstretched arm and sent more wine spilling across the floor. Stalking from the room he roared for more wine and called for "Someone with use in their hands, clean up this mess."

When she hit the floor, Violetta knew better than to move. Each breath felt as though she was being struck again. Tears flowed down her cheeks and her shoulders shook. Slipping her hands to hold her side she allowed herself to gasp at the pain as others came into the room. Once it was clear that Vitus had left for the night there were many eager and friendly hands to help her to her feet and to offer to inspect the injury, but she shook her head and stumbled back to her cot. Sleep was impossible with the ache in her side, but even more disturbing was his words threatening that one day he would possess her. That terrifying reality kept her eyes open long after her body demanded sleep, each breath a painful reminder of what her future could hold.

The morning of the invitation Violetta stood in joint attendance with Meridius, dressing Felix who noted the stiff movements of the usually graceful girl and the bruise upon her back that Meridius stared at intently and so had brought his master's attention to it. "You will attend the feast tonight at the home of Tertius." He said in a monotone that she was sure he did not feel. "There will be entertainment from the ludus as well as the test I am sure. What a pity that Vitus does not enjoy the games and will not be in attendance." When she flinched at the mention of his son's name, she knew Felix would know that his offspring had once again been the cause of her pain that morning.

"It is a shame that he does not share your enjoyment Dominus, for such would increase the love between a father and his son." She kept her eyes down and moved carefully as she tied the belt at his waist. Her relief in his continued stance that his son would not be invited that night was something she could have barely found words for if pressed to do so.

He smiled at the expected response, happy with her eloquence, then reached to raise her chin; gripping it tight but without malice until their eyes met. "I would have the truth from you now. How is it that you came upon the mark on your back?" They both already knew the answer though it was incredibly important that she give the right one when asked, on the off chance that the gladiator or lanista raised the question.

Her eyes darted away from the face of the man that owned her fate, if she told the truth of the night's events would she be denied attendance to the feast for the insolence in her reply to his son or would he be moved to pity? "I fell down the stairs, Dominus. It is my fault for lost footing while my mind was elsewhere." Meridius frowned quickly and she knew that he knew her words for a lie but the Roman smiled and nodded.

"I would have you be more careful in future. It would be most unfortunate if you came to injury or if a scene was caused tonight due to careless acts." He smiled and patted her shoulder as he then stepped past her to join Selenia at the door before making their way out to the waiting wagon.

Meridius met her eyes and shook his head gently to tell her that he knew better than to believe the lie she had given. He was brave enough to have broken word about the deed of Vitus so that his father knew what kind of monster it was that he had beneath his roof, but Violetta feared the man more than he did and suffered his wrath in ways that terrified her. He placed a friendly hand to the small of her back and guided her towards the wagon, his eyes showed his happiness that she did not pull away from him even if it was just so that the Romans did not ask why.

CHAPTER 20

Tertius stood upon the balcony with Jovian beside him and stared down at his gladiators training upon the sands below. His eyes were particularly focused on Proximus as the test approached. The boy wondered who the victor between the former champion of Rome and the current champion of Velletri would be? Even though Cassian had been commanded to see the other man to the mark, the match would still be a grand battle between two incredible warriors to entertain his honored guests.

The smile that lit the lanista's face was devious and bordering on indecent as he mused to himself about the angst that the Celt had to be feeling. He had commanded the man confined to his cell until summoned to administer the test. Three days had passed, and explanation was refused as was his request for audience. Jovian knew it was a good bet that when he was released to the feast and test that his rage would conquer his reason and allow for the biggest spectacle possible.

"Doctore." Tertius called, breaking the boy's thoughts by gesturing vaguely towards the man he had been watching. "Send Proximus to the baths, and then Cassian after that. Have them oiled and dressed for the night. The test shall be administered here in the villa and I would have it be a feast for the eyes." When the man nodded Jovian was surprised to find himself the subject of his Dominus' next command. "I stand curious to the mood of my champion and his opponent for the night. See yourself to the ludus and, without breaking words to any man, find how they fare before the test." It took only seconds for the boy to run to obey the command, secretly excited to be commanded down among the fascinating and exciting men.

He arrived in the halls of the ludus in time to see the boy who tended the weapons approach the Roman gladiator and take his swords so that he could follow the command of their Dominus. Proximus met the eyes of Doctore and they shared a nod of understanding and respect before he stepped from the sands to head to the baths. The room seemed so much larger when it was not filled with the other gladiators and Jovian was amazed as he peered inside to watch and listen as the gladiator talked to himself.

He did not waste time but stripped himself of his subligaria and lowered himself into the steaming water with a groan of satisfaction. "Tonight," He said to the roof "will be my night of glory returned; no longer seen as just a slave or recruit but as a gladiator and one that could take the title of champion from the Celt and all the rights and privileges that came with such a thing." He went on to talk of how he too would have a favored woman and have her brought to the quarters across the sand and all the wine he could drink. It would likely be the cheap red of the lower provinces but still better than the sour swill they drank daily. "Enjoy what time as champion the gods afford you Cassian." He said aloud with a grin "For the time of Proximus approaches and you will not survive my rise."

Noting the intent of the new man to bring an end not only to the reign of Cassian as champion but his life, Jovian made his way towards the cell where the other man had been confined for days. They were not friends as they had been in his younger days, but Jovian still thought of the dangerous man as the one that had teased him as a child with a friendly smile before joining the men of the ludus. He would be saddened if the Germanic giant accomplished his goal, the passing of his sole 'friend' would be a thing he would not easily recover from. He slowed his steps as he neared the darkened cell and hid in a small alcove out of sight of the guards to watch and listen so that his report to Tertius would be detailed.

The passage of time had begun to lose meaning to the man as he waited; hours turning into days of endless solitude not even disturbed by Agrus who should have been training with him. He had obviously been talking to himself for hours and by the sounds his feet made he was practicing his fights without swords. His emotions seemed as much on edge as his patience. His words painted a constant struggle to keep a grip on his control, to hold himself back from releasing his outrage like a wild beast's roar. Even the boy knew it was only years of hard-fought self-discipline were what kept him sane.

"Why does Tertius do this? What could he gain from his champion sitting idle in a cell before facing another man in the test?" Cassian growled to the darkness around him. "Why does he not acknowledge the request for audience so that I might see mind eased if not body?" A shadow stepped past Jovian in hiding and the door of the cell creaked open, the rusty hinges singing of liberation, but it was not real, merely the allowance for the edgy champion to move from one room to another. He was still trapped, caged, enslaved. Had Tertius decided to come gloat over him and the breaking of his will? To remind him that though he stood a champion he was still only a slave? It was only the sound of a friendly voice that raised his head and brought a smile of surprised relief to the unseen boy's face.

"Come, brother." Doctore called gently from the doorway. He had not agreed with Tertius on the treatment of Cassian and Jovian had been impressed to listen to his argument with their Dominus. He had pointed out that to cage a man of the sands was to tell him that he held little worth in the eyes of his master and every one of the men knew that Cassian was worth more coin than any three gladiators that trained that day. "It is time to bathe and prepare yourself to bask in deserved glory at tonight's feast. You shall prove yourself in the administration of the test I am certain." He went on to add that the men did not think Proximus deserved to face the champion in the test. "The Thracian, Tarcarus, had raged when he discovered that his own match was one of the lesser men. Enough of those thoughts for now. Oils and bath await you before the others are afforded their turn. You had best move ass to purpose before they beat you to the water."

There was no need for words between them as he offered a terse smile and stepped past his old friend into the dank hall. Shadows played upon the walls, painted by the flickering torches. He moved in silence as Lucius and Auctus flanked him, he had offered the men Denarii to break words regarding Tertius' plan or thoughts but either they did not know it, or they agreed with it for they would take no coin and broke no words to ease his mind. Jovian followed quietly behind, though he was almost certain that the guard Lucius had seen him. When they entered the baths the German he was to fight in a few hours time, still occupied part of the bath muttering to himself. The Celt made a passing comment to Auctus about the tightening of muscles from tension and the lack of a suitable release. This night might well go as the lanista desired without his making it a conscious effort, Jovian pondered with deep concern, for if Cassian could not move as he should then he might not be able to truly defeat the large German who quickly departed the bathes to leave the smaller man in peace.

He watched in delight as Cassian disrobed, closed his eyes and sank into the water. Banishing the thoughts from his mind and focusing instead upon the attractive man before him the boy listened to every word said. He spoke with his guards about how he would be able to see Violetta that night, even if he was not permitted the chance to break words with her. With his favored gladiator taking up steel in close quarters there was little doubt that the merchant Census would bring the tempting beauty to bear witness to the savagery. He added that he hoped that the son did not attend or that he found himself with other things to occupy his time besides tormenting his woman. Jovian smiled to himself when Cassian grinned at the realization that he had indeed claimed her as his own and would fight for her honor. Even such simple things as this test would be fought for her. He made sure to look both guards in the eye and remind them "Tertius need not know this. It is a vow of my heart alone."

At those words the youth decided that he had enough information to please his Dominus and carefully left the bathing man to his last few minutes of peace. Sure that the Roman would be pleased with what he had learned and would let him choose his own attire for the event that night. It was the greatest reward he could be given, and Jovian fully intended to take advantage of it. He would be dressed, bejewelled and painted to a splendor that would rival Lycithia to her annoyance and his delight.

Tertius stood surveying the scene with his wife beside him, slaves in attendance as they greeted the guests arriving. Each one was greeted by name and welcomed into a room with tables full of the finest wines and sumptuous food piled high to create the illusion of wealth and grandeur. They both wore robes of silk trimmed with gold and heavily beaded, so they would appear utterly confident in wealth that they did not yet possess. It was a fact well known but unspoken that the night's celebration would see their coin increased and position elevated by way of their ownership of the newly re-crowned champion of Velletri and the new man who had a reputation of his own and was all but certain to rise to glory. Once again, the future was looking bright, a seat in the Senate would surely be his sooner than expected. Jovian stood just behind the hosting pair, dressed in his best attire that complimented his master and acknowledged how he was held in high favor.

When Felix and his daughter arrived the lanista stepped down to offer his hand with a broad grin. "Good Census, you are most welcome. Partake, please, and enjoy all my house has to offer." He said, gripping his arm tight, his smile brightening when he saw the woman of the champion descend the cart behind the statuesque body slave that he could not help but notice would have made a magnificent gladiator. "I see you have brought our champion's prize with you this night. I hope her presence inspires an even greater performance from the man." Looking back at Violetta he caught her eyes for a brief second, giving her a glare that warned that she had better inspire as expected.

Grasping his forearm in friendship Felix smiled at the lanista "Tiberius, it is a joyous night indeed to be a guest in your home." Turning to Lycithia he held his hands wide "A vision of beauty to rival the gods as always, Lycithia." Selenia followed her father in greeting their hosts with a warm smile "Gratitude for the invitation. Such an event is not to be missed." They all smiled to each other as though they were the closest of friends instead of acquaintances that were simply using each other for whatever they could possibly gain and turned to join the festivities as the slaves followed behind as the expected shadows of their masters.

Jovian could not help but stare at the tall silent man who ignored him as though he were a pestering child. Turning his attention to the girl he tried to get her to speak, to at least tell him the name of the man who made the final piece of their serving trio, but she was caught up in other things and thoughts, leaving him annoyed by his lack of attention.

Violetta did not seem to dare to look up and take in the scene of opulence around her, even to scan for the face she desired to see. He had to be here somewhere, or he would be if he was not yet. Jovian wondered what would be in his eyes when he saw her? When at last the Romans had their wine in hand and became heavily immersed in their conversations, ignoring the slaves as though they were nothing more than shadows, she raised her head to stare around the room. There were gladiators lining one wall, cleaned and oiled but none of them was the man she obviously hoped to see. A feeling of dread washed over her, and her shoulders slumped; had he been forced to bed a Roman woman was the fearful question in her eyes. He could have relieved the strain, but Jovian was still hurt by her obvious disinterest in him. She was so lost in her fearful thoughts that she did not notice her master's man leaning close until he brushed her hand with his.

Jovian watched her carefully, this was the woman who now possessed the unattainable, a champion's heart? She seemed nervous and edgy as she stood waiting for a summons or command from either Felix or Selenia near the open doors to the patio above the training grounds of the ludus. With a silent, begging look to the mute who nodded in answer to the unvoiced question; he would alert her if her absence was noted by any, she slipped through the gauze curtains that danced slowly in the soft breeze to stand in the empty space. Carefully, taking advantage of the other man's gaze in the opposite direction Jovian slipped closer to watch her, his eyes full of curiosity at what she could want upon the empty balcony. The guests being otherwise occupied indoors with food and wine she moved freely to the edge and looked down upon the sands, her eyes wandering over to the door of the room she had occupied with him so recently.

She leaned lightly on the rail for just a moment, indulging her thoughts with a dreamy look on her face. Jovian watched as the moon illuminated her pale skin so that it seemed as if she glowed and, in that moment, he understood why Cassian had called her divine. Silhouetted in the unearthly glow she stood a vision of Diana herself and he wondered if she might be the deity herself come to entrap the mortal champion so often likened to Mars.

He was about to speak to her, to ask if she was the goddess come to earth when a soft click brought her back from dreams and alerted her to the need to return to her duty. With a last look to the sands below her and the few men in the shadows that she had not likely noticed, she slid back through the silk to stand once again unnoticed as the lanista and her own masters laughed and drank to their own delight. She shared a look with the man beside her and their mutual smile made him feel some certainty towards her humanity. He had been about to step closer to speak words of introduction when her gaze was caught by the appearance of the man, she had desired most to see from the balcony lingering just beyond the doorway of the party room.

Watching the lanista move around the room with a cordial smile upon his face, Jovian knew that all of those that had been sent invitation were there and those who had been strategically excluded to drive their desire to be included were also in attendance. Tertius had learned many years ago which man needed his ass to be metaphorically kissed to earn his favor, how to do so and which of the 'nobility' would never see him as more than a cheap peddler of flesh that could not rise beyond current position. So many of those within his walls were ones whose associations could easily set things in motion to elevate his position and the Roman was driven to ensure that they were willing to extend their hand to pull him up to their level.

Raising his hands to quiet the murmuring and laughter until the house was as silent as the dawn, with Jovian hanging on his every word. "The time has come upon us for glorious combat between titans. The test of gladiatory brotherhood, a noble tradition set in blood for years beyond count, to be delivered here for your viewing pleasure. The champion of Velletri, recently returned to such title, Cassian to test the worth of the former champion of Rome itself; Proximus. Gladiators attend!" He called and gestured the men to enter the room, eagerly awaiting the reaction of the crowd to the proximity of the men they idolized in the arena. Though he knew each of these men from years of watching from the balcony, even Jovian was impressed by the stature and presence of the champions.

At the lanista's words Violetta's head rose and so did the blush on her cheek, simply hearing his name brought a smile to her lips. The curiosity was on everyone's faces; who was this Proximus and what test was it that they were to be put to? He watched her eyes searching the room briefly but then lay to rest solely upon the champion, her champion, as he strode through the sea of Romans, the air of a god flowing from him like a silk robe in the night's breeze. She did not notice when Meridius glanced at her and read the pure emotion in her eyes, or the way that he sighed with resignation, her heart belonged to the gladiator, and it would either be cherished or destroyed as would the man who sought her eyes just as eagerly. A smile lifted her lips when her eyes met those of her lover and Jovian watched her fight her instinct to wave at him with a chuckle that he hid behind his hand.

Every man and woman parted as Cassian strode through the crowd, slave and Roman both, giving wide berth to their demon of the arena. Not sure if it was fear of his rumored savagery or the awestruck adoration that caused the effect, Cassian would not care. An imposing figure glowing in the candlelight caused him to look every inch the bronzed god moving with a grace that belied each rippling curve of muscle. Despite the whispers and gasps he would keep his thoughts directed inwards, only seeing and hearing what he needed to make it through nights like this when at any moment his person could be assaulted by the unwanted touch of those that saw themselves his master. He had to force himself not to glare or cringe when a woman he did not know placed her hand upon his chest to stop his parade into the room with an obvious curiosity that had nothing to do with his skills in the arena. Instead of lowering his eyes as an obedient slave would be expected to do, he made direct eye contact, daring her to stare to her desires content. Jovian was amazed at the boldness of the man, but he was the champion, that meant he had to be bolder than most.

The woman seemed thrilled to have the attention of the glorious creature and lowered her hand to explore him further, the ringlets of her hair spilling forward as she bent to take a closer look at the man before her. He squared his shoulders, despising the inspection and eager to put his mind elsewhere he searched the room for a distraction and that is when he saw her. Just across the room, mere feet from where he had been stopped, she was looking at him and Jovian was watching them watch each other. Cassian was visibly entranced just looking at her and the bemused look on his face spoke of how he wondered why every man in the room was not staring at her as he was. Her soft, slender sweetly feminine body was beautifully outlined beneath the linen of her dress in a way that even Jovian could appreciate.

When the woman put her hands on Cassian Violetta's hands and jaw clenched in silent protest and Jovian thought she would cry out in outrage, but she stilled as the lovers eyes met, words passed silently in that gaze and she inhaled sharply before relaxing her hands, hoping she did not draw notice. The Syrian boy knew that he saw her and the look in his eyes told anyone who could see that he wanted more than just to look at the woman breathlessly staring at him. There had been the instant image in his mind of the two of them together in a stolen moment with tongues and bodies entwined, deep passionate growls and breathy moans as they came together in urgency. His daydream was shattered by the gasp of Violetta at the touch of cold metal on her arm startled her as Selenia tapped her wine glass in silent demand for more of the rich drink.

Though blood and violence appealed to few women and even fewer like Selenia, Jovian was surprised to see the way the woman stared at the pair, it was as though she had appraised them in the market and found these two to be of the finest stock. The German was a mountainous brute but alluring with his roughly shorn dark hair and dark eyes so rich that one could get lost in them. His skin a sun warmed brown as if he had worked in the sun all his days, it was the way he moved though, as though the bulk of his muscle meant nothing. He was as graceful as the large cats that were brought at times to the games of the Circus Maximus.

Wetting her lips, the dangerous beauty turned her attention to the champion of Velletri. The man stood the object of her father's manipulations and, obviously, of Violetta's desire. One look at the girl was all it took for someone to know that there was more than her father knew between them and the knowledge of that could be used to do any number of things. Jovian did not doubt that she would use what she knew to her own advantage. "Good Tertius, I must compliment you on your stock. They are glorious beasts indeed, your titans. My anticipation for the demonstration of their prowess grows with each passing moment." The lust in her eyes told, unabashedly, where she would like that prowess to be demonstrated and the boy was shocked to see the agreeable smile on his master's face.

"You have a keen eye for such things, Selenia." Tiberius said with an unexpected smile. It was rare that a woman not living within a ludus could discern skill from muscle but perhaps Proximus was not unfamiliar to her? "Did you, in Rome, have the opportunity to watch the Titan of the Rhineland upon the sands of that incredible city?" If she had then her tale might add to the amounts that he already knew were being wagered upon the difference of skill between the gladiators. Without looking Jovian knew that Tertius' wife had already begun to make her way towards the other woman in the attempt to bring her, as with her father, into the embrace and draw of the ludus. Though he rarely utilized his wife's aid in securing partners in business, it was an asset he would never be without. Even though he enjoyed taking slaves to his bed, his beautiful Syrian boy more than any other to his utter delight, it was Lycithia who owned his heart and possessed his undying loyalty.

Felix grinned and drank deeply as he watched the pair of gladiators step into view his eyes flickering to the trio of slaves watching them with a variety of expressions. His mind was not upon his fellow Roman's whether friend or annoying acquaintance his eyes were glazed as though he had his thoughts upon something he did not see before him but with a shake of his head his eyes landed upon the dark-haired youth that was staring back at him. Turning his attentions back to the gladiators he scanned the room, taking in each one scattered about the party.

Several of them looked as though they might hold promise for future bouts in the arena, Agrus was as well known to the elite of Velletri as Cassian was though for quite different reasons, but he might do well in the arena as well if trained properly. Jovian dubiously watched an exchange of glances between Felix and Selenia before the merchant began to walk towards the champion, his eyes raking his body; his chest bare and gleaming with each band of muscle though his legs were covered as they had been the night in his house and his forearms wore the leather bracers that he wore in the arena the man was still glowing with raw sexual appeal that any fool would be able to note and a plan began to form in his mind as he drew close and realized that Cassian had a singular focus in that moment.

CHAPTER 21

The power of their connection was incredible and overwhelmed every sense that Cassian had. All he could think about was being deep inside her, burying himself in her heat over and over until they were mindless with the need. It only took a moment for him to let himself fly back to the treasured moments with her and his body responded with the instant readiness to take her if she had been before him. The thought of the sweet as honey taste of her mouth and the blissful pressure of her breasts pressed firmly against his chest. When he thought of their shared ecstasy and her hips pressed tight against his as though they were made to rest against him, he let out a feral groan. The tightening of his lips and shift in the linen at his waist exhibiting his body's need brought a blush and giggle from the woman admiring his physique who thought that she had brought the reaction with her attentions.

Ignoring her simpering laugh and hungry eyes he took a further step on his path only to be stopped by the approach of Felix and his vicious bitch of a daughter. What were they going to do in the house of his own Dominus? Demand him stripped bare to skin so that they could further abuse Violetta for their amusement? His eyes flickered from the intoxicating blue of his woman to the ice of Tertius and knew that should the demand be made after the test they would not be denied. The lanista's pride would always come before the well being of any slave, even the champion of his house and city.

Felix and Selenia each circled one of the gladiators who had paused at their approach. Behind him Felix let the tip of a fingernail drag across Cassian's back, noting the subtle flinch with a smirk he saw reflected in a mirror as the Roman stood behind him to look over his shoulder and view the room as he saw it. Following his last glance, he felt the change in Felix' body language when he noted how Violetta stared at him as if there was no one else in the room. "Tertius, the man stands all but a god does he not? I was not of a mind to admire his perfection when last I laid eyes upon him but this night" He lowered a hand to graze his touch across the cheeks covered by the linen of his subligaria, leaving no confusion as to the depth of his appreciation of his form. "I find myself mesmerized by his beauty and the memory of the legend of his younger days." He stood close for a moment before moving on to give Proximus a similar inspection though the German did not shudder in revulsion as Cassian had which gave him cause to wonder if it was better self control or if the man had been trained not only to fight but to accept any attentions given to his person.

Out of the corner of his eye he watched as Proximus steeled himself for a similar inspection, but the Roman did not lay a hand upon him even though his daughter made her interest known without laying so much as a finger upon him. Cassian wondered if this house was like the one, he had served in Rome if, there, any gladiator could be sent to the bedding of any citizen with the coin to spend? If this woman desired him, did he know what was required of him even if his heart was still in his former house as was rumored. He met the eyes of the inquisitive Roman without flinching, but the Celt could tell that the interest there was not the same as he held for the champion.

When the pair switched targets, Cassian did not know if he should be grateful or not for the woman Selenia was as bold with her touch to him as she had been with Violetta in her own house. She groped and teased as though with the attempt to bring him to a near crippling state of arousal before facing his opponent, but the touch of her hands did nothing but agitate him, there was only one woman in this room that could send his blood thundering through his veins with mindless need and she stood, horrified, by the door. "Trust in me." He said with his eyes, trying to calm her silently from the distance.

Tertius' face said he could not believe the boldness of Felix and his daughter, treating the champion of his house as if he existed for their personal entertainment. Of even more surprise was the obvious state of arousal Cassian stood in. He had never allowed himself to be anything but completely void of emotion once he stood among Roman citizens, it was what made him such a reliable choice when touring the houses of the elite and the lanista took advantage of that control.

Someone had once joked that a man could slice off his balls and he would not flinch and yet here he was fully focused on nothing relating to the test that he was about to administer and completely enraptured in staring at a girl, a delicate flower that Felix had thankfully thought to bring with him. He was falling in love or already had. This would mean things were far more dangerous for him and for her than he had originally thought. If the Romans found out, even suspected, what she meant to him then she would become the target of jealousy, rage and deeper manipulations.

He looked towards Violetta who looked as though she would either burst into tears or run from the room if she was able. Clearly the thought of sharing him with either of the Romans hurt her. It took more willpower than he thought she had to not hide her face in Meridius' shoulder to hide from the showcase but when Cassian once again caught her eyes, she found that she could not look away. Sharing strength between them so they could both endure the torment of the Roman's attentions. She nodded when he whispered silently to her and even though she could not hear him she appeared to calm as she squared her shoulders to try and be brave, to face the horror of the moments of the night.

Cassian watched as a pair of women approached Proximus, each teasing the other to be bold enough to speak or touch the larger man. Grateful for the distraction from Felix and his lecherous daughter for a moment he watched as the pair finally drew close enough for both men to hear their words. "I heard that Titus Claudius desired to purchase the man." The other woman laughed and replied, "Surely if that was the case, he would have done or else how would Tertius have won him in bidding." Their curiosity got the better of them and so they turned their eyes to the gladiator "Find tongue and give answer, slave, how is it that you come to be here instead of the house of a Senator, the wealthiest man of Rome?"

The champion fought a grin when his opponent gave his answer "The choice was given to me as a final favor by my Dominus. I chose Velletri and so whichever man it was that sought my purchase from here as there was no gladiator left in the city of Rome to offer proper contest. I had heard whispers that perhaps there was a man here who might challenge me though I did not know he would stand my brother." When they gave him a bored look he quickly added "I was also told that the women of this city are the most beautiful in all the Republic." He smiled broadly at them and dared the brazen act of winking at proper citizens. "I am thrilled beyond words to find upon my arrival that though the rumors I have heard of Velletri and its peoples were not entirely truth the words spoken of its women did not do their beauty proper justice." The giggle let loose by the women turned more than one head in the crowd as Proximus returned to rigid attention as though he had not just dared to flirt with the pair.

"The man is far cleverer than I gave credit for." Cassian thought as the women blushed and flounced away as though they had achieved something more than a tidbit of gossip. He wondered how it was that a Germanic gladiator would know how to speak with women of the Roman elite. He was a slave, but did he perhaps spend more time breaking words with them than he was afforded by Tertius? Did this mean that other men, other Romans, allowed their slaves to speak to those around them instead of commanding that they stand ever silent in the presence of their masters? His moment of silent reflection was destroyed when his eyes fell on Violetta being summoned to stand at Felix's side to pour him wine. It would have been a sight he was able to bear if the man had not leisurely begun to stroke the tips of his fingers up and down her thigh near the waist of her dress. If his fingers slipped below the fabric, he would lose his control and he knew it.

Before Felix put his hand on her Violetta had been staring at the large man Proximus. He was a giant in comparison and covered in scarred muscles that rippled beneath the touch of the Roman's reaching out to caress him as though he was a statue instead of a dangerous man. Cassian hoped she trusted in his skill and desire for victory. He had to admit that the size of the man that he faced was unlike anything she would have seen before and she would be right to wonder if her lovers' victory was truly possible? What injuries would they both take tonight? The touch of the hand near her hip startled her from the thoughts that had her staring at him, and she almost dropped the jug of wine she held. There were smirks upon the lips of several men that caught the look on her face and Meridius tensed beside her; he must hate it when Felix made a public spectacle of his lust. For the first time the Celt thought he might have something in common with the other man in his woman's life.

The air had become so tense that Cassian could taste it. He could barely recall the last time he had come this close to losing control. He rarely gave a care to his personal dignity among the Romans though where Violetta was concerned his outrage was like a raging fire. His sense of honor called for vengeance, for her defense which no one else seemed to have a care for. As if the touch of her Dominus was not a brand of indignity, the gloating expression in the merchant's eyes as they turned to stare at him while his hand wandered the ivory flesh of her thigh seared his mind with a flash of unbearable helplessness.

She was so frightened and looked to him for help that he could not give her. He drew a deep breath and clenched his fists as he fought to put his thoughts elsewhere to avoid falling into the trap that Felix was tempting him with. They wanted him to lose his focus from the fight, so he would lose the match against Proximus. He would never do that, she was his reason for living, for winning and he would not leave this world knowing that she was still in the hands of that monster.

He had to distract himself before he lost his mind and his control and so he studied his opponent instead. Proximus allowed his eyes to wander the room as the men and women draped in finery made their way around it with more than a few deeply interested glances in his direction. The women whispering and giggling to themselves as they stared, and the men assessed him for his ability to win matches in their name in the arena. It took him a moment before he realized that his eyes kept coming back to the woman who had fear in her eyes and her master's hand upon her thigh.

Her eyes locked to those of Proximus for a few brief moments as though pleading without words as worry twisted her beautiful face. He watched what looked like a wave of compassion for her and the fears she must have on the German's face perhaps there was more to the man than he thought, but Violetta's face... How could she know that they were instructed not to take each other's lives but merely to test the skills to show that Proximus had earned the right to be called gladiator once more? He would stand victorious and pass this test, swearing the oath upon his bent knees before the sun rose, in this he had no choice, but he prayed that what he must do to achieve his masters command did not bring that sadness to her eyes again.

A slave moved to put steel into the hands of the combatants as the Roman's stepped back to clear space for the test to be played out. Cassian met the eyes of Proximus and nodded; there was no harm in showing the man some small respect by acknowledging that he was not the normal unskilled recruit that faced this test. Though he would never acknowledge that the German could possess skill greater than his own he knew the man was trained and should they ever meet in true contest it would be a battle of titans indeed.

When his nod was met with an arrogant chuckle the champion powered his body into an attack stance, ready to teach the man the lesson in humility that he so obviously needed if that was to be his reaction to an attempt at friendly respect. There would be blood shed tonight though it would anger Tertius to see his two prized men damaged. He averted his gaze from Violetta whose blue eyes implored for safety that he could not promise and focused instead on searching for any weakness his opponent might display. "I hope you stand prepared Proximus, for if you are not then the gods will greet you with the rising of the sun."

Tertius grinned as the room drew naturally silent with steel in the hands of slaves. The women drew back behind their men as though seeking protection should the savages decided to break free of their master's command. They all knew there was not a man in the room that would be able to match the skill of either man if they had decided to rebel and if the other gladiators about the villa joined in then they would all be doomed but the armed guards outnumbered the slaves by double and so they would feel perfectly safe. Besides the fact that the gladiators of the house of Tertius were known for their perfect obedience in public, at least until Cassian's behavior in the house of Census.

When at last all eyes were upon the lanista he readied himself to speak, adjusting the draping of his robes to match those of the magistrate before he held out his hands to draw even more attention to himself. "Good people of Velletri, my friends, gratitude to you for joining me in celebration this night. The house of Tertius has much to raise voice in thanks to the gods, not the least of which is the return of the champion of my house, Cassian, to the title of the champion of Velletri. It is this feat that spawned the idea behind the celebration that brought all of you to my house this evening." He preened through the applause before he continued. "Though there is no call for blood to be shed or lives taken this night it may be that you bear witness to the fall of a god this night." He licked his lips and nodded to Cassian, sure of their understanding regarding the test and its results. "Let the test... Begin!"

A roar went up from the gathered crowd as the men moved and began their deadly dance, the candlelight sparking off the sharpened edges of their swords. They shifted and circled each other, each one feigning strikes to test the defence of the other man. They were both powerful creatures but only one had the heart to stand a true champion and he would be the sure victor this night. "Come champion, show us how it is done, if you can." A Roman called across the room. The answering spark in the Celt's eye to the taunt told the audience that they were witnessing something special.

Violetta cringed at the sound of each of the preliminary blows. To her it must seem so much more dangerous than it had from the pulvinus, even though they were not commanded to kill each other in this match it was brutal and violent for one unaccustomed to such things. Cassian saw Meridius reach to take her hand in his, but she could not let him, pulling her hand away from his. She would not allow anyone to touch her that she could help. Here before him she showed all that she was his and his alone, causing his heart and chest to swell with pride and affection. She squared her shoulders and nodded to him, sharing a breath of solidarity before the true violence began and her hand flew to her mouth to stifle a cry of fear.

CHAPTER 22

Cassian's lips spread in a wicked grin at the command to begin battle. Now he would show any that might yet doubt his return to form just how capable he was to defeat any foe they chose to pit him against. It did not matter that Proximus was the larger of them by a significant weight, he was fully capable of sending him to the ground as a corpse. Were it not for the order of Tertius that would have been his intent but instead he had to allow the man the victory while keeping some pride and his life? It was still undecided which of those tasks would be the more difficult to achieve. There was no hatred between him and the German and yet there was not the bond of brotherhood either, it would be easy enough for a blade to slip and end the life of the man it touched. He thought he heard a gasp and saw Violetta out of the corner of his eyes, covering her mouth in fear. Hades could take him if he allowed himself to be killed before her eyes. He was her hero and somehow, even though he was nothing but a slave, he would find a way to save her from the torment of the house she lived in now. A few moves that Proximus made betrayed a favoring of his right knee and brought a glint of victory to his eyes as he smirked deviously.

Proximus met the grin with one of his own and advanced again, swinging the blade so that it struck at the man's thigh. Cassian suspected that he knew one of them held a wound and if he could strike it hard enough it might bring him to his knees, granting victory and the mark of the brotherhood. How he would defeat an opponent a full head taller and inches larger was beyond most strategies he knew, though he had known stranger things to happen in the arena. This was a test though, not the sands, there was no need for death simply Proximus' victory. The steel in his hands felt light and long missed but he was not willing to overlook that this man, the champion of the capitol city, could be able to do damage to him.

Grunting when the flat of the blade struck his thigh, Cassian changed his stance. It was not the wounded leg but there was no need to give that away to a man who obviously sought to use the injury to see him to defeat. It took only a brief second before the blow was answered with a parry and a quick slash with the opposite hand to draw the first blood of the test in a shallow cut to his arm. The crowd cheered but it was barely heard as his entire focus was on the man mirroring the circling tactic that was designed to expose a flank or weakness.

He noted how the German kept his right knee back even when his motion would normally have put it forward and knew that the joint was one that could easily be used against him. Their eyes met and then their blades did the same, the Celt's moving fast enough that a shower of golden sparks fell to the floor to the astonished gasp of those who witnessed it. Even retreating Proximus kept the right leg to the back but the words of Tertius kept his blow in check even though a single powerful kick would likely have brought the man to the ground. A single look to his Dominus brought the reminder back to the forefront of his mind and he took a breath while allowing the new man to circle him once again.

The weapons of the two men struck together, hard and fast, leaving the sound of metal on metal singing throughout the villa. It appeared as if every man and woman there had begun to realize that this was no ordinary match for entertainment as they had expected but it was indeed a clash of titans the likes of which many of them might never see again. Their breath was drawn, and every neck craned to get a better view of the contest. Though the appearance of the men would lead one to believe in an obvious advantage it was becoming more and more clear that the smaller man was better than his size would lend belief to.

The Celt had drawn first blood but Proximus was quick to find a way to return the favor. Surging forward, using his size as a weapon he managed to throw off his opponents footing just enough to let his blade land upon the leg he thought uninjured. His blade opened a bright but clean-cut line of bright red blood that began to flow as the German laughed at his own minor victory.

Somehow Cassian heard Violetta's breath catch in her throat when the bright line of blood showed on his thigh. A gasp, barely audible, escaped her lips and her hand flew to her mouth. Was she afraid she was about to see his loss? His death? Her eyes flicked to Meridius who stood stoic beside her; he shook his head in warning to be still and wait to see what would happen. He had likely seen the gladiators of Velletri fight much more often than she did, but though she looked as if her heart clenched in her chest, he gave no sign of concern. She allowed him to draw her back the step she did not know she had taken towards the men locked in deadly combat. Cassian hoped he would take care of her in that house where no one else did.

Caught off guard when the steel tore his flesh Cassian's face twisted in a rage, the pain mocking his skill and confidence. How in Hades had the man found that advantage? The blood flow was warm and its bright colour in contrast to his skin and the wrappings around his leg brought a flood of anger forth from the depth of his soul. It would be impossible now to hold back, the days spent in unexplained solitude had tense nerves near to frayed. If Tertius wished for his compliant obedience why punish him for no reason? The man clearly wanted a show and he would give it to him though not perhaps in the way that he thought.

He released one blade, allowing it to fall from his right hand to the floor as a singular warning to his opponent and his master alike. He desired above all else to see his woman to his arms, but a loss here tonight could well see it not only denied but her given to the hold of another. She was close enough to touch but kept at bay by the will and word of those who took joy in his suffering and her agony, which he could see written plainly on her face. Though her eyes still shone at him as if he were the hero of some great legend instead of a man commanded to a loss that would not be genuine and any within the room that knew his skill would know it for what it was and think him an obedient dog to be commanded for their amusement. He shook his head in denial of what seemed to be the will of the gods. If they chose to sever the newly forged bond of affection, then it would not be in shame that he watched her torn from his heart. The question now was how he was to avoid the shame and loss of her but keep Tertius from becoming enraged by the loss of the man he desired for the sands?

With a quick thought, he charged in retaliation for the blow, crouching to avoid the strike of his swords he raised his own above his head as a shield before coming up to strike his fist against the German's jaw. While his opponent shook his head to clear it from the blow, Cassian parried his blades to provide the opportunity to leap into the air with a twist that allowed him to land a harsh kick against his foe's chest. Bracing his empty hand to the ground as he landed, he reached to retrieve the sword he had momentarily discarded and rolled to his feet in a predatory stance, his eyes like that of a savage cat seeking the opening which would end his prey. The days of isolation, and the presence of Violetta, were all that was needed to send him into a dizzying blaze of deadly tactics.

Tiberius was watching the two titans with an anticipation that could only be described as gleeful. The elite of the city stood with bated breath to see what would happen next; who would land the next blow or draw blood? The fates only knew. Proximus was as eager to take back what had once been his as Cassian had been only days before. Together as a team or in matches opposing one another they would bring much coin to the lanista's purse and even more sport to those that wagered upon the games. Clapping a hand to Felix's shoulder the lanista raised his goblet in a toast of utter delight. "To mutual gain paired with honored and profitable friendship good Felix. For years to come." The words carrying at a perfect pitch to the Celt's ear, causing a dangerous moment of distraction.

The kick had come as a surprise but Proximus' size was a good defense against that manner of blow. It only took a pair of backwards steps to regain his balance though Cassian suspected he would feel it in his lungs for much longer. He might have even cracked one of his ribs but that could be dealt with after this match which needed a swift ending if he was going to make the victory a decisive memory for all those gathered to watch. He pushed forwards, steel ringing against steel as the Celt twisted his body to block blows which should have sent him backwards off balance. He saw it in his eyes, the second the German made the decision that it would be impossible to win this match with honor; a quick flick of his wrist brought the flat of his blade down in a blow to the fresh wound. He had no intent to make it bleed any worse, but the pain was staggering.

Cassian grunted and cursed when the pain lanced from his leg all the way through his body. The man fought without honor and it would be remembered by more than just himself.

"Maybe Dominus will send your prized little whore to my cell once I defeat you." The German growled in his own language. He must have seen Cassian talking with Argus at some point or else he just did not care who did or did not understand him. The thought of it was all that was needed to change his mind from following Tertius' command with ease to making sure that there was no possibility that the German could think to lay hands upon

Violetta. He doubted that the lanista would have allowed it, but Cassian could not take that chance.

He had made it easy for everyone to think that Proximus could have easily killed him but instead of looking to Tertius for his declaration of the victor, Cassian continued the match with a renewed determination. All it took to remove himself from the kneeling position was a dodge to the side and a flurry of sword thrusts to his stomach. It was expected for the new man to win and thus be branded a member of the brotherhood. He would fight in the arena and, hopefully, earn back the coin for his Dominus that had been spent on his purchase and transport. There would be pain to pay for this defiance in the future but for now he would do whatever was needed to keep his Violetta safe from the lecherous touch of another man. The Romans were beyond his reach but Proximus would never know the touch of her skin while he drew breath in this world.

When he struck back at Proximus, moving out of the expected position of submission, the lanista looked as though he was about to take the whip from the hands of the Doctore and flay him publicly for his disobedience. As Cassian blocked another strike of the German's sword. This was not just about pride now but there was finally a chance to protect his woman. Even if it changed nothing and no one except the two of them ever knew about it, it mattered. He fought with a savagery he had almost forgot himself capable of and, ignoring the anger on Tertius' face, he was sure of his victory even though the other man had stood as a champion not long ago in Rome.

The crowd seemed to be undecided as to who had their favor, the champion that they knew or the man that might be able to defeat him. They were growing louder at each strike, but Cassian had to keep his focus on his opponent who was not the usual recruit to be given this test. Tertius would rage and might even let Proximus kill him for his disobedience but there was nothing that could be done about that now.

The man, Proximus, would bear the mark of the house of Tertius by the end of the night. Cassian had no intention of ending the man's life but now that he had evaded being forced into submission the Roman would be livid and he, as a gladiator, had to find a way to be defeated while keeping his life and, he hoped, a bit of his pride as a fighter. Blocking a dangerously close swing to his head he ducked low and drove his fist into the German's stomach, letting his blade drag across his flesh as he pulled away.

The man bellowed in pain and Tertius, as well as the gathered company, flinched along with the man while Cassian fought to catch his breath and find the best angle to continue his attack, but it was another breath that he heard making him pause in his attack. Violetta looked at him with a strange sense of panic in her eyes. Jovian was just beside her and the silent man that served Felix was on the other side. Had one of them touched her? She had cried out, but he could not see why. He was about to call to her when her hands flew to her mouth and a fist connected to his temple. Just as he opened his mouth to shape her name, he crumpled to the floor. His consciousness was floating around him giving him the sounds of what was around him though he could not open his eyes to focus clearly.

He could hear the voices around him, Violetta's fear rang clear to him first, but it was quickly silenced by Tertius declaring Proximus to be the victor before crouching beside him to hiss in his ears "Fucking fool. I swear to the gods if you do not get to your feet, I will let him kill you here and now before the eyes of the girl." There was no doubt in Cassian's fogged mind that the lanista meant his words and so the champion fought to open his eyes and rise to his feet again, at least long enough to acknowledge the victory of the other man.

He felt Proximus clasp his forearm and when Tertius began speaking to the gathered crowd the new man leaned closer to whisper awkwardly "Apologies for words earlier. The reputation you carry is well deserved, and I will not underestimate you again." Cassian could barely nod but the words needed acknowledgment. He gave a curt nod "That could save your life another night." He blinked hard, trying to focus "Gratitude for not taking mine." He silently added that it had more to do with Tertius remembering his value then it did the choice of Proximus.

It was as if the lanista heard his thoughts. As Proximus stepped forward to accept the congratulations of the crowd the brand that was to mark him as a member of the brotherhood of gladiators was heated by Cirandon who would soon hand it to the lanista so that he could accept the oath that his new gladiator. While the others cheered Tiberius leaned over to hiss angrily in Cassian's ear.

"If you were not worth more alive than the satisfaction your death would bring me, I would be sending you to the cross at dawn. Did you think to defy me? Was the cost of obedience too high for your damned pride? Was it worth your life?"

Cassian turned his head to answer but before he could speak a word the world spun, and his vision went black. He fell unconscious to the floor. He didn't hear Violetta cry out or feel when Proximus lifted his head from the ground. His mind was already departed to the realm of dreams while around him the staff of the ludus scrambled to aid the fallen champion. Was he dead or just injured was what was whispered around the room by the many fans of the games?

His head cleared for a moment, hearing the definitive click of a Roman woman's heeled shoes and the voice of Selenia speaking to her father, who must have joined Tertius, and to the lanista as well. "Father? I wish to know the victor of this match better. The German." The second part of the question had to be directed at Tertius. "That is, of course, if the brute is obedient?" Even dazed as he would Cassian could tell that there would be no chance for any woman in the room to have a chance for the same if they desired it.

Struggling to regain his full consciousness and footing he was surprised to feel the tension in the large hands holding him as Tertius answered the woman. "You desire to test his skills outside the match, dear lady?" There was surprise in the usually unflappable voice, but Cassian paid more attention to the man holding him to the floor. He did not want to be with the woman, despite his earlier taunt regarding Violetta. What secret was the man hiding? Did he prefer men like a few of the other gladiators? Or was it that he had a woman of his own that had been left behind in Rome?

Tertius had the same lack of choice that his gladiator did but summoned a guard with an uncertain voice. "Selenia requests private audience with our victor. Take her to a room where this might happen and see that she is well satisfied but kept safe of course. It would not do for a beautiful flower such as yourself to be bruised by the beast." Both the merchant and his daughter seemed very pleased to be afforded the exclusive courtesy of bedding the newest man to the ludus, and the Celt felt the reluctance in Proximus when he left to follow the command.

Cassian was regaining himself though he almost wished for death as he caught the laughter of more than one of the nobles of Velletri. If it were not for the new-found bliss of burgeoning love his prayers to be taken to the afterlife would have been in complete sincerity. Love; his heart sank with the realization that Violetta had witnessed this foolishness that saw him so defeated. She would likely think him as absurd as he thought himself. She had met him as a champion returning to his title but what would she think of the man who could not defend himself before her eyes. These, and other thoughts like this, whirled in his mind like a cyclone so that he barely felt the friendly hand under his arm or heard the words "Come, I will see you to Arturo." From Cirandon.

Cassian didn't want to leave the room where Violetta was, not until he knew if she would reject him for his foolishness. "No... no. The druid can wait." He grumbled, struggling slightly as Julius took a grip under his arms and hauled him to his feet. When the room began to spin again, and he wavered on his feet he looked at the guard. "Violetta? I need to break words with her. Julius?" His voice was almost pleading before collapsing again.

"Jupiter's cock!" The lanista bellowed, stepping from the center of the room to glare at the gladiator being held up while his head rolled to his chest. "See him tended and brought to my office." Looking to the left he saw Violetta standing by the column, having taken a single step forward when he fell. "You." He called, pointing a finger at her then to the champion "Attend him, and see him to awareness."

Violetta stepped forward to lay a hand to Cassian's arm. Before she could utter a word, she was shoved roughly aside by one of the other guards who snarled "Your tender ministrations can wait, girl." She looked to Cassian and then the Doctore and Julius, both of whom she knew to be his friends, but both simply shook their heads and Julius beckoned her to follow.

CHAPTER 23

Violetta followed after the men who were half dragging, half carrying Cassian from the room where the celebration of Proximus' victory would continue for many hours to come. It was strange to be walking through the dimly lit halls of the villa with the escort of guards and the intimidatingly silent instructor, but she did her best to keep her eyes on Cassian. How bad was the injury and how did his master think that she could help him? She was not a medicus and did not know how to diagnose maladies or mend broken bones. She cringed when they dragged him down the stairs but at the bottom the trio seemed to disagree where to take him.

Julius, the guard who was with him most times she had seen him, wanted to take him to his cell so he could sleep off the blow to his head while the other Roman guard wanted to take him to the baths and use the water to force him to waking. "If you do that the man is likely to drown." Cirandon said, acknowledging Violetta with a slight nod of his head. "Bring him to the platform beside the training grounds. The fresh air there will revive him, and he can be observed by Arturo, the medicus, or this girl that Dominus has sent for that reason while the druid is at his prayers which are not to be disturbed."

Violetta felt that his words of warning regarding the druid were more for her benefit than the two guards. Her breath was tight when the two guards finally realized that she had, in obedience to the lanista's order, followed them down into the depths of this world of violent men.

She thought that Lucius gave her presence a moment of consideration before looking down the hall towards the light of the approaching sunset from the sands and what lay in that direction.

"Alright, the fresh air is the best idea. The girl will stay with him until Arturo returns." The trio of men agreed though the guard that was not Julius did not seem to like the fact that she was there but with the command of the lanista and the permission of Felix Census, who had edited so many games for the man who paid him that he gave in without the words that matched his facial expression.

The Doctore looked at her, she felt that he somehow sensed her nervousness. "There are no other gladiators below the villa tonight until the end of the celebration. No one will bother you, but the druid and he is a holy enough man that you need have no fear of him." He told her softly while they followed the guards to the gladiators dining platform. They heaved the barely conscious Cassian onto the flat top of the thick planked table where he and his brothers ate their meals while the sun set beyond the edge of the ocean that kissed the edge of the city at the cliff base.

"The door at the top of the stairs will be locked but should you need anything, yell for Arturo and he will come to aid you. You must be loud though or he will not hear you." The Doctore instructed her in his calm deep voice. He looked at Cassian with concern. "He was a fool to try such a thing. I pray that the gods do not punish him too severely."

She nodded carefully, agreeing with his last words but not understanding what he had done that was foolish. Violetta sat down on the bench as the Romans left, she thought Cirandon had left too when he spoke from the darkened doorway. "Though perhaps in you, he has found his greatest reward. I pray it is so." He gave her a warm smile before rejoining the rest of the gladiators in the villa above.

His words left her with a warmth in her heart but to look at her champion, unconscious and laid out flat on the table before her like a slab of meat or a corpse, she felt a deeper concern. "Cassian?" She whispered in his ear, leaning close "Wake up. Come back to me."

Whether it was the man or the gods that heard her, she did not know but it was mere moments later that his eyes fluttered, and a pained groan loosed from his lips. "Arturo? I thought I heard a sweeter voice than yours, but it had to be a dream." His hand rose to rub the side of his head where he had been struck. Violetta was tempted to catch his hand in her own but instead she cleared her throat to attract his attention.

"What voice did you think you heard champion?" She asked with a teasing note to her voice. "Perhaps you have indeed been dreaming." She was so relieved that he was awake she almost didn't notice the deepening bruise on the side of his face from the intense blow. "Or maybe you have crossed to the underworld at last and I am Morta, goddess of death." She almost laughed at her own joke of being any goddess, let alone one of such great importance to a warrior like the one before her. Even though he claimed to hold no faith in the gods of any nation it was still unwise to anger them through false claims. "Perhaps you wake to the real world and I am just myself. Adoring though unworthy I may be." She corrected herself nervously.

A broad smile spread across his face as he sat up and caught her chin in his hand. "Better than that. I wake to solitude with the woman who holds my heart. My personal priestess." He brought his lips down to touch hers with a warmth that spread from him to her and she felt a flush rise on her cheeks.

"Shush with such words or the gods will hear you." Violetta murmured. Letting her head rest against his side, sighing with relief when he wrapped his arm around her shoulders to give comfort when she thought she would break down into the tears she had felt stinging her eyes when he had fallen. "I thought they had taken you from me tonight and I could not bear it."

"Did I not warn you of such things that night in the pool? That it would become harder with each match? That deeper feelings would bring a risk of greater heartache?" He told her, gently pressing kisses to the top of her head. His concern for her and his affection were becoming more and more clear with every touch.

Also growing more real was the truth in his earlier warning. If she had thought her heart would break now if he was taken, what would happen months, or years later when he fell in the arena and she was left alone, or, gods willing, with a child of his blood to share the heartache with? What would she do then?

Would she be able to go on living or would she fall into an emotional state so severe that she would be declared mad and put into the street? She pressed her eyes closed and wished away the thought for he was there with her, in the moment. His arm was around her and his face buried in her hair. Her arms wrapped around his firmly muscled waist and she held on as though their happiness might be snatched from them at any given moment by the return of the Romans.

"Cassian, I cannot let such thoughts into my mind. I cannot think of what might happen without you to give joy to my heart." She turned her head to press a kiss below his ribs before she pulled back enough to look up at him. "Please do not frighten me like that again?" She had not known what he meant to do but she was certain that the loss had been planned, at least it had been until the moment that Cassian had been upon his knees. The German giant could have killed him with the blow to the temple, but she believed it was the gods that saw him spared, this time.

"I feel as though I could have fought that giant myself. When he struck you, I felt rage with my fear." She said, leaning into his touch while he stroked her cheek with the pad of his thumb as though he was trying to soothe her instead of the opposite.

"I would not want to think of you fighting, let alone against Proximus. Though there is a form of wrestling you excel at." He said, shaking his head dismissively. Cassian was staring down at her with a warmth in his eyes that brought a blush to her cheeks with his teasing intention.

Laughing at his playful joke, Violetta rose from the bench to sit beside him on top of the table. "I do not think a proper lady would be known to participate in such sport. I am sure that you do not think lowly of me, do you?" She had baited him at his own game of words and wanted to see if he would be as crude as the women of the house said all gladiators were or, if she was right, he was a man of higher birth and knowledge than most thought he was.

"Violetta, my sweet priestess," He said with a warm smile, taking both her hands in his and pressing them into a pose of prayer, "I stand the lowly one before your grace and beauty. You humble me with your presence, and I will gladly risk the wrath of all the gods to have you in my heart, in my arms and one day I hope to have you at my side to stay."

He was staring down into her eyes and his words sounded so sincere that Violetta could not stop herself from believing that he meant everything that he said but how could it be done? Would the gods align the fates so that it could be? Was this why they were brought to each other? "Cassian? How? How could such a thing be done when I belong to another man?" She said, leaning forward to kiss his hands that still covered hers. "I want to believe such is possible but how could it come to pass? I have heard of gladiators purchasing their freedom, but I have no way of accomplishing such a thing." She shook her head "Even if I did, I do not think Felix would grant it and Vitus..." She shuddered at the though of what he would do if he found out she had ever asked the question.

Picking up her slight body to settle her across his lap Cassian smiled at her, pressing their foreheads together for a moment. "I would move the heavens and the earth to see it done. I have not yet thought of how, but I promise you that I will find a way. I want you here, safe from them, from Vitus."

His hands skimmed down her sides and before she knew it, he had pressed upon the wound created by the foot of Vitus. "Oh!" She exclaimed in pain before she could stifle the sound with her hand. He reached to draw it away with an expression near to anger flashing in his eyes.

"What is it? You cannot tell me after the words we have just exchanged, after I have just given my word to fight to save you from that house and the sadist that would possess you utterly, that you do not wish my touch. Tell me that is not what this means? Tell me that I have not made myself a fool with my words? With my heart?" He looked down into her eyes with such hurt as his hands reached for the fabric of her dress where his hand had rested moments before.

"Cassian? Please... it is not your touch, but the blows delivered by the angered foot of another. It will make you angry. I beg you not to look." She pleaded. "Your touch is the only thing that soothes my heart. There is no joy in its absence. Please, believe me."

She sighed with resignation when he shook his head, he was as determined to see the reason for her discomfort as she was to keep it hidden. There was nothing he could do now, as much as she wished that he had been able to be her hero the night before, the damage was done.

"Show me, Violetta. What do you hide from me?" Cassian said with a firmness in his voice that was without a choice for her unless she was willing to risk his deep displeasure. "Please? I would know any injury done to you in that house so that I may pay them back in exact balance one day."

Untying the knot at her side Violetta opened the dress to show him the dark bruise upon her side and turned so that he could see the slightly lighter marks upon her back. "Vitus has let his anger settle upon me of late. Last night he was in dark and dangerous mood. This was how he soothed his temper." She said, turning her head to look away, not wanting to see his face when he examined the bruises.

His touch was feather light over the pained skin, and she heard him suck in his breath before he spread his hand over her side. Maybe he thought that hiding the mark would put it from her mind or maybe he truly could not bear the sight of it. "The pain will fade soon enough. I have suffered worse at his hand than this." She knew that he would not be soothed by her words, but she had to say something to fill the silence.

"He has done this before? Hurt you like this?" Cassian said, his hand finding her chin and turning her face to look at him again. "I want to know everything that happens in that house, even if it breaks my heart to know that I cannot protect you as I want to."

Her jaw trembled at his words, speaking the desire she felt even now to hide in him. Her own words could not pass her lips even though she tried to find her voice. "Cassian..." She began to try to tell him what he asked but her words were stopped by the sudden pressure of his lips against her, softly stifling anything she could have said with the distraction of passion.

Violetta lifted a hand to his cheek, silently inviting him to pursue his passion. Each press of lips washing away pained memories and fears to give way to thoughts of romance and stolen embraces. They were alone and with there being almost no chance of interruption, she was just as eager to come together with him as she could sense that he was wanting to be with her.

He slid his hands around her waist and pulled her into his lap, the evidence of his desire alerting her to the strength of the need he had for her. She smiled and threaded her fingers into his hair, loving the silky feeling of it while she pulled him closer. Angling her mouth against him with a soft moan, she thrilled when he responded with a guttural growl that was followed by a deep plundering thrust of his tongue. There was no need for more words between them, not tonight.

All thoughts of the Romans were pushed aside in the growing heat of the moment. His touch to her skin was like a fire and sent moisture pooling between her legs. His hands had slid beneath the fabric of her dress where she had opened it to show the mark on her side. At first, he simply caressed her back, soothing and exciting her at the same time. When his palm slid to cup her breast Violetta arched into him, pressing her weighted flesh into his massaging grasp.

She broke the kiss so that she could focus what attention she had on the fastenings of the light armor he had worn during the test. She wanted to touch his bare skin and feel his heart racing beneath her touch. She wanted to rake the tips of her nails across his chest to make him growl and wink at her in the devilish way she knew that he would. He was as playful in moments of passion as he could be serious upon the sand which sparked a fever in her to increase the contact between them. Shucking the leather from his shoulders, Violetta bit her lip and stared at the sculpted glory of his chest. She traced the tip of her finger across the muscles that strained under the power of his restraint.

When he gave a slight growl at the scratch of her nail, she looked up to meet his eyes and gasped in surprise at what she saw there. His gaze was filled with a hunger that startled her with its intensity. Everything in his eyes spoke of his desire to consummate the words that he had uttered to her about his wish to have her at his side.

Violetta had never seen such a hunger in the eyes of a man and for a moment he frightened her with his ferocious intensity. Before she could voice her trepidation, his lips were crushing down on hers once again, replacing fear with the heated frenzy of the need she was developing for him. Her lips raced down his neck and her arms wound around his waist as she lowered her kisses past his collarbone. She wanted to devour him and memorize every inch of him with her lips and the touch of her hands. "Cassian," she moaned breathlessly against his thundering heart "We must make the most of this chance together. When will the gods grant us another such moment? Please?" She whispered against his flesh.

He answered her without words, slowly sliding his hands up her arms, staring down into her eyes, his own shining like a golden fire in the sunset. She shivered at the light touch but when his palms reached her shoulders, and he hooked his thumbs under the straps of her dress to swiftly tug the fabric aside until the entire dress fell to her waist as she sat on his lap. Easing her to the table's surface he spun to stand and pull her to her feet. Violetta gasped as the dress pooled at her feet and the cool evening air greeted her nakedness with the embrace of a breeze.

"Sweet Venus in the heavens..." Cassian swore softly, staring so intently that Violetta lifted a hand to cover herself in the light. His hands caught hers and he shook his head "No, I beg you, stand bare before me a moment or two longer. For I have never seen anything so beautiful as you are now, in this light."

She paused only for a moment, the look of reverence in his eyes etching itself in her memory, before reaching to pull him close enough to kiss again. Her arms hooked behind his and her hands gripped at his shoulders to pull him as close as was possible, needing to be nearer and still finding that being pressed skin to skin was not close enough to satisfy her craving for the warrior in her arms. She wondered if there was such a thing as being close enough to him or having enough of him? Surely not for her, and not in this lifetime.

Violetta gasped against his lips when she felt the touch of his fingers between her thighs, exploring her readiness. He knew just how to touch her, how to stimulate her body so that she could think of nothing but joining with him in ecstatic embrace. She nipped his neck playfully when he ceased to tease with his fingers and firmly pushed first one and then a second deep inside her. Her hips rocked in tandem to his thrusting strokes, each one bringing new heights to her arousal.

Moans of a deepening bliss poured from her throat and she opened her eyes that she had not known she had closed. Cassian was smiling down at her as he played her as the musicians upstairs in the villa played their instruments. She propped her hands on the table behind her, biting her tongue to stop from crying out when he pressed his thumb against the nub of nerves that sent her over the edge into orgasm.

"Don't hold back priestess." He growled, looping an arm behind her to pull her tight against him once again with a possessive grin. "I want to hear you, see you, feel you as you come apart in my arms."

He buried his face in her neck, nipping at her to make her giggle and then smile at him while he slid his hands underneath her thighs to pick her up but when her knee bumped the fresh wound upon his thigh and she cringed when he grunted, obviously trying to hide the pain that the injury was causing him.

"Cassian? Your wound?" Her eyes lifted to his, but he shook his head emphatically, stopping her from further words that would break the spell of the moment.

A slow, wicked smile spread across her face. "Lay back, champion." Violetta eased the surprised gladiator to his back upon the table where they had been sitting minutes ago. "You are in need of some tender care, and I am going to ensure that you get just what is needed."

As Cassian lay back Violetta followed his body with her own, straddling his hips, carefully avoiding contact with the injury while reaching to untie his subligaria. "Do you want this as much as I, Cassian?" She asked him, watching his eyes drinking in her nudity as she knelt above him. Though she was sure that he was as confident as ever, there was a look in his eyes that made her curious if any other woman had taken such daring control with him before. Was she the first?

Reaching down she traced a fingertip down the center of his chest. "Are you perhaps too tired? Or the injury causes too much pain?" She asked with a teasing smile, straddling him while his hands reached to grip her hips.

"Woman, I would have to be dead before I could be too tired for you." He answered her with a grin, sliding his hand up her body to thread into her hair and pull her down for a deep and probing kiss while the other pushed aside the unfastened fabric that had kept his cock from her sight. Her mouth gaped at the sight of him, so undeniably, powerfully male. Taking him in her grasp Violetta felt a swell of pride that the intensity of his arousal was for her, that his desire for her was so strong that there was no doubt of the need between them to come together.

His body responded to her intimate touch, his hips rising and falling with each stroke of her hand on his shaft, emotions flickering across his face as she watched with fascination at what power was in her attentions. She inhaled sharply when one of his hands reached up to take her breast in grasp, rolling her nipple between his thumb and forefinger until it beaded into the tightness of a budding flower and she pressed herself further into his hand in an attempt to satisfy the hunger that was building within her.

There were no more words to be spoken, their eyes and bodies said it all. When the hand that had rested on her hip slid down her thigh to pull her forward, she knew that he was as ready as she was for them to finally join. A flush spread across her chest as Violetta used the pad of her thumb to spread the liquid pool at his tip across its broadness, her excitement growing more intense when he gripped her tight in anticipation of her next move.

Sliding herself up his length, the wet of her growing arousal readying him while teasing her aching slit for the fullness to come. Rising upon her knees Violetta paused above him, vaguely aware that his hands had moved from her leg and breast to her hip and beneath her, holding himself poised and ready to pierce her body in their next breath. She wet her lips and nodded, almost imperceptibly, to him. Cassian responded with an upwards thrust of his pelvis at the same time as he pulled downwards on her hip, sinking home with grunt of his satisfaction that matched the gasp that fell from her at the sensation of being suddenly filled, stretched, completed.

Her confidence in her actions faltered for the moment it took for her body to adjust to the size of her lover buried to the hilt of his cock inside her, but soon she moved along his length. Her body instinctively searching for the rhythm that would take them both crashing towards the blissful release they sought. His hands gripped her tight, easing her body into the roll to match the push and pull of his own to stimulate them both.

Letting her head fall forward, Violetta's hair created a curtain, secluding herself and Cassian from all but the brightest rays of the setting sun as they moved together, each return of his body into hers bringing them both nearer to the climax that beckoned them both. They strained together, their bodies rushing towards the divine ecstasy. Violetta could feel her body tightening around Cassian, clenching so that she felt like a bowstring drawn back and ready to let fly into the heavens.

Slowly one of his hands slid from clasping her hip to slide between her thighs and press once again on the bud of nerves with the pad of his thumb. With that touch he released her to fly over the edge of bliss and into the sky of physical bliss. His name poured from her lips in a cry of release, she could not care if there was anyone on the balcony above to hear them, so intense was the pleasure of orgasm.

Her lover's hands held her up as his body surged upwards into her as he released himself, again and again. "Violetta!" She heard him call her name as she collapsed down upon his chest. Her own heart thundered with the same speed as his was beating against her ear.

Turning her head Violetta kissed his chest and slid to lay beside him, her arm stretched across his heaving chest while he wrapped tender arms around her.

"My little priestess." He said warmly kissing her temple. "I shall now have a deity to pray to in earnest." He said with a small laugh. "Arturo, the medicus, will be satisfied at last."

"He will?" Violetta asked, raising her head to look at him with a slightly dazed smile that was the result of their lovemaking.

"Yes, he will." Said a soft voice on the edge of laughter. "Though most priestesses wear more clothing than that, young lady."

Violetta looked over to the doorway and gasped at the sight of a man stepping out of the shadows.

"The Romans await you both." He said with a resigned look in his eyes but a warm smile on his face. "I fear this joy is finished, for now."

To Be Continued In "The Champion's Torment."

"The Champions" Series Characters

Cassian/Otho (*Cass-Ian/ O-tho*): Champion Gladiator, Twenty-Five, Slave since age 12 when captured from Britannia

    Violetta (*Violet-A*): Body Slave to Felix Census, Eighteen, Slave since age 10.

    Tiberius Tertius (*Ti-Beer-Ee-Us Ter-Tee-Us*): Lanista, Dominus to Cassian, Arturo, Argus, Cirandon, Nala, Tarconus, Proximus, Jovian

    Lycithia (*Lie-Kith-ia*): Roman, Wife of Tiberius Tertius

    Arturo (*Art-Ooro*): Celtic Druid, Former General, Medicus to the Gladiators, close friend to Cassian

    Jovian (*Jo-Vee-An*): Favored body slave to Tiberius Tertius, Seventeen, Syrian,

    Argus (*Are-Gus*): Gladiator, Twenty-three, Germanic, training partner to Cassian, secret interest in Jovian

    Tarconus (*Tar-Cone-Us):* Gladiator, Twenty-Six, Thracian, Former champion of Velletri hoping to reclaim the title from Cassian

    Proximus (*Prox-ih-mus*): Gladiator, Twenty-Four, Germanic, Fallen Champion of Rome wanting to earn the mark of the brotherhood and rise to champion of Velletri

    Cirandon (*Key-Ran-Don*): Former Gladiator now instructional Doctore, Thirty-two, Husband to Nala, Close friend to Cassian.

    Nala (*Nall-A*): Body slave to Lycithia, wife to Cirandon, former lover of Cassian, deceased

    Felix Census (*Fee-Lix Sen-sus*): Roman, Silk merchant, Dominus to Violetta, Father to Selenia and Vitus, sometimes friend to Tiberius Tertius

    Vitus Census (*V-Eye-Tus*): Roman, Son to Felix, would-be Dominus to Violetta and Meridius, enemy of Cassian

    Selenia Census (*Sell-En-Eea*): Roman, Daughter to Felix, Spends much of her time in Rome hunting for a husband

    Meridius (*Mer-Id-Ius*): Body slave to Felix Census, Spaniard, Thirty-three, Father figure to Violetta

    Auctus (*Oct-Us*): Roman, Captain of the ludus guard, Superior of Lucius, Friendly with Cassian and Arturo

Julius Lucius (*Jool-Ius Loo-Sius*): Roman, Assigned guard to Cassian, former soldier in the legions, reports to Auctus directly, friendly with Cassian

Titus Claudius (*Tie-Tus Claw-Dius*): Roman, Senator, Wealthiest man in the Republic, Hobbyist Lanista, General of the Legions

Astrix (*Ass-Tricks*): Slave. Right hand man to Tiberius Tertius, Syrian, former gladiator.

Darius (*Dare-Ius*): Older brother of Argus. Sent to the mines after setting fire to the ludus.

Cicero (*Sis-Ero*): Slave attendant to the weapons on the sands

Maximus Textus (*Max-ih-Mus Text-us*): Roman soldier rising swiftly through the ranks, known as The Wolf.

About the Author

Born in Hardisty, Alberta Monica developed an undeniable love of reading at an early age. Homeschooled during her primary years, her mother not only taught the basics to her five children, but she also read to them at least twice a day. From Anne of Green Gables to Tolkien's Lord of the Rings the stories and the people behind them instilled a love of the written word.

As soon as she could hold a pencil Monica began to write her own stories. Her first complete work was 'Monkey Millionaires' in which a pair of monkeys became millionaires by selling ice cream. While it was a huge hit among the kids in the neighborhood it was just the beginning. After discovering the TV show Spartacus, and full immersion into that fandom, Monica was disappointed to find there was very little fiction to satisfy her desire to indulge a love of Roman era romance. The spark was then lit to write the stories she wanted to read herself.

Despite some eye-opening experiences (it's not as glamorous a profession as the movies would have you believe) she would not change her journey in the slightest. When she is not working or writing, Monica is a single parent to a little girl. Nothing makes her happier than when her daughter tells her that she wants to be a writer, "Just like you, Mommy." So, to keep inspiring a very special little girl, and to bring some elements of romantic Rome and the romance of real life to some not-so-little girls, she is pleased to be writing as M. Francis Lamont and brings you "The Champion's Prize" the first of her centurion saga and many more stories to come. She encourages everyone to "Live with Passion. Live with Purpose. And most important of all, Never Lose. Welcome to the beginning of something wonderful.

Book 2 of The Champions, "The Champion's Torment" Coming Soon!